SOUL GOBLET
LEGENDS OF THE FALLEN BOOK 7

J.A. CULICAN

H.M. GOODEN

Soul Goblet © copyright 2019 J.A. Culican

All Rights Reserved.

No part of this book may be reproduced in any form or by any electronic or mechanical means, including information storage and retrieval systems, without the express written consent from the author, except in the case of a reviewer, who may quote brief passages embodied in critical articles or in a review. Trademark names appear throughout this book. Rather than trademark name, names are used in an editorial fashion, with no intention of infringement of the respective owner's trademark.

The information in this book is distributed on an "as is" basis, without warranty. Although every precaution has been taken in preparation of this work, neither the author nor the publisher shall have any liability to any person or entity with respect to any loss or damage caused or alleged to be caused directly or indirectly by the information contained in this book.

The characters, locations, and events portrayed in this book are fictitious. Any similarities or resemblance to real persons, living or dead is coincidental and not intended by the author.

Paperback ISBN: 978-1-081211-55-4

Hardback ISBN: 978-1-949621-13-6

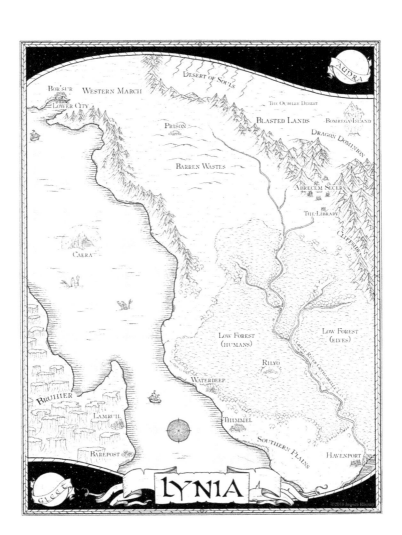

CHAPTER 1

"This is not well written," I grumbled as I glared at the ancient book in front of me, before letting out a groan of frustration.

Pushing back from the table, I stared at the expanse in front of me. The heavy oak surface was large enough to accommodate twenty scholars and able to support a great deal of weight. That was a good thing. During my search for answers I'd managed to occupy every square inch of the golden surface with a mountain of books.

Biting my lip, I absently tapped my fingers on my green dress. Blotches of ink dotted the thick silk. My mother would be upset if she saw it.

"None of these books tell me anything." I mumbled under my breath.

Normally, I enjoyed doing research for its own sake, but this was different. I considered my options carefully. Maybe there was another book in the stacks I hadn't yet discovered.

Ever since the news had arrived, on the panting gasps of an exhausted emissary to the town of Cliffside where I lived, that the prison holding Dag'draath had broken, I'd been frantically searching for any information I could find about the history of the Dark War.

While I was tucked away from the action for now, I knew we weren't completely sheltered. Dag'draath was being released from his prison. The greatest enemy our world had ever seen, and the only hero who could protect us, Onen Suun, was long gone. It was only a matter of time until the fight came to us.

There had been a brief mention of an artifact and a ritual which had been used to trap Dag'draath. The only problem was the details about what exactly the artifact and the ritual were happened to be incredibly murky.

Why were all the old scribes so vague? Was it deliberate? I assumed it was to cause frustration in the researcher, or to keep the artifact from falling into the wrong hands. I stood up from the chair and stomped to the shelves, passing a map of the Low Forest on my way.

I'd never traveled beyond the Low Forest. I knew it was silly, but I felt as though I'd already explored the world through my books. If I'd had the chance, I would have been happy to spend every waking moment in my library. But this news had shaken me out of my books and into a state of near panic.

I *needed* to find more volumes with information about the Dark War. I returned to the table with two more texts, stumbling into the chair as an idea hit me like a bolt of lightning. My eyes went wide and my heart picked up its pace.

It was written in code!

I stood, almost knocking over the heavy wooden chair in my excitement. But when I thumbed through the pages of the books spread out in front of me, I was disappointed again.

None of the other books seemed to contain what I was searching for. Of the twenty or so texts on the table in front of me, only two had been useful, and only when read together.

CHAPTER 1

Pushing the other books out of the way, I lined both volumes up side-by-side, following the words with my finger, as if they would somehow impart more wisdom.

They were written in the same awful handwriting. I wasn't the best at graphology, but when I examined the script, it appeared the ink, as well as the swirling loops and hurried pace it seemed to have been written in, were identical.

"Aha!"

The moment I put the paragraphs together, my idea was supported and bloomed. One spoke of an artifact used in a ritual but didn't call the ritual by name. It mentioned the qualities of the artifact, but not enough for me to identify what it was.

The second text, however, spoke of a ritual named the Beheratzi Dokuzgen. It only briefly mentioned the artifact used, instead focusing on what had been required to activate it.

"Interesting." I absently scratched the back of my neck.

Sel abruptly interrupted my moment of clarity by placing another book on the table. Normally, his silence and stealthy movements tended to make me jump, but in this case, I was too distracted to be startled.

"Sel, you're just who I need." I pointed at the two black books on the table. "I think there are a few more books matching these at the top of one of the back shelves." I flipped one of them closed, tucking my finger in to hold the page as I showed him the spine.

I hadn't seen it at first, but the books I'd been drawn to were both bound with a thick, black, leather-like material. The color absorbed the light and was different than any binding I'd seen before. Instantly, I decided it was an omen. A black binding that absorbed light, covering volumes with information about the Dark War. It was fitting and made me think I was on the right track at last.

He bowed, not as deeply as he would have if he'd been

4 SOUL GOBLET

ordered to do something by anyone else, then left in the direction I'd pointed without a word.

We had a good relationship. Even though he *was* technically a slave.

Humans in Cliffside were often mistreated by the elves, but I didn't understand why things had to be this way. I'd been taught since childhood humans were a lesser species, not as smart, unattractive, and certainly not as good at fighting. I didn't know many humans, but the ones I'd met had never struck me as lesser in any way, merely different.

While I waited for Sel to get the books I couldn't reach, I walked over to the large arched windows that let light into the library. I could see my brother in the courtyard, preparing with the other elves for battle. They'd been working longer and harder since the emissary had arrived, and I'd hardly seen him in weeks unless it was through a window.

I was terrified and wistful watching them, wondering if I'd been allowed to train if maybe my life would be more exciting. As it was, I wasn't supposed to be spending my time in the library, but my mother viewed it as the least objectionable activity I could get up to while remaining marriageable, which seemed to be her sole desire these days.

My brother's friend paused and looked up. I ducked away from the window, hoping he hadn't seen me. He was nice, but I didn't find him interesting. I didn't want to encourage him or my parents.

The rustle of movement drew my attention and I was surprised to see my younger sister enter the library. She was dressed as elegantly as usual, but her movements were jerky and her face was pale. When she saw me beside the window, she narrowed her eyes and headed straight for me.

"What have you found? Have you heard if we are going to war?"

I held my hands up, unable to back up any further from where I'd placed myself against the wall. I considered her

CHAPTER 1 5

words carefully. "I haven't found anything yet. And I have no idea what Father has planned, but based on the fires in the distance, my guess is we'll be at war soon."

Her face crumpled and I sighed, looking back out the window toward the now ever-present fires on the horizon. Ur'gels were everywhere, or so I had heard from the younger elves in the military. They spoke in excited whispers, but the elders were tight-lipped.

"You'll tell me if you find anything, won't you?"

The hope in her voice made me wonder what the world was coming to. Usually my sisters viewed my "hobby" with a patronizing air. To see her looking at me with such pleading was almost more frightening than the smoke in the air.

I gave her a brisk smile. "Of course. Now, I have to get back to my books if you want me to do that."

"Thanks, Rhiniya. Oh—don't be long. Remember, you still need to change."

I managed to hold back a groan and waved as she swept off in a cloud of anxiety and roses.

I sat back down on the chair, the hard wood making me squirm. At least my dress was more comfortable than what my sister had been wearing. When I remembered the condition of my dress I grimaced, knowing my mother would be unhappy.

I shivered slightly, beginning to feel the chill in the library. I'd been here all day, and realized it had been many hours since I'd eaten. But when Sel returned carrying not just two, but three large books with the same black leather spine, all thoughts of hunger and discomfort vanished.

I reached out my hands, standing to accept them. He passed one over, carefully placing the other two in an empty space beside the ones I'd been comparing. Once again, he'd perfectly anticipated my needs.

"Thanks. Have I ever told you how brilliant you are?" He truly was the best research assistant I could have hoped for.

He winked. "No, you never have, Rhin." We shared a silent

6 SOUL GOBLET

moment before he turned on his heel with a quick nod, returning to his ready position by the door.

An elder entered and he bowed deeply. I caught the way he was ignored, as if he was a piece of furniture. My stomach twisted, as it did every time I saw the casual cruelty humans received from my people every day. He was my friend, but there was nothing I could do.

He caught my eye and shook his head. I knew he didn't want me to say anything, so I turned back to the books, feeling guilty. He did so much for me and I let him. I knew how privileged I was, but suddenly I wanted him to understand.

I waved him over and he approached, eyebrows knitted together.

"My lady?"

I pressed my lips together. "I want you to know that you're the reason why I want to know everything."

His eyebrows shot up. "Excuse me?"

I smiled at the confusion on his face. "When you were given to me at fifteen, I was on my way to being as obnoxious as the other fair elves."

Sel began to object, but I shushed him. "No. It's true. When I got you for my birthday, it was the first time I realized how different life was for humans. I didn't know that you had no choice in serving, or that you'd been born into a position."

He shrugged. "It's not that bad working for you."

I shook my head. "Still. I wanted to find out what led to such gross inequality. No one should be able to own anyone else. It's wrong. As wrong as the Dark War and what Dag'-draath wants to do with the world."

Suddenly embarrassed by my outburst in the face of his quiet consternation, I turned to the textbooks that had so efficiently been placed before me, and he returned to the door.

The new books were large, and must have weighed at least twenty pounds each. They shared the same dark spines and

CHAPTER 1

when I trailed my fingers along the back of one, another shiver coursed down my back. This time, it wasn't from the chilly library air.

"Excuse me, Lady Rhiniya."

I looked up, my brow furrowed in irritation. I'd just started reading, but stifled my disappointment when I recognized the slight figure. Dara, my shy chambermaid, stood beside me, with her head bent low as she waited.

"What is it, Dara?" I smiled, biting back my frustration at the interruption. She was already too timid, regardless of my many attempts to reassure her I wouldn't have her imprisoned or executed for poor service, so there was no way I would snap at her. Apparently, her last mistress had been ... well, cruel was the only word that came to mind. Most of the humans in Cliffside were relatively well treated even though they were second-class citizens, because good help was hard to come by.

She bobbed her head, keeping her eyes downcast as she smoothed the front of her dress. "Your lady mother requests your presence upstairs. It is time to change for the festival. Remember, your presence is required."

I dipped my head slightly, forcing false cheer into my voice. "Thank you for reminding me, Dara. I guess I should get going, so my mother doesn't become upset. After all, appearances are important!"

I wasn't sure how my mother had obtained Dara's services, but I suspected she'd found her being mistreated and had negotiated her transfer to me. My mother had firm ideas about what a lady did and did not do, and I never doubted the kindness within her heart. That was why, even though I'd been raised with the usual biases, I was able to understand they weren't justified.

Dara bobbed her head again, letting the barest of smiles out before standing to the side with her head down as she waited for me to pass so she could follow.

I stood up, feeling stiffer than I should. It was good for me to take a break before I lost myself completely in the books. Sel remained beside the door, staring placidly ahead until I'd passed him. I caught his eye and gave him a meaningful look. He smiled in response and I readied myself to face a battle of another sort.

CHAPTER 2

The hallways stretched in a series of elegant loops and twists as we walked back to my chamber from the library. By the time I ascended the stairs to my wing, my body had received plenty of exercise.

I loved our home for its history and beauty. Some might consider it a castle, but I thought of it more like a family estate. It had wide, arching hallways that were ornately decorated with tapestries on every wall unadorned by portraits or paintings. Significant events in either my family's personal history, or elven history in general were prominently displayed at every turn. My mother had picked the current locations for most of the decor, but most of the art was centuries old. A few even dated back to the time before the Dark War, before either of my parents had been born.

An idea struck me as I passed the stern-faced ancestor elves who seemed to glare down from their vantage points, judging me as my steps echoed loudly on the marble floors. Maybe one of the older paintings or tapestries contained answers to solving the riddle of what had happened. Perhaps some of what was so coyly hinted at in the volumes I'd found would be depicted in art, as well as text.

All thoughts of the riddle in the library vanished when we arrived at my room. Dara rushed around muttering under her breath while I sat meekly on the dressing stool. I'd caught her disappointed look at the condition of my hair, but as she hadn't commented, neither did I.

I'm sure she was used to the fact I was a mess almost every time she had to prepare me for dinner, but she'd never once complained her time was wasted on me—at least, verbally. I allowed her to tug and primp my hair and skin without complaint and gradually she seemed less hurried.

The dress my mother had picked for the festival tonight was objectively quite gorgeous. It was the height of fashion. The ice-blue color would highlight my eyes and hair, while the cut would flatter my slender form perfectly.

I was sure my mother didn't use magic to make the dresses, but she may as well have, given how each new addition to my wardrobe always fit me without requiring a visit to the seamstress, for which I was eternally grateful. If I must dress in a style as elegant as my mother deemed necessary, at least she wasn't forcing me to spend the time I could be reading to maintain the look.

Which, of course, was the reason I'd accepted a lady's maid in the first place. I was hopeless at doing my own hair, content to leave it down or throw it back in a quick tie, both styles which my mother deemed unacceptable for a high-ranking female. Even the warriors kept their hair tied back in tight plaits or knots, styles which eluded my hands entirely.

Basically, I had no skill with hair. At least my behavior was acceptable, due to a nanny I'd had as a child who'd thoroughly drilled manners into me prior to the time I'd discovered my love of accumulating knowledge. It was a good thing, otherwise I'm sure I'd have received even more disdainful looks from my family and peers than I already did. Not that I cared, much.

Dara fluttered around, gently tugging, primping, and

styling my hair into a style that managed to gather all of my hair into a swirl that defied reason and remained off my face and neck, except for a few tendrils trailing down the front of my dress. After my hair was finished, she readied my face. Nothing too obvious, of course—my mother would be horrified if I wore anything but the most ethereal makeup.

Once she'd finished the minute details, I stood, allowing her to tighten and smooth my undergarments before finally, carefully, placing the heavy dress on top. I held my breath as she fastened the back, tightening it to show off my waist to its full advantage.

I caught a glimpse of myself in the mirror along the far wall and knew, on the outside at least, I was every inch a sheltered princess. To so many of the elven folk, it was all I'd ever be. A woman to be traded for matrimony, for alliances. Not a person in my own right, not even a warrior, allowed the freedom to come and go and die for what I believed in.

The second that emissary had arrived and the elves had begun preparing for war, something had changed inside me. I may not be a fighter, but I was a scholar, and my brain was as sharp and well-honed as any weapon. I wasn't willing to sit back and allow my parents to trade me to make alliances. I wanted to be useful beyond simply getting married.

"There, milady. What do you think?" My maid's timid voice interrupted my rebellious thoughts. I smiled, lightly touching her on the shoulder as she'd bent into a deep bow awaiting my response.

"You've done a marvelous job, as always." I waited for her to look up, but she continued to curtsy, keeping her eyes down. I wondered how long it would take, if ever, for her to look upon me as a friend, the way I hoped Sel did most of the time. We remained like that, my hand on her shoulder while she remained subservient, until finally she looked up and saw my pensive expression. Her eyebrows raised with alarm and I removed my hand from her shoulder and waved it in dismissal, trying to allay her fears.

"I was just thinking how lucky I am to have you. I wish you believed me when I tell you I would like to have you think of me as a friend."

Her cheeks pinked slightly, and I caught a ghost of a smile. "I know, milady. But it is so strange to me it may be almost against my nature." This time, she looked at me full in the eyes and added softly, almost whispering, "I'll keep trying, milady."

She bowed again quickly, this time a mere bob of her head, then disappeared. I smiled, feeling as if maybe I'd broken down a barrier. I didn't have many friends, since others my age and station either thought I was strange, or I found them irritating and shallow. It would be nice if my personal assistants would trust me, so I could trust them back unhesitatingly in return.

The door swung open, and Sel smiled down at me. He followed me to the banquet hall, remaining one pace behind always. As I was unmarried and we were hosting the dinner for the festival tonight, I took my place at the head of the room, at a large table raised on the dais looking out on all the others below. I hated these events but smiled the way Mother had taught me.

I allowed him to pull my chair out and push it in once I was seated. The men at the table stood until I had taken my place, then sat and resumed their own conversations. A quick scan of the table showed the faces I'd expected. My mother and father, my brother and two sisters, as well as most of my extended relatives. My aunt and uncle, cousins, and a few high-ranking and important visitors. I smiled broadly, unable to hide my delight when I realized I had been seated next to my great-uncle, Jorel.

"It's wonderful to see you here tonight, Uncle!" The last time I'd seen him had been at least five years ago. His eyes

CHAPTER 2

sparkled as brightly as ever, but he seemed older than I remembered. Or perhaps it was I who had changed.

He smiled back, tipping his head slightly. "Lovely to see you as well, my young Rhiniya. I was asking your mother about you earlier and she expressed some dismay at your most recent *past time*."

I could tell from the look on his face he meant no judgment, and in fact, appeared intrigued instead, his bushy eyebrows drawn together as he waited for my answer.

I inclined my head, unable to resist the chance for a willing ear to discuss my latest idea with. I hadn't even bothered mentioning it to my parents, let alone my sisters. My brother was so busy preparing for battle with the other elves I'd hardly seen him around the house at all, so he was also out as a confidant. But I could tell my uncle was interested in what I had to say when he leaned forward and rested his elbows on the table.

"Ever since the news came, I've been looking in the old textbooks in the library, trying to figure out what it was Onen Suun did to trap Dag'draath in the prison."

He quickly looked around, then leaned closer when I stopped, feeling dumb. I sounded like a naïve schoolgirl recounting an assignment. I flushed, ready to turn away and change the subject, but he dropped his voice to a whisper meant only for my ears.

"Have you found anything? The library at Cliffside is one of the best in all the elven territories. Anything in there to help defeat Dag'draath?"

My temporary fit of nerves abated at his clear interest. I leaned closer to answer in a conspiratorial tone. "There were two books I found, each with black leather bindings. They seemed to have paragraphs mirroring each other, only they were slightly different. One spoke of the High Dragons, while another spoke of an artifact. I'd found a few more, but..." I cast an exasperated glance toward the head table and the guests below.

"Then duty called, did it?" He laughed again, before shaking his head. "Never you mind. I'm sure you've planned some excuse to slip away later." He slyly looked over his shoulder to where my mother sat, engrossed in conversation with a traveler.

I pursed my lips but didn't answer. It was true I'd already planned my way out, but I didn't need to share that with anyone and confirm their suspicions. I changed the subject, keeping my voice low. "What do you know about how Onen Suun ended the Dark War? I've only found hints in those textbooks I mentioned, but you've been around a little longer than I have. Perhaps you've heard something?"

As delicacy wasn't always my strong point, I'd asked a little more bluntly than was necessarily polite, but he didn't seem to mind. He leaned back, stroking his long silver beard, then allowed his hand to drop to an old amulet he wore around his neck. He fiddled with it for a moment as he considered my question. Just when I was ready to scream at the suspense, he finally bent his head back toward mine and answered in a whisper no one else could hear above the din of the festival around us.

"I do remember a few tales, but likely not important enough to be of any great assistance. I believe it was the dragons who did most of the work in sealing the prison of Dag'draath." He paused, raising an eyebrow. "That's actually where the Bruhier Elves started. A group of elves known as the deep elves joined the fight on Suun's side, but almost all were lost in the attempt."

His face was solemn. Sadness at the loss of elven lives was deep amongst my people because we were such a long-lived group. To lose any prematurely was a great tragedy, let alone to lose an entire tribe at once. I vaguely recalled hearing of them before, but it was obviously before my time.

"Are those the same ones the forest elves call the Dead Clan?"

CHAPTER 2

15

He pressed his lips together. "The very same. The deep elves who lived became known as the Bruhier Elves, but because only a handful of the original force remained, many of the elven clans began to refer to them the Dead Clan. They prefer being called Bruhier Elves." He sighed. "Many good men, elven and otherwise, were lost in that dark time. It breaks my heart to think the same circumstances are unfolding again."

My heart twisted in agreement. I was about to ask another question about the dragon connection, but my aunt leaned across my uncle to glare at me instead. "Rhiniya, *darling*. I couldn't help overhear what you and Jorel were talking about." She gave me a look of disappointment, her entire head sparkling with jewels, while she wiggled her shining hand at me in disapproval.

I took a deep breath and managed to compose myself. I had to hide my judgment, but it was hard to prevent an eye-roll when I realized she was wearing a tiara. She looked like a princess four decades past her prime. Aunt Bhārjini was not my favorite, and I considered her a perfect example of what happened when you encouraged women to look pretty and marry well above everything else. Not for me.

I gritted my teeth as I gave her a smile I hoped passed for polite, responding as mildly as I could. "I was just asking Uncle Jorel about the lost tribe and the Dark War. I read—"

She snorted, a surprisingly crass and unladylike sound, waving her hand airily in front of my face. It smelled like meat and I pulled back slightly. "Oh, my dear, no wonder your cousins think you're so odd. You need to stop putting your nose in those musty, dead books and settle down, get married already. No one wants a wife who spends all her time in a library. You'd make better use of your time if you acted more like your sisters." She looked pointedly at my polite, demure, and wonderfully ladylike sisters, seated beside my mother.

I could see they'd placed the most honored guests close to them. My sisters would be doing an admirable job entertaining, faking laughter at every sentence oozing from the diplomats while batting their eyelashes incessantly. I had to bite back a snort of my own, as I wouldn't have made my mother nearly as proud if they'd tried the same thing with me. Tact wasn't one of my strengths, let alone buttering up puffed-up politicians. Oh well. I'd rather sit next to an interesting old elf than a diplomat I needed to simper for.

I tried to focus on my breathing and not embarrass my parents as I responded to my aunt through gritted teeth. "Yes, Aunt Bhārjini, I'm working on it, but I thank you for your concern. How is Uncle Leil these days?"

And she was off. No longer concerned about my marriage, as I'd hoped, she was instantly distracted. Unfortunately, that meant the rest of the supper was filled listening to her as she droned on while Uncle Jorel and I interjected the occasional murmur to prove we were still present.

In the distance, the chime signaling the end of the meal sounded and filled me with a mixture of frustration and relief. While it did mean I could escape my long-winded and shallow aunt, I was disappointed I'd run out of time to ask my uncle any further questions about the Dark War.

Servants moved around the room as they cleared the tables of plates. As people below the dais stood from their tables, other servants efficiently whisked them away, leaving the space open for the traditional after-dinner dancing for the festival. Strains of harp and flute music began, and I forced myself to be strong. Each time we hosted a festival dance I was besieged by invitations, each time progressively more painful than the last.

Dancing wasn't natural for me. I could dance when pressed, but it wasn't my favorite pastime. If my father hadn't been who he was, I would have been left in peace to sit along the sidelines with the other socially awkward elves. Even now, my father was surrounded by young elves lined up at the table where he still sat. When a few cast speculative glances my way,

CHAPTER 2

I groaned. Why couldn't they ask me instead of my father? Or better yet, just leave me alone?

I fondly remembered the spell I used as a child to hide from my parents but ruled it out immediately. Someone in the room would certainly be able to see through it, including my mother and at least one of my sisters, which would draw more negative attention to me when I was caught. And if I was going to escape, attention was the last thing I wanted.

Instead, I searched for my co-conspirator among the servants who were darting in and out of the revelers who'd begun to dance. When I spotted Sel waiting patiently beside the door, I felt relieved. We locked eyes. I widened mine, giving him *the look*, which was basically me looking panicked. To the casual observer, he appeared to simply be going about his duties, but the faint twitch of his nose and the minuscule upturn at the corner of his mouth as he walked toward me told me he was able to both recognize and be amused at my desperation.

Just as my aunt was about to launch into another story, he miraculously appeared by my left elbow, bowing deeply, and keeping his eyes turned to the floor.

"I am sorry to interrupt the festivities, milady, but there's an important missive waiting for you in the library."

I quickly jumped to my feet, flashing my aunt a look of apology while doing my best to suppress a smile. "I'm so sorry, Aunt Bhārjini, Uncle Jorel. I've been waiting for this letter all day and it cannot wait. Please, excuse me. I shall return as soon as I'm able."

My aunt raised her eyebrows so high they almost touched her perfectly styled bangs, but when I leaned forward to whisper, *"It's from a boy,"* in a conspiratorial tone, her suspicion melted away to be immediately replaced with more excitement than the sentence warranted.

"Well," she said, her left hand fluttering to her throat. "Don't make the man wait! This could be your only chance."

She shooed me away with the other hand, the flickering of her gemstones almost blinding me again. "I shall look forward to your return."

I gave her a grateful look I didn't have to fake, curtsying before hurrying off. Sel and I strode through the almost deserted hallways toward the library. It was silent away from the great hall where the banquet was being held, and I relaxed at the absence of noise. It was just the way I liked it.

The dancing had just begun, but my head was already pounding from the noise of so many elves in one place. I looked around surreptitiously, expecting someone to catch me and tell me I needed to go back to the dance. But no one did. When we arrived safely at the library, I nearly slammed the door behind me as I leaned on it to catch my breath.

He shot me a mischievous smile, which I answered in kind.

"Well, that was the most fun I've had all evening," I chuckled, walking away from the door and back to the table. I was pleased to note none of the books had been touched. While I hadn't expected them to be taken, there was always the chance an overzealous servant could have put everything away and lost my place in my selections.

I sank into the hardback chair I'd been in earlier, wincing as my elaborate dress crinkled, creating hard, uncomfortable lumps underneath me. I wistfully remembered the plain dress I'd been wearing earlier, thinking how much more comfortable it had been. I didn't have much time, but Uncle Jorel's words had inspired me to keep looking in the texts. Before I called it a night, I wanted to see what was inside the books I'd not yet had a chance to look in.

I spread them out, fashioning a rough triangle. I flipped one open and began to read, but as every moment passed, I became more frustrated. "How in the name of Onen Suun himself could anybody understand what any of this means?"

I gritted my teeth, looking for anything related to the ritual, the artifacts, or the Dark War in general. I reviewed the pages on which I'd found the original information, finding the two complementary passages, then moved on to the other three books.

I remembered chapter headings, which seemed to correspond to the ones in the first two and began by focusing on the book to the left of the bottom row. The paragraph briefly touched on the artifact, but once again with irritatingly vague details, mentioning a sacrifice as well, but also not in any detail. What was different about this book was the mention of the Temple of the Suun.

I leaned closer, squinting as I tried to make out the words. It appeared to have been written in the same hand, but it was even harder to decipher, as though this person spoke another mother-tongue, and had translated the text into this language. It was also irritatingly vague, without the specific information I needed to figure out where to go next. I sighed, moving my attention to the book in the middle, and found the same chapter heading corresponding to the other three books.

"Oh, for the love of…"

The sound of muffled laughter greeted my ears. I turned to glare at Sel, still standing at his perch beside the door. He looked relaxed and amused, which made me even more irritated.

"You wouldn't think it was so funny if you were the one who couldn't figure this out."

He raised a shoulder, giving me a half smile. "Perhaps it's time to put the books away for the night." He turned, pointedly looking toward the banquet hall. "Your lady mother will have noticed your absence by now."

He was right, but I couldn't help feeling I was missing something. Each passage showed me a glimpse into what may have happened when they'd finally succeeded in trapping Dag'draath. But I didn't have enough to go on.

Having memorized the passages I needed and allowing myself notes as well, I took his advice. We carefully packed the books I'd need into a safe spot for morning so that they wouldn't be disturbed, leaving the others on the table. I couldn't be sure the books wouldn't be disturbed in the night by a serving cleaning. I stretched as I sat down at the table, then remembered something my uncle had said.

At the time, it had been a throwaway sentence which I'm sure hadn't meant much to him. But now, amid my frustration, his words came back to haunt me.

"Your library is one of the best in the elven territories."

It wasn't the statement which had been important, but it had reminded me my answers could lie elsewhere. Perhaps the reason I was so frustrated wasn't because of my lack of knowledge, but because the information I required was hiding somewhere else. At least, I hoped it wasn't my own deficiency making this so difficult. I slumped in the chair, glaring at the books in front of me for a moment before carefully cleaning myself off. I nodded to Sel as I stood. It was time to return to the festival before Mother sent servants to find me.

She would not be pleased to find me in the library instead of at the banquet being a dutiful daughter. For now, responsibility called. Mysteries must wait.

CHAPTER 3

After we'd cleaned up, I'd gone back to the festival and behaved as politely as possible, acquiescing to my family's suggestions. I had danced with each eligible suitor my parents placed before me, recognizing several from the line of supplicants who'd been vying to speak with my father when the dance had begun.

I wouldn't have minded so much if they were actually interested in me, but half of the time they wanted to know if my father was looking for a new protegé, or asked about one of my sisters. I may not be interested in marriage and romance, but it was still insulting to have a dance partner ask nothing about my interests. When I wasn't dancing with the young elves, I was stuck faking laughter at stories from boring old elves at the correct intervals, wishing it was my uncle instead of foreign diplomats who smelled strongly of drink.

By the time I managed to escape, it was late, and my feet were sore. I gratefully accepted Dara's help getting ready for bed, not even attempting conversation. I had just enough energy left to put my notebook in the drawer of my bedside table before I fell into a dreamless sleep.

When I awoke the sun was already high in the sky, which

meant I'd wasted valuable time. Dara helped me dress, and I didn't bother to eat, instead heading straight for the library before I was required to do something else.

Grateful for the reprieve from questions and interruptions, I painstakingly laid out the books again. As I'd expected, the rest of the books had been put away at some point during the night. Pleased at our cleverness, I settled into the chair and set to work.

Laying my books out, I placed my notebook on the table. The sound of my quill tapping the page echoed around me as I considered what I knew so far. I had five books with matching bindings, which appeared to have been written by the same unknown hand. Each book had a chapter with the same passage, alluding to paragraphs in the other books, but each passage was slightly different and didn't touch upon the things in the other chapters in much detail.

The creak of the door startled me, and I tensed, only relaxing when Sel's calm face poked around the large wooden door. I gave him a sheepish grin.

"I had a feeling I'd find you here." He assumed the relaxed, watchful position he favored.

"I feel like I'm close to something. I just can't quite decide what." I wrinkled my nose, "Were there any other books? Anything else in the back room we might have overlooked?"

He walked over to me. "Was there something in particular you were looking for?"

I scratched my head. "I'm not sure. Do you see here, this part?" I tapped the passage that mentioned the Temple of the Suun, "I feel like this part is important, but I don't have it sorted out in my head yet."

"Let me look. I think I found a book mentioning the Bruhier Elves yesterday."

My head whipped around. "The Bruhier Elves? Why would you mention them now?"

He raised an eyebrow. "Just a feeling I had." His words

CHAPTER 3

sounded smug, but when he looked at me, he relented. "I watched you having a conversation with your uncle. If anybody knows old stories, it would be him."

I absently bit on my quill, immediately spitting it out. "Yuck," I brushed my mouth off, but I was certain it was stained with the ink. By the time I'd finished removing the taste, Sel was gone. I tried to see where he'd vanished to, but he was already returning from the stacks with another ornately decorated blue book.

It wasn't as massive as the black ones, but it would have still made a decent weapon if you wanted to hit someone over the head. Like maybe my Aunt Bhārjini. I grinned as I allowed myself to imagine a scenario which involved me hitting her over the head when she told me to get married to make my parents proud.

"Thank you. Wow, this book looks ancient."

I ran my hand over the binding, enjoying the way the blue seemed to almost ripple in the warm light of the library, the shade fluctuating between the blue of the ocean and the darkness of the night. Yellow jewels were arranged in a diamond shape on the front cover, and as I flipped it open, I discovered the identical, difficult handwriting I'd seen in the black-covered tomes.

My heart began to pound with excitement. Could this finally be what I needed? I placed the blue-covered book in front of the black-covered ones. When I squinted, I realized the handwriting was subtly different even though the language was the same. I didn't know if it was because of the dialect, or simply due to the passage of time since it had been written, but it felt almost as if I was reading a foreign language.

I immediately lost track of time, immersed in trying to decipher the words in front of me. It wasn't until the familiar *click, click, click* of high-heeled slippers sounded on the tile just beside me that my head snapped up. My eyes widened and heat crept over my cheeks.

"So, this is where you've taken yourself off to?" My mother looked at the books on the table, wrinkling her nose.

She rubbed her arms, and I realized with some surprise it was chillier than usual in the library. I looked down at the table, wondering what she would think if she knew what I was trying to find. Somehow, over the course of the morning I'd managed to fill the table with books again.

"I was reading something last night, Mother, and I wanted to see if I'd understood it correctly." I followed her gaze to the books spread in front of me. "I must've lost track of time." I shrugged. "Did you need me for something?" I wasn't surprised when she answered in the affirmative.

"Yes. A few of the guests from last night are staying for supper. I wanted to ensure you were available and prepared to entertain them this afternoon. One of them, Sjen, has professed an interest in discussing our library's holdings. I would like you to be polite to him, and if he were to happen to find you personally interesting, I do not think I need to tell you your father and I would find him acceptable." She absently checked the fingernails on her left hand, then looked over my clothing, wrinkling her nose. "I'd like you to be ready within the hour. Dara can assist you with the appropriate attire. I've already spoken with her about what I would like you to wear today."

My head dropped in defeat. "Yes, Mother. I'll finish here, and be ready within the hour, as you wish."

My mother gave me a cool smile of approval before she walked away.

I loved my mother and knew she loved me, but we were completely different. At times, I felt as if my family and I had drifted so far apart we'd never find a way back. Over the last year, I'd fallen deeper into my books as the noble elves and warriors had fallen deeper into preparing for a war we didn't want. I was looking for an answer that would save my people from fighting and dying, and my mother was looking for an advantageous match for marriage. Apparently, the best way

CHAPTER 3

she could think of to ensure the survival of our people was for me to spend the rest of my life as a broodmare and a figurehead.

Well, I didn't think so.

I got up, closing the book I'd been reading with a snap, and walked over to the window, unsurprised to see only half the warriors in the courtyard today. They were still preparing, but the celebrations last night had left some with headaches, I was sure.

I'd already painstakingly copied out the important passages from the five black-bound books, and sometime during the morning, I'd added the important bits from the blue one as well. Sel, as swift and efficient as always, replaced the books on the shelves almost as fast as I was able to close them.

I was walking between the window and the table, hoping that the act of moving would jar something loose in my mind, when a passage in an old history book caught my eye. It spoke of a lost manuscript, written by Piotr the Elder. My hand fell away from the text as I recalled what I'd read over the past few days and what my Uncle Jorel had mentioned about the Bruhier Elves.

This particular manuscript was no longer lost. Instead, it had been discovered in the Library at Abrecem Secer only a year earlier.

I jotted down the title of the manuscript and the words "Abrecem Secer" and reluctantly headed to my duties. Even though I'd done so grudgingly, I was ready within the hour as I'd promised. I loved my parents and my family. I just didn't want what they wanted.

It was difficult for me to explain even to myself how I felt, but I was a dutiful daughter. I joined my mother and sisters to fulfill my obligations, even if the idea of the afternoon ahead made me cringe.

On the surface, the guests we were entertaining were interesting. Several younger elves were present for a change, having come along with the elder statesmen, so it wasn't all boring, lecherous old men. One was even attractive, and I watched with amusement as both my sisters vied for his attention.

Luckily for me, the elf my mother had wanted me to entertain was older and more studious than the others and clearly as interested in matrimony as I—not at all. He had kind violet eyes that he wore spectacles to brighten and we had just begun discuss the Library at Abrecem Secer. I was excited to hear what he'd thought of it and whether he knew of the book written by Piotr the Elder when my mother's alarmed voice cut through our discussion.

"Do you hear that?"

I'd never heard my mother's voice sound anything other than sedate and polished, even when I was in trouble. But now, fear was the only thing I could recognize. A split second later, the early warning alarm deafened me, and I clapped my hands over my ears.

I'd never heard it before, but there was no mistaking what it was. Within seconds, every available warrior was racing past the sunroom to the ramparts and the armory, including the handsome elf my sisters had been swooning over.

I stood, knocking my chair over behind me. My heart raced as I watched in stunned silence as activity erupted. My father, who'd been discussing politics with another guest, jumped to his feet and rushed out of the sunroom, along with every other able-bodied man in the room. The elder elf I'd been conversing with had a wistful look on his face, and I frowned when he stayed seated. Other than him, it was only my sisters and mother who had remained in the room.

"What's happening?" My heart was still racing from the unexpected excitement, but at least the volume of the alarm had decreased enough that I could hear myself.

He pointed his chin toward the men who'd now vanished from sight. "That sound means we are being attacked by

CHAPTER 3

ur'gels." He regarded me solemnly. "If I'm not mistaken, it isn't just Cliffside being attacked, but the castle as well." He stood, his hand resting on a decorative cane which I hadn't noticed earlier. "If you ladies will follow me, we should move to a safer location."

I critically examined the bright, sunlit room with its large windows. If we were under attack, this room was not a great location to be. The inner courtyard was the most secure location, in the very center of the castle.

My room, as well as those of the rest of the family, were organized around it, with all our windows facing inside. The idea that I would be trapped if the walls were breached made my chest clench. Surely, there was another option.

I pressed my lips together as I waited for my mother, sisters, and a few of my cousins, along with my irritating Aunt Bhārjini, to stop panicking and follow Lord Sjen. Our manservants met us outside the door and flanked the women in front and behind. It was the first time I'd ever seen any of them walk in front.

When we finally gathered in the courtyard, I watched as the others milled around, crying and shaking. My youngest sister even managed a decent swoon at one point after she'd worked herself up enough. After only a few minutes, I knew I would be ill if I had to stay and watch them wringing their hands and wailing.

"Please, Mother, I'm not feeling at all well. I'd love to return to my room and rest. I promise I'll send Dara out if I need anything."

My mother dismissed me with barely a glance, nervous and visibly paler than usual. "Fine, fine, go rest. We should all retire to our chambers. You may send Dara or Sel if you would like to speak with me."

I curtsied, leaving before she changed her mind. Once back in my chambers, I turned to Sel the second the door shut. "I need to get out of here. If we're under attack already, we're no longer safe at Cliffside. We're running out of time and I can't wait any longer. I have to do something before it's too late."

He looked at me, eyes full of concern, and I remembered how young he was. "I'm not sure you know what you're proposing. You've never been outside these walls alone. You won't last five minutes if someone sees you, let alone if an ur'gel gets to you first."

I clenched my fist as irritation and impatience outweighed my fear. "I can't just stay here, simpering and wringing my hands like my stupid sisters and cousins, waiting for a man or an alliance to save my people. I may not know how to fight, but I have a brain, and I'd like to think it's a good one. I found something I believe means I need to go to Abrecem Secer. I'm positive I can figure out what the ritual and the artifact are if I can just get there. If I can find the information I need, maybe I can stop this war before too many lives are lost, and send Dag'-draath away for good this time."

He grimaced, running his hands through his floppy hair and causing it to stand up, and I knew he was considering helping me.

I pressed the advantage my words had gained me. "Come on, help me escape. I couldn't live with myself if someone I love dies because I just sat here and did nothing. What if the answers *are* in Abrecem Secer? I must go, I need to find out if my theory is right. I'm useless here, but if I can get there... Please, help me?"

He sighed and dropped his head, and I knew I'd won him over.

I grabbed him, squeezing his thin, gangly frame in a giant hug. When he stiffened in surprise, I realized I'd never hugged him before. He was even thinner than he looked. I pulled back awkwardly and gave him a sheepish smile.

"Sorry. Don't worry, I won't make hugging a habit. Tell me what to pack. If you can point me in the right direction and keep my mother distracted long enough for me to get a head

CHAPTER 3

29

start, that would be wonderful. You can tell her where I've gone after I leave."

He raised an eyebrow. "Do you really think I'm going to let you leave here unescorted?"

"What do you mean? I'm capable of looking out for myself." I felt my hackles rise, which transformed into full-blown irritation when he started laughing. I crossed my arms, glaring at him.

"I'm sorry, but you've got no idea how to read a map, and hardly even know how to ride a horse." He crossed his arms, mirroring my stance, his jaw set stubbornly. "I'm coming with you."

When I opened my mouth, he held up a hand.

"There's no point in arguing. I may only be a slave here, but I'm making it my choice to come with you on this hare-brained mission." He raised an eyebrow. "While you've been a decent mistress, I wouldn't be going with you if I didn't believe you knew what you were doing. If anyone can find a way to trap Dag'draath, it's you and your quirky brain."

I blushed at the unexpected praise. "Thanks. But as I'm sure you're aware, we may be heading to our death. I don't want you to sacrifice yourself for me."

He gave me a mischievous smile. "Don't worry, I've got no intention of dying. Besides, it's time we both see a little bit more of the world, don't you think?"

My face split into a grin, unable to believe my friend was willing to throw his lot in with me. I was terrified at my audacity but somehow, having Sel at my side made it feel like an adventure.

I changed into an old pair of leggings and a tunic my brother used when he'd first begun his training. I was positive my mother had no idea I'd had Sel steal them for me, and I'd kept them hidden away at the back of my closet for several years, hoping to one day use them.

Today was that day.

I packed an old leather satchel that had been my father's when he'd been a messenger for my grandfather a century ago and took one last look around my room, spotting my notebook and writing implements. Grabbing them, my heart skipped a beat at the possibility I could have forgotten them.

Scribbling a note to my mother on a sheet of paper in my notebook, I tried to explain my reasoning, but gave up. Instead, I told her that I loved her and Father, and to let my brother and sisters know that no matter how much we fought, they meant the world to me.

I sighed, feeling as if my love of words had somehow failed me, then placed my notebook and quill carefully within my satchel. I looked at Sel.

"Ready to go?" He held out his hand. I placed mine in his and squeezed.

"I'm as ready as I'll ever be. Now, let's go stop this war."

I placed an envelope with the note for my mother on the bed, turned my back, and walked away from my life.

CHAPTER 4

I was extremely relieved Sel was with me. When it came to sneaking away from the castle without being observed, I knew that he would be far better at it than I. As I'd noticed more than once, no one ever looked at the servants, and he was more adept at appearing out of nowhere than most.

He led me from my wing of the castle away from the center of the castle, away from safety. I'd hardly ever left Cliffside and hadn't been past the Low Forest before, and I knew it was why my heart was racing with a strange exhilaration.

The first step was getting out of the castle. With the castle under attack, the usual exits weren't an option. I'd never tried to leave without notice before, but Sel appeared unfazed as I followed him silently down the servants' stairs, acting as if it were a regular day and he was going about his work.

Surprisingly, the servants' stairs led all the way down to a hard-packed earthen cellar which smelled of harvest and root vegetables. Once we arrived, he flashed a quick smile. "Keeping up okay, Princess?"

I glared. "I'm not a princess. As for your actual question, I'm fine. How are we going to get out? I was under the impression that everything was locked up tight."

He smirked. "All of the known exits and entrances are. But, no one ever notices the comings and goings of servants on their daily errands. There's a small window over here the kitchen boys like to use to sneak out at night."

I tilted my head, narrowing my eyes suspiciously. "How did you discover that?"

Sel wiggled his eyebrows. "I've been around. I may or may not have used it when I was younger and smaller." He hesitated, and it was like a cloud hiding the brightness of the moon. When I saw the size of the window he was referring to, the reason for his sudden uncertainty was clear.

"You're not sure you can fit through it anymore, are you?" Amusement colored my voice and earned me a surprised look.

"I'm pretty sure..." He paused, looking around the empty storage room before he leaned closer, admitting his real concern. "I'm worried one of the kids will see us and try to follow. As much as you don't want me on your conscience, someone else getting hurt is not something I'm eager to deal with."

I knew that his sense of responsibility would make him worry, but the basement was empty. I assumed everyone else was acting more cautiously than I and were all in the middle of the castle. I should be there instead of contemplating running away from home, yet here I was, about to escape through a window.

I held my breath as Sel went first. He climbed the boxes stacked along the wall, and I was amazed that none fell as he scrambled up. He went legs-first once he reached the window, but it was a tight squeeze, and when he reached his shoulders I thought for one horrible moment he would get stuck, but he made it through after a pause to wiggle his shoulders.

After that point, his exit went smoothly, and he dropped out of sight. When his hand appeared over the windowsill and gestured for me, I let out a sigh of relief.

"Come on, there's no one out here. Quickly, we don't want

CHAPTER 4

that to change." I shivered as his disembodied voice gave me an intense feeling of unease.

I climbed up the same path I'd watched him take to reach the high window without anywhere near the same amount of grace or skill. My arms muscles strained to pull myself up the foot or so between levels of boxes, and I wobbled horribly, almost losing my balance several times.

By the time I reached the ledge, I was uncomfortably sweaty, with loose tendrils of hair plastered against the side of my face. His hand was beckoning faster, so I reached out with my right hand and grabbed on. It was a good thing he was with me, as I relied heavily on his strength to pull me up. Inelegantly, I wiggled far enough across the ledge until I had my legs over, then I fell headfirst into his waiting arms, almost knocking us both over.

Once I was back on my feet, I gave him a quick nod. "Thanks," I huffed, trying to catch my breath. "Apparently, lifting books doesn't give me upper body strength the way I'd hoped it did."

He bit back a chuckle as he looked around. "I'm sure we'll have plenty of time to work on your muscles, if we're headed to the Library at Abrecem Secer." He squinted, not waiting for a response as he pointed his chin. "Come on, there's a path through the woods at the back of the castle we can use to get to town. I've never seen anyone other than humans use it."

"Hopefully, the ur'gels will be busy with their attack on the front of the castle, not planning on a double-pronged assault." I swallowed at my words, falling silent as I considered the possibility.

I hoped he was right about the path being secret. If the ur'gels figured out there was another entrance, they might be able to get in the same way we'd escaped. The first stop on my journey was the Low Forest community outside the castle walls. I wasn't sure they'd received word of what had happened.

34   SOUL GOBLET

I vaguely recalled my brother telling me the alarm had been enchanted to ring throughout the entire community in case of attack to rouse as many warriors as possible. Maybe the elves there would be able to help, or at least be prepared to defend themselves. With that thought in mind, I became even more determined to reach my destination.

The reason I headed for the Low Forest community first wasn't just because it was on the way. Over the last few years, I had struck up a friendship of sorts with another elf around my age. Her name was Gwennael Fuur, a wolf-walker. She wasn't a scholar the way I was, but she was the only elf I could think of who could help me reach the Library.

I'd first seen her when I was much younger and out exploring with my older brother, back when I'd wanted to be just like him. She'd been alone except for a single wolf, and I'd been surprised to see her. It wasn't common to see someone so young all by herself. I waved, but she'd quickly darted away.

Instead of chalking her up as a town elf exploring the forest as we were, something about her had struck me as sad and alone. Over the following weeks and months, I'd deliberately gone searching for her, sometimes with my brother when he'd been in an indulgent mood, but usually with a servant. In time, she'd stopped running away and we'd struck up an odd friendship in the way that only outsiders can. But even then, she'd been tight-lipped about her reason for living in the forest, away from the other elves. The only thing she would say was that her family was the wolves she lived with.

I felt connected to her because of that oddness. Both of us were apart from society in our own way. I'd seen the looks people gave us when we'd meet at the Low Forest market-place, and the way her face would fall before she quickly assumed a blank expression to hide her emotions. She usually had an excuse about something she needed to do and left whenever it happened.

I recognized the look because I'd felt that way frequently

CHAPTER 4

35

when people interacted with me in the castle. It may have been my slightly more acceptable love of books which made me an outcast instead of wolves, but it didn't change how alone I felt. Finding someone else who understood had been indescribably wonderful.

Beyond our mutual solitary status, I'd always admired how she never reacted to the disdain others showed her. Her almost magical ability to connect with wolves and live in the forest was something I wished I could do, and the reason I was trying to find her now.

I ducked a branch that seemed to come out of nowhere and winced at my clumsiness. I would definitely need her to come with me to Abrecem Secer if I wanted to get there in one piece. It was a huge ask, as it was at least three hundred miles away from home. It was just as likely she'd refuse to come. But I needed her help to survive. She had practical knowledge of animals, hunting, and living off the land that would be required to get there. Otherwise, branches would be the least of my concerns.

I trudged along behind Sel, thinking about how many times I'd wished I could throw aside my life at the castle, and now here I was. I still cared about what my family thought, but finding Gwen and reaching Abrecem Secer was the most important thing I could do to protect my loved ones from death at the hands of ur'gels.

While I mulled over how I'd reached this point in life, we traveled swiftly. Sel surprised me by unerringly knowing where to step to make the least amount of noise. Each time I stepped on a twig, I flinched. I was an elf—wasn't I supposed to be naturally more graceful?

I doubled down, working on being aware of my steps, and after some time I was happy to notice I did seem to be making less noise, if not as little as him.

The downside to all the walking was I wasn't used to phys-ical exertion. Soon, my legs and arms were aching in ways I hadn't anticipated. The burning in my thighs reminded me of the time I'd had a fever, and the rivulets of sweat that stuck my tunic to my back were sticky and pungent.

It felt harder than the last time I'd walked to the Low Forest town, but I couldn't remember how long ago that had been. Apparently, the research I'd been doing had left my muscles soft and ill-prepared for what I was now attempting to accomplish. Wistfully, I thought of the drills I'd watched the warriors doing every morning and regretted not trying harder to join them.

I swung my satchel to my back for the millionth time, as it had fallen over in front of me and was impeding my movements again. Sel looked back, noticing my discomfort when I bumped into a small shrub that snugged my pants. I grimaced at the sudden sharpness from a thorn and that must have convinced him I needed a break.

He pointed out a flat spot underneath a large tree beside the path. "We should be far enough away from the castle that the ur'gels won't be near, and I don't think anyone else followed us. Here, have a sip of this."

He threw me a flask, and I was grateful he'd thought ahead far enough to pack food and water. I took a large swallow, feeling even more unprepared that such an important detail hadn't even crossed my mind. What had I been thinking? To pack a small bag with my books, a change of clothing, and head off on a quest to a Library three hundred miles away? With my confidence dropping to my boots, I handed the flask back.

"Thanks. I don't suppose you have any idea how far we are from the Low Forest village?" I felt strangely alone and yet alive for the first time in a way I never had, realizing how much I depended on him.

"Only about another twenty minutes or so, I think. We're taking the long way to town, through the forest. If we'd taken the road, we would've been there by now, but I assumed

CHAPTER 4

secrecy was more important than speed. Unless I was mistaken?"

"No, this route is good. We made it away from the castle unseen, and no one knows which direction we went. Ur'gel or family." I cracked a small smile, wishing I felt as confident as my words sounded.

He nodded, drinking from his flask before recapping it. "I brought food, but if it's all the same to you, I'd like to get to the Low Forest before we stop for a real meal."

I stood, wincing at the soreness of my muscles. "I agree, better to get there and relax after..." I trailed off. I'd never told him why we were headed there. "I was hoping —"

"That Gwen would join us? Don't worry, no one said anything. I like to observe."

When I narrowed my eyes, he chuckled.

"Not like that. I just meant I watch people. Humans and elves. I've noticed in general that the smartest person in any room is the person watching without speaking. I'm hoping to one day be that person. "

He'd never said anything so introspective before, but looking back, it made sense. I'd always thought him quiet by nature, but he was saying he was quiet because he was practicing restraint and trying to learn wisdom, not because he didn't have anything to say. I felt even more confident in his skills now.

"That sounds like something I need to practice." I laughed for a moment, before returning to his original statement. "I was hoping to find Gwen because she's brave, confident, and knows how to survive in the Low Forest. I'm just not sure she'll want to come on this mission, especially since I haven't seen her for a while."

I looked away from him into the trees so I didn't have to meet his eyes, then admitted my weakness in a quiet voice. "I wish I were more like her. Maybe I wouldn't let everyone push me around so much." I tried to hide it, but I could hear the sadness leaking out.

He put a hand on my shoulder and patted it reassuringly. "Nonsense, you've got your own kind of bravery. That's a big part of why I came with you. I have to say this is the craziest scheme you've ever come up with, but I trust your reasons. If I help you get to Abrecem Secer, you'll stand a good chance of achieving your goal. Which, based on the timing of the attacks, I'm assuming is to find a way to stop the upcoming war everyone is worried about?"

"Yes, it is. If I could just figure out a way to lock Dag'-draath back up in his cage, the way Onen Suun did after the Dark War, I think we could end what is promising to be another era of devastation before it begins." I looked at him, pressing my lips together as I considered the fate of my world if I failed.

He stared into my eyes for a moment before he stood. "Then I guess it's time for us to get moving. Are you ready?"

With my aching muscles protesting, I got to my feet with difficulty and followed him through the narrow cow-path through the forest. The break had helped, but I shivered as the cool breeze dried my damp clothing. Luckily for my poor, deconditioned body, he'd been correct when he'd told me it was only a short distance away.

I'd never entered the Low Forest town from the forest path before, having always taken the main trade route with a caravan of traders, on foot with my brother, or in my parents' luxurious traveling coach.

When we arrived, the town was quiet. From the way the sky had darkened, I imagined everyone was tucked into their houses, eating supper with their loved ones after a day's hard work. I wondered how my family was doing. I bit my lip to hold back a sob, hoping that they were safe from the ur'gels, trying to brush my worry aside. There was nothing I could do for them back there, but if I was able to get to Gwen and the

CHAPTER 4   39

leader of the Low Forest elves, perhaps I could still help them.

He halted abruptly, causing me to nearly collide with his back. He held up his hand without turning as he continued to peer blindly into the darkness behind us. "There's something out there." His voice was barely a whisper.

I tensed. "What do you mean? Aren't we safe here, within the town?"

He tightened his lips. "We're still on the outskirts, nowhere near where we need to be to notify anyone important of an oncoming attack. I can feel something in the woods, something that wasn't out there a little while ago."

He looked worried but at his words I relaxed. The only creatures I knew who could be so quiet and who hung out in the area we were currently approaching were with the very elves I wanted to find.

I turned, looking into the darkness falling around us. "Gwen? Are you there?"

"Shush! How do you know it's her?" He glared, looking at me as if I'd gone crazy.

"I don't, but I can't hear anything. If you can feel something we can't hear, it probably means there're wolves nearby."

Sel scowled. I'd never seen him angry before. It wasn't a good look for him.

"You don't know you're right," he muttered, crossing his arms.

I turned and glared at him. "Look, if there is somebody or something out there who wanted to kill us, they already know we're here. We're standing directly under the lights. If it's Gwen and her wolves, they know we're here as well. Either way, I don't think it's going to change anything if we announce our presence." I gestured at the houses we were passing. "If nothing else, someone might hear us and help us if we are attacked. Assuming they hear us, which they won't if we don't say anything."

He relented, but I noticed his shoulders remained tense. "Fine. But the next time you feel like shouting into the forest when we're trying to be quiet, don't."

I suppressed a smile. Yelling into the wilderness could have been suicide. I probably would have been too frightened to do it if it hadn't been for one small thing he hadn't noted. A tuft of grey hair, just behind the tree to my left, which was the exact same color as Gwen's bonded wolf, Swift.

With hardly even a crackle of the dried leaves on the ground, Gwen stepped out from the trees, followed by Swift so close to her left knee they practically touched. He was a large, majestic animal with ice-blue eyes that seemed to look into my soul. I often thought part of the reason the villagers shunned Gwen was because of how wise he looked.

Swift reached just past Gwen's waist, which was the perfect height for her to rest her left hand comfortably on the back of his neck. She tossed her golden hair back over her shoulder and cocked one eyebrow at me. In that moment, she looked like a savage queen, with her dark green eyes flashing with curiosity.

"Rhin? What brings you out here? And without an entourage." She looked around in confusion until I pointed at Sel. Now she looked shocked.

"Wait a minute, let me get this straight. Princess Rhin—"

"I'm not a princess," I corrected.

Gwen rolled her eyes. "Okay, Rhiniya of the Cliff Elves, daughter of the Lord of the Cliff Elves, is in the woods of the Low Forest with a single human servant to protect her. What alternate universe have I walked into?"

I wrinkled my nose. "Okay, when you say it like that, it does sound a little out of the ordinary," I began, causing Gwen to give me a look. "Fine. Cliffside was attacked. Everyone else is still in the castle. I escaped with Sel and we're on our way to Abrecem Secer to look for a book in the Library to stop the oncoming war. I have a bad feeling what's

CHAPTER 4

41

coming will rival the Dark War, and I'm not sure any of our people will make it this time if I don't do something. I came here looking for you and to warn the villagers to be prepared."

Gwen's expression changed to wide-eyed disbelief. "Are you okay? What do you mean, 'attacked'? Who attacked Cliffside? I thought the castle was impenetrable."

I took several deep breaths to compose myself as the memory of the alarm going off and the frantic action afterward caused my heart to race the same way it had the first time. I realized I didn't even know if my family was alive and had to bite back the sting of tears.

"Yeah, so did I. We were attacked by ur'gels, right before we took off. I didn't want to chance getting stuck inside the castle when I know there's information out here that could help us win, help us defeat Dag'draath for good this time. I know it sounds silly, but I can't explain it any better."

Gwen's face shifted, a series of unreadable emotions like storm clouds passing over it. In reality, we didn't really know each other all that well because of the distance between our lives. I knew I was asking a lot of her, but I was hoping she'd find my idea exciting and come along.

Her long fingers tightened in the fur around Swift's neck, as if she was gathering his energy somehow, and two more wolves appeared from the trees to flank her. They were smaller, and looked younger as well. Gwen smiled down at the wolves, communicating wordlessly with them as I waited.

When she looked at me again, it was with an intensity that made me redden.

"Rhin," she started, pausing to bite her bottom lip. "You've got interesting ideas and you love your books almost as much as I love my wolves. If you think there's something in a far-away Library to prevent all of Lynia from going to hell, I'm in."

"Really? I mean, I'd love it if you joined me, but I didn't think you'd say yes, let alone volunteer yourself. I mean, I have no idea what I'm walking into, and there's a huge chance I'm not going to make it home."

Gwen shrugged, exuding strength as she stood, legs hip-width apart in her forest-green leggings and oak-colored tunic, looking exactly how I imagined a goddess of the forest would look. She had a face that on first glance I'd thought sweet and innocent, until I'd noticed the stubborn jaw and warm green eyes that had shadows of pain in their depths.

"Let's face it, Princess. If we don't do anything, no one will have a home to go back to. From what I've heard, the last time Dag'draath was free it almost destroyed our planet. If you have a plan to stop him, I'm willing to take my chances with you and your big brain."

From the corner of my eye I caught Sel shaking his head and muttering something under his breath. It sounded suspiciously like, "She's as nuts as Rhin. What have I gotten myself into?"

I shot him a glare, but he pretended not to notice, avoiding my eyes by looking at the path. I ignored him, thinking instead about what Gwen had said. She was right. If we didn't do anything, there may not be anything to go back to.

From what my brother had shared with my sisters and me against my father's wishes, the ur'gels were completely merciless and enjoyed killing for the sake of it. I'd only ever seen pictures, but that had been enough to fill my veins with ice. I could only hope Cliffside held out long enough for me to have a family to go home to after I found answers.

"Thank you, Gwen. I was hoping you would come." I cast my eyes down, kicking at the forest floor as I hid my lack of confidence. "I was hoping your animal and forest skills would complement my knowledge base."

Gwen snorted inelegantly. "You think I'd let you travel by yourself? I know you don't like it when I call you 'Princess', but you basically are one. I also suspect you think you know

CHAPTER 4   43

more about the world than you do because of your book learning, but the real world is quite different."

She looked down at the wolves surrounding her. Once again, I couldn't hear a word, but watched curiously as the three wolves scattered.

"Where did they go?" I was impressed by the soundless exchange.

Gwen shot me a smug glance. "I told them to go eat something. I'm not sure when the next time I'll have ready food for them will be. If the ur'gels are attacking the castle, they'll be here soon. We need to get moving, or we won't make it to the Library. You mentioned you wanted to raise the alarm?"

"Yes, I was hoping to notify the Low Forest townsfolk, maybe get extra fighters for the castle and Cliffside."

Gwen looked at my bag, raising her eyebrows. "Do you have something I can write with?"

Reluctantly I passed Gwen my notebook and winced as she ripped a page out. I handed her my quill and ink and she quickly scribbled a note, folding it several times. She repeated the process twice more. When she was finished, her wolves had returned. To my surprise, each wolf was wearing what appeared to be a leather collar, but as Gwen placed a letter in each of the wolf's neckbands, I realized they were functional as well as identifying.

The wolves raced off, splitting into three directions as Gwen watched. Once they were out of sight, she turned to me and inclined her head, gesturing for us to follow her.

"Come on. I've sent Swift, Kiya, and Daimyo to the people who need to be notified. By the time they return, I should be packed. We need to leave immediately if the Cliffs are under attack."

Sel and I followed without question and I realized one of the large trees I'd completely ignored on our way through the forest had ladder-stairs fashioned into the large trunk. There were rope handholds, and the slats were directly inserted into the tree itself. It looked sturdy, but I climbed up hesitantly, having never been in a tree before. My thighs groaned at the new exertion almost loudly enough to drown out the pounding of my heart in my ears.

When Gwen looked back at me to make sure I was okay, I gave her a bright smile. I didn't want her to know I was nervous about the height, but I was sure that I looked like a trapped animal. If she looked at my hands, white-knuckled on the ropes, I was certain she'd know but I was oddly reluctant to show my fear. I wanted her to be proud of me, which was something I'd only worried about with my family in the past.

My thoughts were distracting enough that I was able to get to the top without difficulty. When I reached the platform where Gwen stood, I looked around, impressed by how comfortable her place was. From the ground, I hadn't known anything was even up here, but Gwen had done an excellent job making the place look homey.

There was a wide platform for sleeping. Did she sleep with the wolves? Wait—how do the wolves get into the treehouse? Wolves generally didn't climb trees. Or did they? I hadn't read anything about that, but I'd never researched wolves, so maybe it was possible.

The rest of her home was small. A small cook stove in one corner caught my attention. It appeared well used and there was a small shelf beside it with plates and utensils. Next to that was a contraption with buckets I imagined she used to bring water into the house. It was rustic and yet the entire setup was perfect for her. She seemed to have everything she needed in the small space, and nothing extra.

I turned to see what Gwen was doing to find her in the act of tying up a small leather bag that she quickly threw over her shoulder. She took one last look around her home before coming back to me, a solemn expression on her face.

"I'm ready. If the castle being attacked is true, I think we need to travel now, even though it's almost night. But don't

CHAPTER 4

worry, my wolves will be able to help with spotting any unfriendlies. Let's get moving. You want to go to Abrecem Secer?"

"Yes, the Library there contains the rarest and oldest books on magic as well as everything known about the Dark War. I'm hoping the answer to stopping Dag'draath will be located somewhere in there."

"You realize the Library is several days' travel from here, right?"

"That's one of the reasons I wanted you to come along." I looked down at my feet, noticing for the first time how scuffed and muddy my day shoes had become. No wonder my feet hurt so much. I should get a better pair of shoes, or maybe leather boots like Gwen wore. As I looked at our feet, I realized again just how sheltered I was. When I looked up at her again, my cheeks were hot. "Look, we both know I'm not really a princess, but I've spent my life sheltered. I know how to do a lot of things, albeit only from what I've read." I wrinkled my nose at the admission. Maybe it was because I saw her as strong and self-sufficient and I wanted to be more like her, or maybe it was because it was embarrassing to admit my lack of practical experience. It was silly, but part of me felt I should be good at everything.

"It's okay. We can't be good at everything. I mean, I'm not great with people. So, when my only friend asks me for help, I don't want to let her down."

With her reassurance, my insecurity melted away. It was like she'd read my mind and I was both startled and soothed. She was right, we couldn't all be good at everything. I was good at researching, and my memory was second to none of the elves I'd met, so what did it matter if I wasn't experienced? Wasn't experience something that came with time and doing things, anyway?

A loud yell came from below. "Rhin? Gwen? Your wolves are back and they're looking at me."

I pressed my lips together and looked at Gwen, and then we both started laughing at his nervous, shaky words.

"Come on," she said, tilting her head toward the ladder. "My wolves won't hurt him, but I don't want him having a heart attack before we even leave the forest."

"He's braver than he seems, not to mention a lot stronger than he looks," I remembered the way he'd hefted books almost half his weight in the library the other day. "He may be young, but he's as loyal as they come, and he's a quick study. I didn't want him to come along at first, but I was glad when he insisted." I pushed my braid over my shoulder. "It's always nice to have friends with you when you do crazy things like try to cross a country with ur'gels after you."

"I wouldn't have it any other way myself. Now let's go."

Descending the same way we'd entered, I felt excitement stirring in my chest. I had my two closest friends at my side. I was more hopeful about our chances of making the long journey safely, but above that, I was happy they believed in me. I was about to put into practice everything I'd ever read and I couldn't wait. Even if all I had to bring to the table was a whole bunch of theoretical knowledge, something told me I was about to get a lot of practical experience.

CHAPTER 5

I couldn't get over how much happier I already felt, just knowing that I was traveling with Gwen and her wolves. I'd expected I'd feel safer, but not how much having her with me would lift my spirits. I'd planned to let Gwen lead the way, as she was better with directions than I was, not that I had a map or more than vague directions to the Library to go on.

The wolves joined us minutes after we left her treehouse. Clearly, they had a direct connection with her that went beyond words. I had expected to see them already waiting for us below the way Sel had reacted, but it had just been Swift who'd been waiting below.

His tongue had lolled out of his mouth and he almost appeared to be laughing at Sel's alarm. Based on the quirk of Gwen's lips when she'd locked eyes with him, maybe he was. We began walking without waiting for the other two, but they soon caught up. As the other two wolves emerged through the trees to join us, Gwen checked their collars, her lips curling up with a smile of satisfaction when she found the notes gone and the wolves in good condition.

I looked at her with my head tilted in question at the way

she'd checked them over so thoroughly even though it had been only a short time since they'd been apart.

"My wolves and I aren't always welcome among other Low Forest elves, no matter how useful we can be. I prefer to stay out on the edge of the community, alone, as a consequence."

I was unable to think of anything to say in response. I understood what it was like to be different, even if I'd never lived alone, but I didn't think solitude was something I was built for. I'd initially planned to leave the castle and set off alone, but I hadn't fought extremely hard to keep Sel from accompanying me. If I had given him a direct order he may have stayed behind, though.

We'd been walking for about a half hour while Gwen reviewed what she considered "basic" skills. I took mental notes, but my spirits sank when everything she told me was something new.

"So, does that make sense?" Gwen turned, her face open and interested. When she saw my defeated posture, she stopped and clicked her tongue. "It's okay not to understand how to do everything the first time. Especially without actually doing it."

"Yeah, I know. But I never realized how much I didn't know, you know?"

I scratched the back of my neck, noticing a new bite. I didn't recall getting bitten, but it was entirely possible my other physical complaints had distracted me from the event. I'd been trying to focus on putting one aching foot in front of the other and avoiding complaining about how sore I was while Gwen gave me my crash course in surviving.

We were in the thick of the forest by now, but before Gwen could respond, the wolves' ears pricked up. Until that moment, they'd been content to rove nearby, taking turns disappearing into the underbrush while always keeping at least one with our small group at any moment. It was astonishing to me how having a fierce predator at my side could make me feel so much

CHAPTER 5

49

safer when I knew that if I'd come upon any one of them by myself, I likely would have been paralyzed with fear.

Gwen spun around, reacting to something I couldn't appreciate. Dropping low to the ground, she pulled out a wicked-looking blade and surveyed the small clearing where we stood without speaking. Sel and I froze as we waited for instruction.

I looked into the trees, but couldn't see anything in the darkness. The only noises were the forest night birds, nothing that struck me as out of place. She exchanged a glance with Swift the second I realized the birds had fallen silent.

Before I could process what was happening, she'd turned and pushed me behind her, protectively standing where I'd been a moment earlier.

"What is it?" I wished I'd thought to bring a weapon. Another thing I'd missed in my inexperience that now seemed obvious.

She didn't answer, just gestured for me to be quiet with two fingers of her unoccupied hand.

I reviewed everything I could recall about combat from what I'd seen from the library window, but other than the drills I'd watched from a distance, I had zero experience. At least I was dressed practically, which allowed me to move better than if I'd been in my usual attire, but that was all I had going for me.

I scoured the area for something I could use as a weapon, and spotted a fallen branch. I reached down, grateful it was light enough for me to swing. But when they came through the trees, I wasn't remotely prepared. I'd never seen an ur'gel up close, and these ones were terrifying. They swarmed toward us, causing me to let out an involuntary yelp as all my blood rushed to my head, causing me to feel light-headed.

I knew from my brother's stories and pictures I'd seen that these weren't even the enormous ones. They may have been foot soldiers or lower ur'gels, but they were still horrifying. They skittered on four or six legs, vaguely resembling misshapen spiders, but were larger, as if they'd been left in the sun too long and melted before some evil baker stretched them until they were somewhere between the size of a dog and a horse.

They ranged in color from the pink of a human with a sunburn, to a deep, iron brown, and were covered in blistered skin. I was rendered motionless as they approached, even as my brain screamed for me to run.

Gwen, however, had no such problem. Her movements were lightning fast and vicious. She stabbed, twisted, and lunged, taking on three at once. Sel was also being attacked, but his nimble body allowed him to dodge one of the slower ur'gels rushing at him. I was surprised to see he had a knife. It was smaller and not as deadly in appearance as the one Gwen held, which was now coated in a sticky-looking substance I assumed was ur'gel blood. Even though both of my friends were in front of me, it didn't mean I was protected.

I shrieked and tumbled backward as an ur'gel lunged at me, grateful I'd been unfrozen but unable to move quickly enough to duck the attack. My backside smarted from the way I'd landed on the forest floor, but I hardly noticed as I focused on the ur'gel now on top of me.

Kicking and flailing, I gasped for air as I tried to get the creature off me. It was heavy and I knew I was panicking. I couldn't get it off and my chest hurt from its weight. From the corner of my eye, one of Gwen's wolves appeared. The ur'gel flew off my chest. Before I could get up, another one attacked.

My mind clicked back into gear, and I managed to grab my stick. With one hand, I swung as hard as I could. It moved slightly, just enough for me to use two hands and the stick. I hit it harder, dislodging it completely. Struggling to my feet, fighting my own knees which trembled and tried to give out, I brandished the stick and bared my teeth, trying to look fierce instead of terrified.

I fought another one, more purple than the last but with

CHAPTER 5

what looked like ten legs. I lunged and jumped back before it hit me, catching it under what looked like a chin and surprising myself when it rolled onto its back, legs in the air like a dead bug. Victory!

Emboldened by the unexpected success, I kept them at bay with the stick. I knew I wasn't strong, but I seemed to be fast enough now that the shock had worn off to dodge them one at a time, hitting them with the stick whenever they got too close and using it to push them back the rest of the time.

Just when we seemed to be making headway, a second wave appeared, with double the numbers we'd already dispatched. I wanted to cry, but couldn't catch my breath long enough to manage it. I wondered if I would vomit from the way my stomach lurched when I sucked in air. I'd never been in a fight before, and it was so much harder than anything I'd imagined.

I tried to look at our situation logically. There didn't seem to be any communication or organization as they swarmed us, and that weren't as fast as I'd first thought, but as the hideous monsters charged again, I had no idea what to do. The only thing I was sure of was I wasn't going to make it out of this alive.

I took several deep breaths to slow my breathing while I told my inner pessimist to shut up. I bent my knees, just as two of the larger spider-dogs hit me at the same time. A solid crack echoed into the night as I connected my branch with one of the hard-headed creatures. Before I could celebrate or prepare for the next attack, the other one chomped down on my right shoulder.

I screamed as the needle-sharp teeth tore through tendon and muscle. I'd never felt anything so painful. Even as the burning spread from my shoulder down to my arm, I accepted it was the end. This is how I was going to die.

But just then, the same white wolf who'd helped me with the first ur'gel leapt into the fray, yanking it off my shoulder.

The sharp teeth severed tissue again on the way out, and my pain increased tenfold. I looked down at my hand, numb from the shoulder down. It was covered by blood that was raining down from a gaping wound that resembled raw meat.

"Rhin!" Gwen shouted at me.

I turned blankly, recognizing horror on her face as she saw the blood running down my arm and onto the other hand. I looked at her, trying to convey how sorry I was I'd gotten her into this through my expression alone. I was too overwhelmed to find any words.

She was beginning to sweat from the exertion, and her dark gold hair clung in strands to her face and her neck as it sprang free from her braid, but she looked amazing as she continued to fight two and three ur'gels at a time only a few feet away.

I couldn't see Sel anymore. The last I'd seen of him he'd jumped into a tree as the first ur'gel attacked me. I hoped he was safe. The edges of my vision began to flicker, sparkling with black and white lights. The ground shifted, and I felt as though I was falling into a mist. The distant sound of him shouting my name seemed far away, but I smiled. He was alive.

This time, when I hit the ground, it was soft. It was as if I'd fallen into my bed, and the fight and ur'gels had all been a dream.

"No!"

Gwen let out a primal scream, and the fierce look on her angelic face seemed out of place in the fogginess of my head. Why did she look so angry? I let my head fall to the side and watched as three small ur'gels came toward me. I should do something, but what? I was so tired. She shouted, and the anger pierced my fog, waking me enough to understand her words.

"Swift, Kiya, Daimyo. Keep her safe."

The wolves moved in unison, and I lost sight of them. She pulled out a second, smaller knife from her boot and bran-

CHAPTER 5

dished it in front of her, looking like a warrior queen as she bared her teeth at the ur'gels who'd reached me. These ones were smaller than the first ones we'd fought, only about the size of a small beaver and barely came to her knee.

I struggled to sit, knowing I needed to help, but she continued to fight without me. The angle was perfect for the wolves, but I could see it was hard for her to get them in a place to keep them down because they were low to the ground. She searched the clearing and her face sharpened, eyes narrowed as she looked at something I couldn't see from where I lay.

Even in my half-conscious state, I could tell she had a plan when she suddenly changed direction and strode away, calling out for Sel. I had no idea what she was doing, but wasn't strong enough to ask.

I slumped back onto the deliciously soft ground, now fighting to keep my eyes open. I wanted to sleep so badly, and it took all my strength to keep my eyes from getting dragged shut by the weights pushing them down.

As my eyelids fluttered, Gwen's wolves took up positions around me. I couldn't see much beyond the varying shades of white and grey, but felt strangely safe for the first time since we'd been ambushed. Gwen had told them to protect me, and I was certain nothing would get by their snarling teeth and claws.

I caught of flash of color as Sel dropped out of a tree beside Gwen, uninjured and hardly breathing fast. I smirked despite my haze, unable to believe that's where he'd been this entire time. Brilliant. Once again, he'd proved how smart he was without saying a thing. Why hadn't I considered using the trees? Stupid brain. I'd been too overwhelmed by fear to notice earlier, but none of these ur'gels could fly. I could have sat in a tree and knocked them down.

A trickle of blood burned my eyes and I tried to wipe it away, but my shoulder screamed at me and the nausea crested.

I rolled, emptying my stomach toward my uninjured side as spasms racked my body. I felt Gwen's eyes and looked away.

"What do we do now?" Sel was panting now. The sound of his stick crashing on the head of another ur'gel caused me to look, catching a glimpse between Swift and Kiya just as he lobbed it several feet into the air. As it descended, it smashed against the trunk of a nearby tree and went still.

Gwen's eyebrows rose before she answered as calmly as if they were discussing supper plans. "We need to get out of here. Trappers leave animal snares about ten feet away from here. Do you think we can lead them over there? I know where they are, so if you follow my lead, you shouldn't accidentally set them off. We need to get her out of here and seen by a healer right away."

I could see the determination on his thin face as he raised his chin. He was such a good boy.

"I'll protect her with my life. What do you want me to do?"

Gwen pointed toward the space between the trees. "Underneath the tree with the knobby bark, there's a lever. If you can cut the rope with your knife, it will release the whole mechanism, causing a trap to fall which should cover the entire clearing. But you need to make sure you don't step anywhere other than a straight line between here and there."

She demonstrated the path he needed to follow and he narrowed his eyes.

"I can do it."

He kept a firm grip on his stick and tightened his hand around the small knife. It didn't look as useful for fighting as the stick, which he'd used effectively to keep them at a distance since he'd jumped out of the tree, but it would be perfect for accomplishing the task Gwen had given him.

"Then go," Gwen shouted.

She was amazing. I wish I were that good under pressure. I sighed and closed my eyes again, the last thing I glimpsed as I drifted off was an image of Sel dashing into the trees. A loud

CHAPTER 5

whistle pierced the air, and I listened as if from a great distance as Gwen taunted the ur'gels.

"Hey, uglies. See the little boy over there? I bet you he's tasty."

Did they speak the same language as we did? I forced my eyes open again. It didn't seem to matter if they did or not though, as once they saw her standing alone, her knives out with a strong, bring-it-on stance, with him apparently running off in the distance like a scared boy, they were off.

A few stopped to fight her, but she dispatched them with her knives, their blood spraying everywhere as she slit about five throats before the rest gave up, chasing after Sel, who must have seemed like a much easier target than the fierce warrior in front of them.

I looked at my furry wall, smiling against the pain in my shoulder. I was now sure the ur'gels were pretty dumb, based on the way they'd been attacking, but even they'd realized three large wolves weren't as easy a meal as an escaping human boy. How much he would change away from Cliffside and the rules we lived by if we made it out of here? I shifted slightly. Pain sharpened my mind.

My friends needed my help. How long had I been on the ground? Everything was so blurry. I blinked and forced myself to sit, gritting my teeth against the pain and waiting as the ground and sky wobbled for a few moments. When it finally stabilized and stood still, I knelt and was surrounded by soft fur in varying shades of white, grey, and brown. Swift, Kiya, and Daimyo moved closer to support me as I worked to right myself.

I met Swift's intelligent eyes with my own and tilted my head in acknowledgment of their actions. "Thank you."

I put a hand over my heart, bowing my head only slightly and right it immediately when the world spun again. When my vision cleared, I pondered if it was possible for a wolf to smile. Swift calmly watched me, but before I could decide, his ears perked up and his head swiveled. I followed his gaze toward the clearing, realizing I was now alone with the wolves. There were no ur'gels, but Gwen and Sel were out of sight as well.

I struggled to my feet, knowing I needed to keep moving, keep fighting. At least until my friends were safe.

The sound of fighting pushed me to continue on. After a few staggering steps forward, I regained my knees and headed toward the noise to find them. They were fighting off two ur'gels apiece, and I could see they'd captured at least twenty or thirty underneath a large net too heavy for them to wiggle out of. The ur'gels were struggling, their shrieks of rage futile against the trap. I breathed a sigh of relief. They appeared to have matters under control until another group of ur'gels exploded from the far end of the clearing.

"No, no, no!"

I struggled to move faster, knowing my friends needed as much help as they could get, even if I wasn't great at this and hardly mobile.

"Gwen! Sel! To your left!" I shouted, picking up another stick as I limped toward them. Sel reacted first, scampering back up the tree beside him. He moved effortlessly, as though he was floating, and I wondered if Sel had something more in his background than just human lineage.

Once back in the tree, he began to pick off the ur'gels one at a time as they swarmed up the tree after him. Confident he was okay, I turned my attention to Gwen. She looked vicious and beautiful, with both knives coated in greenish-black blood, her eyes narrowed above a snarl. She looked almost feral, as though she were part wolf herself.

I moved closer to her, placing myself on her right. She turned, and a flash of relief crossed her face when she saw me beside her. I felt a fierce burning in my chest, pride that I'd forced myself to come this far giving me the strength to continue.

The wolves had beat me and already taken up defensive

positions in front of their elven mistress. My right shoulder screamed obscenities in the form of burning knives of torture, but I somehow managed to beat off the ur'gels attacking from my side. Grateful these ones were smaller than the one who'd taken a bite out of my shoulder, it unfortunately meant they were faster as well. Each time I made contact, I could feel my energy lag further. Breathing hard, I grunted with each swing, lancing pain shooting through my injured arm at each blow. I couldn't keep it up much longer. Desperately, I turned to Gwen.

"I don't know how much longer I can do this. There's too many, and they just keep coming." I spoke the words one at a time, gasping as I barely batted another ur'gel off my leg.

Gwen's expression was grim. "I know. I'm trying to think of something else we can do, but the only thing I can think of is to climb a tree the way Sel did. Maybe we'll stand a better chance from above."

I caught her worried grimace as she regarded my shoulder. She winced as her eyes met mine.

I tried to smile reassuringly, but we both knew better. "I'm not sure I can climb. But it's okay. I got you into this, so—"

She glared, twin points of red on her cheeks. "Absolutely not! I'm not leaving you behind. You didn't get me into this, your home was attacked by ur'gels and you left. Cliffside isn't far from the forest or the village. They would have been here within a day even without you here. If anything, you might be the reason any elves or humans make it out alive. Thanks to you, I had a warning, as well as everyone the wolves dropped off those notes to. Hopefully, they got everyone to a safe house before the ur'gels descended."

I couldn't feel proud, even with her vehement defense of my actions. Maybe it wasn't my fault we'd been followed, but either way, it was hard to feel proud when you were getting your butt handed to you by ur'gels and certain you were going to die any second.

We didn't say anything else as we continued to fight the never-ending stream of dog-sized monsters with grunts and rasping breaths. I was sure she was still trying to come up with a solution, the way I was. We weren't any closer to winning and it was only a matter of time until one or all of us were killed.

A loud trumpeting came from the direction the ur'gels were attacking from. I squinted, turning to see what the noise was. The ur'gels were still coming, but now their numbers were decreasing, and the ones who were still coming seemed to be escaping rather than attacking. When a large centaur burst into the clearing, my mouth dropped.

I'd seen a few before in passing, but I'd never been this close to one. He was beautiful, with large, well-muscled flanks covered in hair the red of a blood moon, and a bronzed and well-muscled upper body. His face appeared to have been chiseled out of granite, all hard-edged and deep-grooved, while the hair on his head was long and flowing down his back. He had a matching beard that had been trimmed neatly around his jaw. Intricately tattooed arms gripped a wickedly sharp sword with a hilt bedecked by a single ruby.

A smile crept over my face. Regardless of whether I knew him or not, centaurs and elves generally had good relationships. Gwen had noticed the pause in my fighting and turned to make sure I was okay, her worried eyes running over my body to see if I was injured. When I pointed at the centaur emerging through the woods, she cast her eyes skyward and exhaled with relief.

"It's about time!" Gwen shouted.

I was startled to hear her speaking to the centaur in such a familiar way until he shot her a rakish grin in response.

"My dear Gwen! What have you been up to? Staying out of trouble, I can see."

He was quite clearly teasing her, but her reaction confirmed while they knew each other, they weren't necessarily

CHAPTER 5   59

friends. She was always quick to tease me, but ever since I'd met her, I'd known she didn't take well to teasing herself.

"Ha, ha, Loglan. Glad to see you're still as funny as ever. Hopefully, you fight better than you tell jokes." Gwen arched an eyebrow.

Loglan roared with laughter. "Luckily for you, I can. Not to mention I just happen to have a little something up my sleeve to take care of these little buggers for you."

I frowned, looking at his chest and arms. Up his sleeve? Did he mean the tattoos? As I waited, Loglan closed his eyes, muttering something under his breath. A split second later the forest seemed to explode as ur'gels shot up into the sky, completely disappearing into thin air.

I turned around, looking to see if they were behind me. Nothing. I tried to process what I'd just witnessed. All the ur'gels, including the ones we'd already killed, had vanished without a trace. Gwen leaned over, gently closing my mouth. I swallowed, staring at her blankly, but she shrugged.

"Loglan is the protector of this area of the forest. We've met many times in the past, as I spend most of my time out here. Because he's the protector, he has a few..." she paused, shaking her head while she considered her words. "Why don't we just say he has a few extra abilities. Apparently, one such ability is disposing of things which don't belong in the forest, a category I'm assuming ur'gels fall into."

I could only nod dumbly as I looked at Loglan. Gratitude swelled in my chest now that I processed what his presence meant. I wasn't going to die after all—at least, not yet.

Sel jumped out of the tree, and on his face was a hero worship I hadn't seen from him before. "Thank you, sir. How can I repay you?"

He smiled down at Sel, who barely reached his shoulders, eyes twinkling at the awestruck expression on the boy's face.

"I was just doing my duty. My name is Loglan, what's yours?"

"My name is S-Sel," he stuttered. "I'm the human servant for Lady Rhiniya. We were on our way to Abrecem Secer when we asked Gwen to join us. Then we were attacked by ur'gels."

Loglan gave his hand a solemn shake. "Nice to meet you. I think if the Library is your end goal, you should move quickly. The woods aren't a safe place for you tonight, but with what I can see brewing in the stars, I'm not sure if anywhere in our world will be safe for long."

Loglan stared at the wolves, neither greeting them nor letting them out of his sight. I realized it was entirely possible wolves and centaurs were not the best of buddies. But whether they were friends or not, I could see at a minimum Loglan and Gwen had a mutual respect. Which was possibly why he had just appeared and saved our lives.

"What did you do with the ur'gels?" Part of me was still waiting for them to fall out of the sky.

Loglan winked. "I just returned them to where they came from. It's simple, when you know how."

"I don't suppose you can teach me how? It seems like a handy thing to know, in case we get attacked again." I looked up at him hopefully.

"The spell I used is one which requires time and talent to perfect. While I'm sure you may possess the talent, it is clear you don't have the time. If this many of the ur'gels found you so quickly, you would be wise to continue posthaste." He turned to encompass our group, pursing his lips, and I followed his gaze, trying to see us from his perspective.

Gwen and Sel appeared slightly worse for the wear, but the smallest wolf, Kiya, the one who'd leapt into the fray early in the fight to save me, was lying on the ground, barely moving. Her white fur was matted with dirt and the familiar rusty dark brown of blood on her chest, like a badge of honor.

My heart sank.

At some point during the last few minutes while we'd been

CHAPTER 5

talking, she'd lain down. Her chest heaved and Swift now stood next to her, nuzzling her. He whined at Gwen, and once she saw what he was looking, the worry on her face eclipsed anything I'd seen in the past, including when I'd fallen to the ground.

"Kiya!" Gwen dropped to her knees beside the wolf, resting her forehead on the wolf's head and received a weak lick on her cheek in response. Gently, Gwen ran her fingers over the wolf, murmuring soft words as she assessed the damage. When she looked up, her eyes were swimming with tears. "Loglan, Kiya needs help. Is there a healer, or someone nearby who could help? She can't travel far like this." Gwen pressed her lips together, then tried to lift the wolf up.

I rushed to help, but Loglan stopped me.

"Allow me, Gwen."

He moved beside Kiya, kneeling low enough so he could scoop up the wolf, which seemed tiny in his massive arms. He placed her gently on his back and stood carefully.

"I know a healer who lives at the edge of the forest, not far from here. We can go to her. She should be able to help." Loglan looked at my arm, the sleeve now soaked through. "It would also be wise to have your arm looked at as well, young elf. What is your name?"

I realized I hadn't introduced myself and bowed my head, trying to keep my arm from moving as I did so. "My name is Rhiniya, from Cliffside, but call me Rhin. I came to find Gwen when the castle was attacked, but it appears the battle has already found us."

Loglan sighed, looking into the sky that was now full dark. "I have known for some time this day would arrive, and yet I find myself still unprepared. You are heading to Abrecem Secer and the Library, correct?"

"Yes, we are. I found some things in my library, which makes me believe there may be a way to stop this before too many lives are lost, but I'm missing details. I discovered the lost textbook of Piotr the Elder is housed there. I'm hoping it will point me in the right direction."

Loglan half-closed his eyes, considering me almost sleepily for a moment before inclining his head. "Very well. If you need to head to Abrecem Secer, your way will not be easy. I can guide you to the edge of the Low Forest as far as Sunglen if you wish, but you'll be on your own afterward. Be prepared. The way is long and even more dangerous now than it has been at any time over the last several centuries."

I inclined my head, wincing as the movement jarred my shoulder. "Thank you, for everything. I'm ready to move now, we could be expecting more of the ur'gels."

Loglan looked at Gwen and Sel. "And you as well? You are prepared for the path ahead?"

She narrowed her eyes. When she gritted her teeth, I could see the simple question had set her back up, but she breathed through her nose and abruptly nodded.

Sel was wide-eyed with awe, still staring at the powerful centaur and didn't respond at all.

I bit back a smile at his sudden boyishness, seeing another side yet again to my silent yet competent servant. The moment of levity was nice under the circumstances, and was what helped me make it the rest of the way to the healers before collapsing.

CHAPTER 6

The edge of the forest wasn't far from where we'd confronted the ur'gels, but every step jarred my shoulder a little more. By the time we arrived at the healer's cottage, my hand was completely numb. I'd been experiencing a weird burning in the area and it crossed my mind that I could have been infected by the ur'gel's teeth.

My mind began to conjure thoughts of poison, a deadly fluid that could cause my arm to shrivel up and turn black. I checked my hand constantly, hoping to reassure myself it was still there. It was the first real injury I'd ever received, so I tried to convince myself it was possible the burning, pain, and numbness were to be expected, but no amount of logic could make me worry less, even the sight of my pale hand cradled next to my chest.

I mentally noted each sensation, replaying the battle we'd just survived. I was disappointed with my performance. I thought I should have been better at fighting after watching my brother train, not to mention everything I'd read about in books throughout the years. But reading was no substitute for learning how to fight, which I'd discovered the hard way.

I chanced a peek at my shoulder, wincing at the jagged

mess beneath what was left of my shirt. Bile rose in my throat and I forced it down with difficulty. I'd already embarrassed myself once, and I didn't want to vomit again.

My thoughts were interrupted by a village appearing unexpectedly through the trees. I'd never known there was another village here. The Low Forest encompassed a large territory, mostly comprised of plains, but we'd now reached a deeper area of woodland where all my familiarity with the landscape ended.

This village looked similar to others I'd seen, but something struck me as odd. It took a while, but as we neared the houses, I realized what it was. Each building was proportional to Loglan's size. It was instantly clear that this village had been specially designed for centaurs. Only a few centaurs stood guard around the periphery, which seemed strange considering the time of night. When they saw Loglan arriving with an entourage, they merely acknowledged him with a slight dip of their chins, betraying no sign of surprise or interest beyond what would be expected at the presence of newcomers in the village.

Everything was eerily familiar to what I was used to seeing in the elven village of the Low Forest. With the exception of the size, the houses, stores, and village square were arranged in a similar fashion.

The healer's cabin was at the far end of the village, just passed the last row of houses. It was tucked away unobtrusively in the trunk of a large tree, half dug into the ground, instead of inside one of the larger cottages we'd passed.

At first, I didn't realize it was even a house. I thought Loglan had forgotten to turn when we'd passed the last row of houses, then had decided the healer lived on a farm instead of in the town. So, when Loglan had paused to knock on the side of a tree, it had taken a moment for me to understand what was happening.

The inside was surprisingly spacious, with a ceiling high

enough for Loglan to walk straight in while carrying his wounded cargo.

The healer was nothing like what I had expected. In my own village, the healer was an elder, with several apprentices who did most of the work. She was only seen if you required help beyond what they could provide, and considered wise, old, and wise, and silent.

This healer was a strikingly majestic and powerful female centaur, with flanks of pale silver glowing like one of the moons. Unlike Loglan, her upper body was covered with clothing, with muscles every bit as well developed which emerged from underneath her sleeves. Maybe all centaurs were naturally muscular, or perhaps it was the type of work she did which led to her having more than the average upper body strength for her kind as well.

She took one look at the wolf Loglan was carrying, immediately instructing him to place her on a large table in what appeared to be a kitchen. Her face appeared concerned but betrayed not even a hint of discomfort at the sight of the injured wolf or Gwen, who was pacing in a wolf-like fashion beside the still figure of Kiya.

While I waited for her to assess the wolf, I allowed myself to slump in the corner next to the fireplace. The cold which had begun to overwhelm my body slowly melted away under its heat. There was no chair there, but I was so tired I was just happy to have a wall to rest against.

I must've dozed, because the next thing I saw was Gwen sitting beside me, gently patting me on my good shoulder.

"Huh? What, oh, hi. I guess I fell asleep. Is Kiya okay?"

I looked back at the table where I'd last seen the wolf, surprised to find it empty.

Gwen sighed, giving me a small smile. "Sweetgrass, the healer, thinks she'll be just fine. She bandaged her wounds and gave her a potion to drink which should apparently restore her energy."

I smiled back, narrowing my eyes when I noticed Gwen's searching look. "What? Are you okay?" Was she mad at me because her wolf had been injured?

"Yeah, I'm okay. Those tiny demons didn't manage to do much more than scratch me a few times. They weren't as fast as I was expecting, luckily, but there was a lot of them. I'm just worried about you. Are you sure this is what you want to do?"

It was nice, feeling as though someone was concerned about me for a change. I reached out, resting my hand on hers. "This is something I have to do. But I understand if you've changed your mind after what happened to your wolf."

Gwen blinked at me as though I'd grown an extra head. "Are you kidding? After what we just went through, there's no way I'm leaving you to face this alone. If I'd ever had my doubts, after seeing the way you performed in battle, you need me more than I need you. So, if you're planning to go ahead with this, you better believe I'll be right there by your side."

Unbidden, a smile crept over my face at her words. They were practical, supportive, and a little insulting all at the same time.

"That means a lot. Today showed me I really don't know what I've gotten myself into. But it's also taught me a couple of other things. One of those is that you're even more amazing than I realized." She snorted, but I stopped her before she could say anything. "Another thing I discovered is even though Sel has always seemed so young and dependent on me, when it came right down to it, he fought better than I did. I need to start giving him more credit. He's surprised and impressed me so much in the brief time since we left Cliffside. I have no idea how much he's capable of."

My eyes searched the room for him but came up empty. I turned back to her with a puzzled expression on my face and she chuckled.

"I think your young servant has a crush on Loglan. Or hero worship, one of the two." She shrugged. "Honestly, it doesn't

CHAPTER 6

make any difference which it is. He's pretty struck by him. They're out back, looking at the stars."

I felt my heart lurch in concern even as she rushed to reassure me. "He wasn't injured, but he was too excited to go to bed. So, Loglan took him out back to teach him about stars and navigation." She lifted a shoulder as she admitted her weakness. "I also figured it was a good idea because I may know more about navigation than you do, but I'm not very good at it, especially at night. I figured if he knew more about star navigation it may be helpful on our journey."

I absently touched my shoulder as I considered her words, the lack of pain just registering on my senses. How had I not noticed it earlier? I moved it cautiously, taking care to keep my movements slow. It felt a bit stiff, like I'd had a poor night's sleep, or carried a pile of books wrong. I wasn't sure how I'd ended up so lucky. When the ur'gels had first attacked, holding my own was one thing. But when they'd kept advancing inexorably and when I'd been injured, I'd been certain I wasn't going to make it out of the forest alive.

"Did Loglan mention traveling with us?" My head was fuzzy on details about our walk to the healers. "I remember him saying he would take us here, but was it just my imagination when he promised to take us to the land below the forest?"

"No, you heard correctly. He must've felt pretty bad, or perhaps..." Gwen trailed off thoughtfully.

When she hadn't spoken for a few minutes, I nudged her. "Perhaps what?" My impatience prompted me to speak.

She looked at me, her eyes suddenly dark and worried, all sunshine gone. Moonlight had instead replaced it, swirling behind the rich green. "Sometimes, I see things about the future." She bit the inside of her lip. "I think maybe Loglan does, too. Centaurs are known for their wisdom, but they're also known for keeping prophecies. If it had just been me and my wolves, I know Loglan wouldn't have given us a backward glance had my wolf not been injured. Even though he probably would have helped us, he wouldn't have brought us here. I think seeing you both, especially with you talking about the Library, well, Loglan's face ... shifted. His eyes became thoughtful. I think perhaps he knows something."

She had never mentioned anything about being able to see the future before. I knew we could be important to each other, but until now our lives had been too different to allow us time for deep confidences of this nature. Foretelling dreams and magic weren't unheard of among elves, but I had a feeling she was reticent to share her secrets with me because of her past experiences with others in her village.

"Did he say anything to you about what he'd seen?"

Her face confirmed my suspicions. "We ... Well, we know each other from passing in the forest, and we tolerate each other. But we're not friends."

I caught a wistful sadness in the way she uttered "friends." I reached out my hand, placed it on her knee, and gave it a light pat. "You've got me for a friend. I may end up being more dangerous than either of us expected, but you can count on me for anything."

She pressed her lips together, and then relaxed them into a sweet smile. "If you're saying you want to keep going, you can count on me as well." She put her hand on top of mine and squeezed it gently. " Friends till the end."

I smiled back at her, feeling a tingle of warmth inside my chest. If this was what having a friend felt like, I could really grow to like it.

"Gwen?"

A soothing voice interrupted the moment. We both turned as though we'd been caught misbehaving, and saw the healer standing a few feet away, smiling warmly down at me.

"I'm glad to see you're awake again. You appear to be recovering from the event. How does your shoulder feel?"

I rolled my shoulder tentatively, still amazed by how normal it felt after the searing pain which had been my

CHAPTER 6

69

companion all the way to her treehouse. "Almost as good as new, thank you. I'm sorry." My cheeks flushed with embarrassment. "I didn't mean to fall asleep before introducing myself. I guess I was more tired than I'd realized."

She raised an eyebrow, gesturing at my shoulder. "Or perhaps it was because of the blood loss. Not to mention that the particular variety of ur'gel you encountered has the tendency of leaving behind nastiness in their bite."

I looked at my shoulder with concern, remembering how I'd wondered if they had poison in their bite when the burning had spread out. "Like what?"

She chuckled at my wide-eyed look. "No, luckily for you it's not poison. But they aren't the cleanest of creatures. Their teeth can cause wounds to fester, even with prompt medical attention." She smiled without modesty. "In your case, my skills are better than average. I cleaned the wound thoroughly before patching you up. We managed to get a small amount of blood broth into you while you were out, but I'd like you to have another glass now."

"Blood broth?" I wrinkled my nose suddenly grateful I'd been unconscious. I'm not sure I would have drunk anything with blood in the name otherwise.

Gwen rolled her eyes at my squeamishness. "It doesn't actually contain blood." She sounded as though she was reassuring a child.

"She's right. We use it to strengthen the blood and accelerate the normal replacement schedule. Everyone's body circulates and recycles blood. I estimated you'd lost at least a quarter of your usual supply. It would be prudent to have you drink at least three glasses of blood broth between now and when you leave. I'm confident your stores will return to normal within a day or two if we succeed, instead of the normal one to two months."

I wasn't eager to drink it, but her explanation helped me understand why it was necessary. When she handed me an earthen mug almost as big as my head, I gave her a weak smile. "Thank you ... erm, I don't believe I caught your name." I sipped the drink while I waited for her answer, and had to choke back my disgust. It tasted like dirt mixed with peppermint and lavender, if they were used to flavor a cleaning solution. I took a breath and kept sipping as she spoke.

"Your friends told me all about you, but I forgot the favor wasn't reciprocated. My name is Sweetgrass. I'm the healer for the people of my village. From time to time, I also receive a stray human, elf, or animal, such as Kiya." She turned to Gwen. "I've just returned from checking on her. She's still sleeping, but I believe she'll be good to go by tomorrow as well. She lost a lot of blood and collected a few nasty bites of her own, but luckily, nothing I couldn't fix."

Gwen stood up, moving over to Sweetgrass. She appeared positively tiny in comparison, barely reaching shoulder-height on the female centaur. Tears sparkled in her eyes and she placed a hand over her heart.

"Thank you, so much, Sweetgrass. I know wolves aren't a centaur's favorite creature, and it means a lot to me that you'd help us despite that. They are very special to me."

Gwen didn't say anything else, but I observed with interest as the two women exchanged a look of understanding. After a moment, Sweetgrass replied, her voice soft.

"With what we believe is about to come, we must keep our allies close, and our loved ones even closer. My people have been seeing portents for some time now. If you believe you know something to aid the light in fighting back the night, I would do anything it takes to help in your search for justice and goodness. If you ever require help from the centaurs, regardless of where you are, give them this. Tell them we have vouched for you. It may not be much, but perhaps it will be enough in a moment of need."

Gwen accepted the small gift from Sweetgrass, turning it over in her hand. It appeared to be a small piece of jewelry, but

CHAPTER 6

other than a brief flash of bronze I didn't get a good enough look at it to know what it was. Before I could ask about it, Sweetgrass brightened, then gave both of us a smile.

"Come. Rhin, you can drink the rest in your room. I've arranged a space for you to sleep tonight." She looked at Gwen. "I hope it's acceptable to share with the wolves and Rhin?"

"Yes, thank you. I don't like being separated from my wolves, and I'd feel better watching over Rhin tonight." Gwen bowed her head.

Sweetgrass turned and waited for us to follow. The moment I stood up, even though I felt better than I had upon entering her home, I could tell I was still in need of rest and time. She led us down a hallway with hard-packed dirt floors and walls that looked as if they'd been hewn directly into the tree to a room a few paces down the hallway where she pointed out what we'd need for the night.

Gwen sat down on the pallet, nuzzling nose-to-nose with Kiya. It was clear the centaur wasn't set up for housing elves, but she'd done a decent job making the room comfortable, as well as accommodating the needs of the wolves.

Kiya opened her eyes, letting her tongue fall out in a canine half-smile when she saw Gwen. For a long moment, the wolf and Gwen locked eyes, communicating without words. When she gave the wolf a small scratch under her chin and the wolf closed her eyes, I decided they were finished and spoke.

"Is everything okay?" I still felt guilty her injuries were my fault, but Gwen gave me a tired but reassuring smile.

"She's fine. I was just telling her how brave she was for keeping my friend safe." She flushed as she looked away.

"Is there something else?" Her reaction was unexpected, but her answer didn't shed any light.

"She just told me she knew you meant a lot to me, that you resonate with me."

I raised an eyebrow. "What do you mean?"

"It's just a wolf thing. She also told me the horse-woman is nice and she's feeling better. She just needs sleep, as do we."

Too tired to pry any further even though I didn't understand her cryptic answer, I gratefully sank onto my pallet on the floor beside them. I meant to say thank you, but it was difficult to order my words.

I took another sip of the blood broth as a warm tingling sensation overwhelmed me. Placing my mug on the floor just as the darkness grew from the outside of my vision moving in, my consciousness faded, catapulting me into a deep and dreamless sleep.

CHAPTER 7

I groaned at the rock jabbing my spine. It felt like something trying to pierce my skin and with my eyes closed I groped for the disturbance. My bed was usually much more comfortable. I'd have to get Sel to fix it. Awareness filtered through when I was finally able to pry one eye open. Gwen was across from me, on the floor, cuddled into a mass of white and grey fur.

I struggled to sit up as memories flooded back. It wasn't my bed at home giving me such trouble. I was on a pallet on the floor of a centaur healer's home. Why was that? Oh, right. I'd run away, fought ur'gels, and became injured. I snorted. It sounded like I was still dreaming, except for the hard object which had woken me.

I glared at the bed, finding the source of my discomfort. It was a stone, as I'd suspected from the way it had felt, and had been hidden beneath the pillows. My bed had been comfortable when I was exhausted, but I would have slept longer without it. I succeeded in achieving a cross-legged position, hampered along the way by the shifting of my sleeping surface which made movement difficult at first. I stretched, feeling my stiffness ease.

Sweetgrass was a miracle worker. I looked down at my shoulder, remembering the pain from the night before, grateful it seemed to be gone. I touched and tested it, rolling it, and turning it from side to side. It was only a little tender, nothing remotely like the searing agony it had been right after I'd been bitten.

As I tested my shoulder, I made the less pleasant discovery I was the one emitting the unpleasant, pungent odor. I'd noticed it previously, but assumed it was the wolves until I'd stirred the air. Wrinkling my nose, I found my shirt to be a crinkled and disgusting mess. Dried blood had made what remained of the sleeve and shoulder area stiff and hard, creating a fabric more like burlap than the soft cotton it had been before blood had reinforced the threads.

I wanted nothing more than a chance to wash away all the grime and blood and put on new clothing, but I couldn't wait. Now that I'd discovered how bad it was, I had to change immediately. I struggled to remove the shirt, wincing as it ripped away from areas where the blood had dried it solidly to my skin. Once I'd succeeded in lifting it off, I crumpled it into a ball and grabbed my only other shirt from my bag, which someone had placed beside my pallet.

How had it gotten there? I didn't remember. It could have been Loglan or Sweetgrass, but I didn't think I'd carried it. Then again, last night had several sections missing or blurry. I hadn't felt well, that I did remember, but Sweetgrass had worked her magic and my shoulder was as good as new. A few missing memories was a small price to pay.

Allowing my gaze to wander back to Gwen and the sleeping wolves, bits and pieces of our conversation from the day before returned. I vaguely recalled being insulted when she'd thought I would give up after being attacked by ur'gels, but also how grateful I'd been when she had refused to bail on me.

As she slept, her breathing was almost inaudible. Her

CHAPTER 7

75

eyelashes flickered from time to time, and in the silence of the room I felt closer to her than ever before. We were sisters-in-arms now, an experience I'd thought had bypassed me when I'd gone the way of the researcher instead of a warrior. It was a crazy thought after what had happened so soon after leaving my sheltered home, but in a way, I felt invigorated by it all. Maybe it was the adventure itself, or maybe it knew I had a friend like her at my back. I moved slowly, trying to keep the noise I made to a minimum as I crept out of the room.

Kiya lifted her head, giving me an indecipherable look. I raised my finger to my lips, unsure if she would understand, but she placed her head back on her paws and closed her eyes.

Following the curving hallway, I reached the room with the large table I remembered from the day before without difficulty. Surely, if it had a fireplace there would be food nearby.

A burst of noise erupted from my stomach as it chimed it. Reflexively my hand went on top to shush it, and I looked to see if anyone had heard the sound. Apparently, I was even hungrier than I was smelly, which was astonishing. Maybe I would look for food before washing up, after all.

At the entryway of the room I was able to see Sel sitting at a tall chair beside Loglan. They both had bowls in front of them, though Sel's appeared to have been forgotten as he sat with his elbows on either side of his, resting his chin on the heels of his palms as he listened to Loglan. I'd never seen him act this way before. It was as plain as the nose on his face he'd developed a serious case of hero worship.

Before I could hear much of the conversation, Loglan noticed me and stopped telling his story.

"Good morning," I entered the room hesitantly, feeling uncomfortable under his stare.

Loglan gave me a thorough once-over, looking pleased once he finished. "You're awake earlier than I expected." He lifted his mug toward me in a toast. "And looking better than I expected, as well."

I smiled, demonstrating my regained ability to move my shoulder. "Yes, Sweetgrass is brilliant. My shoulder feels almost normal. I'm a bit more tired than usual, but I feel pretty close to my usual state of wellbeing."

"I imagine you're hungrier than usual, too." He gave Sel a look, who nimbly jumped off the chair and went to the hearth, coming back with a third bowl which he placed at an empty place at the table before clambering back onto his stool to continue eating.

"Yes, I could most likely eat an entire cow for breakfast. I seem to have a sudden craving for red meat. I'm not sure if I remember correctly, but I think Sweetgrass mentioned something about wanting me to have another glass of blood broth?" Before he could answer my question, the same voice I remembered from last night spoke from the other side of the room.

"I did." Sweetgrass held out another large mug of the disgusting drink and wiggled it at me.

I winced, remembering the medicinal dirt taste, and she began laughing.

"Don't worry, you won't be the first and you won't be the last to dread the taste. But the fact you are asking for another cup means the effect outweighs the less pleasant aspects of the potion."

Her words were mild, and her smile was easy. Sighing, I drank it as quickly as I could.

Loglan began laughing, and I turned, cocking my head with surprise once I'd drained the mug.

"You've done a better job drinking her vile magic than most of the centaurs I know," he leaned over, pretending to whisper in Sel's ear. "She's a great healer, but not much of a cook."

"I don't see you cooking. Perhaps next time you show up uninvited at my house in the dark you can take over the meals and healing? You would clearly be a suitable replacement."

He threw his head back, deep laughter erupting from his belly. Sel howled along with him and my lip twitched. The

CHAPTER 7

77

comfort of their interaction sank into my soul and soon I was giggling as well.

Sweetgrass made a valiant effort to remain stoic, keeping her arms crossed and her lips pressed together, but had just curled into a smile when Gwen entered the room.

"Well, looks like I slept in and missed all the fun." She looked bemused, but quickly sized up the room, making a beeline for where I stood with Sweetgrass, holding the thankfully empty mug.

"How do you feel?"

"Almost back to myself. Thankfully, Sweetgrass says this is my last dose of medicine."

"That means we can leave as soon we're packed." Gwen removed her hand and moved to where Loglan and Sel were watching our interaction. "Are you still able to take us to the edge of the Low Forest?"

"Yes. I believe you three are on an important quest. I wish I could go to Abrecem Secer with you, but my duties are here, in the Low Forest. And after what we encountered yesterday, I will be needed." He shot Sweetgrass a somber look. "When I first came upon them in the woods yesterday, they were swarmed by hundreds of the smaller ur'gels we've been expecting. If it hadn't been for the vanishing spell, it's possible none of us would have made it out of the forest alive."

Sweetgrass closed her eyes, sighing. "So, the time we've feared is at hand."

Loglan unfolded his legs from beneath the table and came to stand beside her.

"It has long been foretold. It isn't as though we haven't known this day would come."

"Knowing and seeing are two different things. I had hoped the soothsayers were wrong, and events wouldn't unfold in our lifetime." She turned to look into the fire before her words echoed sadly through the room. "But such is prophecy."

For a moment, no one spoke. I still held on to the empty

mug, Gwen sat at the table with Sel, and we all watched Loglan and Sweetgrass, who had both drifted off, staring into the fire. I wondered what it was the centaurs knew, and if he would share it with us on our journey. When I chanced a glance at Gwen, she looked thoughtful as well, and I remembered something I'd heard her say last night.

When she caught me watching her, she spoke. "I can be ready to leave within the hour."

"As soon as I'm finished eating, I'm ready."

Sel scooped out the remnants of his bowl and jumped off his stool seconds later, bringing the bowl back to Sweetgrass, who gave him a half-smile.

Loglan took a deep breath, looking at each of us in turn. "We'll leave within the hour," he began, pausing when he caught me staring. How could he not smell me? I refused to travel anywhere without at least washing the blood off, along with whatever ur'gel blood had been left behind. "What is it?"

"Is it possible for me to wash before we leave?"

Sweetgrass let out a bark of laughter. "Of course. I imagine it must be hard for someone such as yourself to go without washing daily, even without the extra amount of filth you accumulated yesterday."

I wasn't sure if her words were meant to be a compliment or an insult but tried to brush them aside. They had done so much for me it hardly seemed appropriate to become offended about something true, even if I wanted to object. I found it strangely hard to accept how others viewed me outside of the castle, perhaps even harder than being seen as an oddity within the walls.

By the time I returned from Abrecem Secer, I vowed that people would no longer think I was so entitled. I would be someone worth knowing, for more than my value as a marriage piece to be transferred for status or to create an alliance.

Even with the delay to eat and wash up, packing was swift, and we were soon ready to leave. Sweetgrass had even found an extra set of clothing that fit me reasonably well, explaining they'd been left by a previous patient and she'd kept them on the off chance they'd be needed. With Loglan in the lead, we bid farewell to Sweetgrass. We had enough provisions for a week, which should be enough to last the trip to Sunglen, and I was eager to begin our journey. The sooner we reached Abrecem Secer, the better.

Daytime in the centaur village was truly a remarkable sight. We skirted around town, but still caught glimpses of centaurs going about their regular duties. Fixing holes in roofs, selling their wares as we passed a marketplace, even herding livestock. It was surreal when we passed a young centaur leading a flock of sheep. He was so much bigger than they were, he appeared to be an adult until I caught a glimpse of his face.

But for all the novelty of the village, we quickly left it behind. We were already on the periphery so it soon became apparent that the centaur village was at the very edge of the forest. It was a bit of a misnomer to call where we lived the Low Forest, as much of the area was actually plains. I was ambivalent about the sudden shift in landscape. On the one hand, it would be easier to see if anyone was coming to attack us, but on the other, we would also be easier to find by others, which kept me on edge even as the grasslands stretched peacefully in front of us.

The next few days wound together. Both Gwen and Loglan seemed to have decided to make me do as much of the work as possible. I understood their reasoning by the end of the first day, even if every muscle in my body ached. Not only was I carrying my own bag, but I'd been given the bulk of our food as well. When she'd passed me the large backpack, Loglan had smiled approvingly.

"That should help develop some of her muscles," was all he'd said. After that, no one offered to help me carry the cargo, no matter how much my body wanted to give out beneath me. Even Sel, who looked at me with a wrinkled brow from time to time when I lagged and fell behind. He didn't want to disappoint Loglan, and neither did I.

Gwen taught me how to build a campsite on the first night.

We found a sheltered area with scrubby mulberry bushes to block the wind. By now, we were far into the rolling plains and it was the most cover from the elements we could find. Loglan seemed happy with our progress, but I had no idea how much ground we'd covered. Between carrying and walking, I was exhausted and more than happy to stop for the night. When I put the food and my bag down and exhaled in relief, she merely pointed to the load Loglan had been carrying.

"You need to build that."

"Build what?" I'm sure I looked as confused as I felt. I had no idea what the pile of sticks and fabric were supposed to be. My expression of dismay must have amused her, or maybe it was a dumb question because she broke into peals of laughter.

"You need to learn how to do all of this on your own. We likely won't need it tonight but it's helpful to be able to build a shelter in case of rain or when it gets colder. You won't always have someone who knows how to do it for you available, and I want to make sure you can be self-sufficient." She paused, tilting her head slightly as she looked at me.

Instead of complaining, I sighed and set to work. She coaxed me along, showing me where to put the poles to reinforce my structure. When we stretched the thick tarp overtop, I was pleased with my efforts. Even though it took me twice as long as it would have taken her and with my hands aching and back sore from the lifting, a sense of accomplishment held me up long enough to curl into my sleeping sack, where I instantly fell into sleep.

When I woke to the feel of hands on my shoulders gently shaking me what felt like only a few minutes later, I groaned in protest. "No." I refused to open my eyes and accept reality. I

CHAPTER 7

tried to burrow into my coverings, but the shaking continued until I gave up.

"It's your turn to tend the fire," a deep voice sounded beside my ear.

My eyes shot open to see Loglan watching me as he waited impassively for me to wake up. If it had been Sel or even Gwen, I might have tried to argue, but he didn't strike me as someone I'd win against. I groaned once more, rubbing my eyes, and rolled out of my makeshift bed. The moons were bright, ergo it was not daytime. I stomped over to where he was reclining beside the fire, my face likely a grumpy picture of childish rebellion which he simply ignored.

"It is wise while traveling to have one person on fire duty. This is not only to tend the fire, but also to keep a watch for animals, or anything else that could mean you harm." He poked at the fire before unwinding his long legs and standing, handing the fire poker to me.

"Because you had a hard day yesterday and I imagine today will not be much easier, I saved the last watch for you. I know it doesn't feel like enough sleep now, but in actuality, you got more than your friends as you had an uninterrupted sleep. When the sun crests the hill over there," he pointed to the east, "it will be time for you to wake us. It is also your duty to have breakfast ready, the extra chore of the final watch as a gift to your companions for getting the best shift."

I accepted the poker with numb hands, my brain still half-asleep, and watched as he made comfortable across from me on the other side of the fire. There was space in the shelter, but he'd told us he preferred to sleep under the stars.

He pulled a blanket around his shoulders and closed his eyes, leaving me alone with my thoughts.

I'd never watched a fire before, nor made one. I had done a lot of things I'd never done before in the last few days. I'd fought ur'gels, been injured, walked farther than ever, carried more weight than I'd ever carried, and last night I'd built my first shelter. Now I was mesmerized by the dancing flames.

The world was so quiet and so large in the darkness. For a moment, it felt as if I was the only person alive and an unexpected sense of peace settled into my heart. This was what I'd been waiting for all those years studying my textbooks, I realized. A chance to see the world I'd dreamt of exploring for so long. I smiled, looking up at the sky. It was still dark, but the faint lightening in the east told me daylight wasn't far off. I decided to be proactive and gather all the supplies I needed for cooking.

By the time Gwen woke up, the sun was almost where Loglan had told me to look. At the look on her face I felt pride sweep over me. The mixing and measuring were done for the porridge, and it was warming in the fire, and I had already cut two slabs of meat off the salted ham and laid out the utensils and plates.

"You've been busy."

"I don't want to hold us back. This is my mission and I've enlisted you to help me with it. I'll try harder not to complain, but I can't promise I won't be whiny at times."

She sat down and put one arm around me, giving me a tight squeeze. With her warm green eyes locked on mine, she disagreed. "I'm sure you feel overwhelmed, but you've done brilliantly. In fact, within the first day, you'd already achieved more than I expected from you. I've always liked you, but you've always been, well, for lack of a better word, sheltered." I narrowed my eyes at the description, but she continued. "I never thought you were a bad person, it's just that your life was so different and so easy, I didn't give you nearly enough credit. You've got a lot more fire than I expected, which gives me hope we'll succeed in getting to our destination, and you'll find whatever it is you're searching for."

I ducked my head at the praise, then remembered something. Tilting my head, I looked at her. "Did you mention

CHAPTER 7

83

something about seeing the future, or was that part of my post-injury confusion? Is that why you said you'd come with me?"

Her arm fell away, and I felt its absence with an unexpected pang. It had been warm and soothing. I hadn't sat like that with anyone that I could recall and I regretted asking the question even before she moved away from me.

She toyed with her long golden hair for a few moments as she bit her lip. "Sometimes, I see things."

I drew my eyebrows together, wondering what things she meant, even as her shoulders drooped.

"In my dreams. I think maybe it's part of my connection with the wolves. That's why I agreed to come so quickly when you asked me. I've already had time to get used to the idea that something is coming, I just didn't know what until you showed up in the forest." She looked into the distance.

I followed her gaze, noticing the sun had now risen to sit just over the gently rolling horizon. For a moment, the light was blinding.

"War is already here. I can't share anything that would help you find what you're looking for because the images are still too jumbled. I do know we need to be as prepared as possible."

She searched my face, her eyes full of emotion, then lightened the mood by smiling suddenly. "I promise, I'm not trying to torture you by making you do all the work."

I snorted, amused even while I continued to think about her previous admission. "I know. I'm smart enough to realize it's my mission, but I'm the weak link in the group. Even Sel knows more about fighting than I do."

I looked at the shelter where he was still sleeping. It was time to wake him, but I was enjoying the alone time with her and wanted to delay changing that for as long as I could. "I've always been impressed with him, even more so now. I think someday he's going to be a formidable man. I just hope I'm around to see it."

Gwen smiled. "Yeah, I was impressed with the little guy, too."

We sat there for a few more minutes, watching the sun make its climb. Once it was higher, I stood reluctantly.

"You can get started, if you want. The porridge is warming in that pot and should be finished. I'll wake up the guys. Just make sure there's enough for all of us," I warned. She blinked, her eyes wide and innocent as I turned to wake the others.

I watched as they ate, hoping I'd done a decent job making breakfast. It was the first time I'd ever cooked for anyone and I was unexpectedly proud of myself. It tasted fine to me, but maybe I was fooling myself. "How is it?"

Sel stopped with his spoon halfway to his mouth and nodded, continuing without speaking. I looked at Gwen, who'd fashioned herself a sandwich with the bread and meat. Loglan grunted, eating the porridge. Although it wasn't much, I assumed it tasted all right as they kept eating, even if they didn't say anything. Once we'd finished our breakfast and packed up, Gwen and Loglan narrowed their eyes and turned to me as one unit.

"What?"

I didn't know him well, but the look on her face was one I'd seen before, usually when she was considering something particularly mischievous. I knew I wasn't going to like what was coming, but to my surprise, it was Loglan who responded to my crossed arms and suspicious glare.

"We'll reach the edge of the Low Forest and the city of Sunglen within the next few days, which is where I'll leave you. As part of your education, it would be prudent for you to learn how to hunt for your food. I'm not worried you'll run out on this trip, but I see much traveling in the future for you." He turned to Gwen. "As my diet is mainly vegetarian, I will defer to you for the appropriate way to go about such a thing. What is your recommendation?"

A smile crept over her face. "I think hunting is a great idea.

CHAPTER 7   85

Perhaps we can look for our meal while you set up camp tonight?"

My eyebrows shot up in surprise. I'd expected to be given that chore again and hunting suddenly sounded like a reprieve.

"It is still early, so we should continue on. I'm hoping we can make some ground today and when we stop for the night, you can take her then."

I swallowed hard at what they were suggesting. Once the elation at one less chore had passed, the reality of what it meant to go hunting struck me. I'd never killed anything before, unless ur'gels counted, but that had been a matter of life or death. I had never killed something not trying to kill me and was clueless how one even carried out such a thing.

"I ... can try." I gave both Gwen and Loglan a weak smile, relieved to see they both seemed pleased with my answer instead of disappointed at my hesitancy.

"Perfect. Let's get moving then. It's going to be a long day." Gwen tossed the backpack with the food in it over to me and I caught it with a grunt, securing it as I took a look back at the place we'd spent the night.

The only trace was the fire, which had been doused with water then covered over with dirt. Prior to today, I wouldn't have even known anyone had been there. It was amazing how much my life was changing.

THE DAY PASSED SWIFTLY, my legs settling into a rhythm which became easier as we walked. They still hurt, but I had become accustomed to the sensation and it no longer made me grit my teeth. Perhaps I was getting stronger, or more likely, some of the morning stiffness had worn off as the blood circulated with the exercise. Still, by the time Loglan halted and turned to Sel with a smile, I was ready to rest.

"Are you ready to learn how to make a campsite?" He

looked down at Sel, who was bouncing on his toes. I bit back a smile at his eagerness.

"Yes, sir! What would you like me to do first?"

I bit my lip harder, certain laughter wouldn't go over well, but when Gwen caught my eye it was almost too much for us both. I feigned a coughing fit, for which she passed me a flask of water.

"Are you okay? You aren't getting sick, are you?"

Her tone was solicitous, and on the surface she seemed concerned. But the smile crinkling the corner of eyes made it obvious she was as amused as I was.

"I'm fine."

Once we'd calmed down and Sel and Loglan were occupied with the camp, she showed me what to pack for our hunting trip, which thankfully allowed me to leave the rest of the items I'd been carrying at the campsite with the guys. Our home for the night was an area not far from the river, sheltered by willows and peaceful in the late afternoon sun. I paced the beside the spot Gwen had designated for the fire and turned to look at her for direction.

"We'll need to go far enough from here that our prospective game won't be frightened off by Sel and Loglan. As lovely as it would be to hunt nearby, there's too much action here."

"But isn't it important to stay close? What about the ur'gels?" The thought of another ur'gel attack worried me, especially without the guys for assistance.

She shook her head. "We won't go farther than necessary. The river has plenty of brush and trees that shelter small creatures, but I'm hoping for a larger one. It's also important to be as silent as you can. Any noise can startle a small animal. Not to mention our scents."

"What else do I need to do? I mean, should I do anything special?" I had no idea what I was asking but wanted to take her instruction in hunting seriously. I figured asking questions would show I was trying.

CHAPTER 7

"Well, the first step is to make as little noise as possible. Become aware of where you step, as even the smallest crunch of a leaf or crack of a twig can frighten away an animal. Their hearing is far keener than ours. The second crucial part is to stay upwind."

"Upwind?" I had no idea what she meant.

"Animals tend to congregate near water or sources of food. We want to make sure we approach our prey from a place our scents won't blow toward them. Ideally, their scent would blow toward us. Does that make sense?

"I think so. But how do we tell which way the wind is blowing?"

She raised an eyebrow and I blushed, instantly feeling stupid.

"If you can feel the wind blowing on your face, your scent will be blown behind you. If you can't feel the wind, you can wet your finger and hold it up. The colder side is where the wind is coming from. And if all else fails, my wolves usually know." She smiled down at Swift, who had perked up his ears and come over to her side during our conversation.

"Anything else?"

"No, those are the big things. Be stealthy, stay downwind, and if something passes by, try to kill it."

We remained silent as we left our campsite. She found a spot she thought animals would congregate, making a hand gesture for us to wait. We hid under a tree and could see the river from where we crouched. I couldn't tell if we were upwind or downwind, but she seemed happy. The wolves had been silent companions, but hadn't stuck as closely to Gwen's side as I'd thought they would.

They roamed widely, occasionally returning to touch base with her before disappearing into the bushes again. When a sudden loud rustling of leaves and the cracking of branches as something trampled through the brush at a rapid clip headed in our direction, she tapped my arm and stood, half-crouching as she pulled out her knife.

I followed her lead with shaking hands, taking a deep breath, and letting it out as quietly as I could while I drew the knife I'd only used once before. I tried to will my hand into stillness, to no avail. It appeared trembling was the best I could do, so I bit my lip and hoped it was enough.

Seconds later, a frightened deer burst into the clearing in front of us between the trees and water, followed by her wolves nipping at its heels. The wolves were intent on their prey, snarling and working as a team to herd it away from us and onward. I caught Swift's sidelong glance at our hiding place at the same instant Gwen leapt forward. I jolted up then ran after her, somehow managing to stay close behind.

"Now, Rhin!"

She shouted and I lunged at her command. I had no idea where to strike the deer, but it was heading straight at me so I had no time to ask. I sent out a prayer, hoping I didn't end up trampled for my effort, and then stood still with my knife held out. At the last second, I ducked to the right and closed my eyes, stabbing wildly as the deer rushed past.

My blade made contact and I pushed it deeper. As warmth gushed over my hand, I opened my eyes, widening them when I saw it had entered into the deer's neck. At first, it attempted to continue running. I was nearly knocked down as it thrashed, but managed to twist further to the side, which caused the knife to plunge even deeper into the animal's throat. I still had no idea what I was doing as the knife proceeded to slice through flesh, stopping abruptly in something hard. Bone. A sudden warm spray of blood coated my hands and face, and my eyes shut reflexively again.

Everything moved fast after that. The deer stumbled, eyes wide with confusion. It was as though I was under a shower of hot rain, as the blood coated my arm and part of my face. I

CHAPTER 7

closed my mouth, but not before a few drops of the tangy, iron-rich fluid had baptized my lips.

The deer attempted a few more steps but its speed had disappeared. It faltered, and I stared as the front legs buckled and the entire weight of the deer pitched forward onto its neck. It lay in an awkward position, eyes blinking at me before slowly glazing over and remaining still. I'd never seen anything die in front of me, but I instinctively felt the second the spirit left the body.

My mouth must have fallen open at some point because when Gwen came up to me, she clapped me on the back, took one look at my face, and gently pushed my chin up.

"Nicely done, Rhin! I've got to say I was fairly sure you were going to be trampled with that move." She glanced at the deer, shooting me a grin when she looked back at me. "That was a nice strike. Probably one of the quickest and most effective ways to kill an animal. You see?" She pointed at the spot my knife had entered on the left side of the deer's throat. Blood was still oozing from the site, but the spray effect had ended as the deer had died. "That means you hit the artery. The nice thing about this particular death blow is that we've already drained a good portion of the blood." She knelt beside the deer, checking it over. "Now, we need to dress it to take it back to camp. Are you going to be okay to help?"

"Tell me what to do and I'm yours."

CHAPTER 8

The next morning, I was still riding high on my success at taking the deer down single-handedly. In the last week, I'd experienced more than I had in my entire life previously. I was beginning to understand how different book learning was from the practical application of information.

Loglan had gone out of his way for us, but at the same time he hadn't gone easy on me. Gwen had been tougher on me, but he'd been instrumental in teaching me many of my new skills. So, it was a disappointment when he announced at breakfast he was leaving.

"We've reached the edge of the boundary to the Low Forest. I must leave you here, as my duties lie within the Low Forest. It has been a pleasure."

"Thank you for everything, Loglan. I can't express how much you've done for me, for us." I smiled, offering a hand. He inclined his head as he accepted it and we clasped hands for a moment. He turned to Gwen, who gave him a jaunty salute, then grinned at Sel, ruffling his hair. Sel didn't appear to mind, although disappointment Loglan was leaving was written on his face.

"I'm sure we'll see you soon," Gwen offered.

CHAPTER 8

91

"I hope so. Be careful. Although your mission is worthy, darkness is spreading over the land and Lynia is becoming far more dangerous than it has ever been." His words were solemn, and a chill rippled down my spine as if he'd spoken a premonition.

He slung his bag over his back, and we watched without speaking for several moments as he galloped off.

"Well, I guess it's just us now." I turned to see Sel on the verge of tears. He looked like his hero had just died instead of departed, and I felt bad for the boy. Gingerly, I patted him on the shoulder.

He blinked rapidly as he threw his narrow shoulders back, brushing my hand away as he tried to look tough. "We'll be fine. I mean, he was nice and experienced and all, but we can do almost everything he can."

I'd never heard him try his hand at swagger before and it didn't really suit him, even though the bluster in his tone made me suspect he was trying to convince himself more than he was trying to convince either of us. I shared an amused glance with Gwen.

"Oh, absolutely. We're going to be fine. Especially since he gave us directions to get to Abrecem Secer from here."

I turned to her, surprise making my voice come out higher than usual. "He did? When?"

Gwen wiggled her eyebrows. "Last night. After you fell asleep, I traded off guard duty with him, and he gave me a map."

"I was under the impression he was directing us by the suns, moons, and stars? You mean to tell me he had a map this entire time?" I snorted, crossing my arms. All this time I'd thought he was doing something special.

She laughed, lightly punching my shoulder. "Yes, of course. Centaurs are excellent celestial navigators, but they still carry maps. What do you do if it's a cloudy night or you can't see the sun during the day?"

What she said made sense, except for one thing. "But it was cloudy the first day and I didn't see him looking at a map."

"Yes, but I don't think he needs a map for the forest. After all, he's one of the Guardians. I'm pretty sure he could navigate the route we traveled from his village to here without being able to see anything in the sky. His map will be important for between here and Abrecem Secer. In fact, he said if we continue walking, we'll be at Sunglen by dusk."

My eyes widened. Happiness flooded through me. "So, I don't have to build a shelter tonight?"

This time, both Sel and Gwen laughed.

"That's great!" Sel weighed in. "That means I don't have to hear her complain tonight."

"I wouldn't go that far. It means we should be able to get lodgings someplace with a roof and soft bedding. As to whether she complains today, only the gods can answer that question." Gwen shrugged, smirking at my open mouth.

I glared at both of them. They were teasing, but still, it hurt my feelings.

He recognized my expression and became instantly apologetic. "I'm sorry, I wasn't serious. No one would ever mistake you for a pampered princess if they could see you now."

I looked down at my clothes. "I'm absolutely filthy. No one could mistake me for a pampered princess, but I don't think it has anything to do with what I've learned over the last few days. I look like one of the roving nomad people."

Her mouth twitched again. She was trying to hold back laughter for my sake. "You're right. If you'd looked like this when we first met, I wouldn't be calling you 'princess'. Homeless, maybe. Traveler, absolutely."

As much as it chafed to have my friends laughing at me, a tingle of delight replaced some of my irritation and I relaxed my jaw. Gwen thought I looked like a traveler? They were the toughest and most resilient guests we'd ever had at the castle. I stood straighter with pride, looking around the campsite and

CHAPTER 8

changing the subject. Loglan was far from sight now and I stood, beginning to clean up the remains of our breakfast by the fire. "If Loglan thinks we can get to Sunglen by nightfall, we should start moving. I'll take down the shelter if someone else wants to make sure the fire is doused."

Sel and Gwen got to their feet and we divided the chores. Consequently, everything was packed away within half an hour. The wolves had been absent during this entire time and I'd begun to wonder if they'd make it back before we left but as we started off walking, Swift and his sidekicks came loping into view. Amusement welled as I looked at them. Gwen caught my expression and tilted her head.

"What?"

"I'm impressed, I guess. The connection you've got with the wolves is something I've never seen before and don't quite understand."

Gwen looked down, her amusement fading.

"What is it? Did I say something wrong?" I was caught off guard by her reaction.

"No, you didn't say anything wrong. I wonder if I didn't have this connection with the wolves if I would've been better off at times. I'd never trade them for anything, but maybe I would have fit in better. Maybe I could have been normal."

"I can't believe I just heard you say that."

I pressed my lips together while I searched for the right words to support her while convincing her she was being stupid. "Look, we both know we're different from other elves. You're different because of the wolves, sure, but there's more to you than just the animals." She didn't answer, but the flicker of her eyelids told me I'd struck a nerve. "That's not a bad thing. I'm different too. I think it works for us." I smiled and placed a hand on her shoulder. "If it wasn't for you being different, I wouldn't be alive now. So, forgive me if I think what makes you different is also what makes you incredible."

Gwen's eyes sparkled with unshed tears. I was sure I'd

completely blown my attempt at reassurance when a smile crept over her face.

She launched herself into my arms and I almost fell backward before I braced myself and returned the hug.

"Thanks, Rhin."

I smiled at the sound of her muffled voice against my shoulder, catching Sel's eye and seeing his relief.

She sniffed, stepping back briskly, as though her moment of weakness had never happened.

"We should keep going. If we want to make it to Sunglen before nightfall, we'll have to move quickly." She narrowed her eyes, assessing the distance before turning and giving us both a look of caution. "Moving fast will also help if there're any more ur'gels looking for us.

Without any further conversation, we headed onward. I was still sore from the previous days' travel, but I could already feel my stamina increasing. Every muscle I had was still aching, but each step was a bit easier than it had been when I'd first left the castle. Now, an entire day of walking was only as hard as the first walk through the forest to find Gwen. My muscles felt tighter, larger, and stronger somehow. I was carrying the packs with more ease today, so when Sunglen appeared on the horizon near midday, we shared triumphant looks.

We broke for a light snack, filling our water bottles at a fast-moving river, then continued on the path which was now clearly defined. All the while, the watchful eye of the spires grew larger the closer we came to the city.

When we finally approached the stone outer gates, I was elated. The city I'd dreamt about seeing for so long! We entered easily, without any guards checking us. I was relieved but surprised. At Cliffside, we were cautious about newcomers, even before the ur'gels became rampant.

Maybe the sheer number of people made it impractical, or perhaps the danger hadn't made it this far yet. I'd never been

CHAPTER 8   95

surrounded by so many people before. My mind was flooded by the sights and sounds of so many of them in close quarters. The roads were a wide grey cobblestone, but the buildings were a mixture of wood, stone, and brick.

I hadn't expected the city to have a smell, but as we wove our way through the busy thoroughfare onto smaller side streets, we passed vendors selling food and other items. The aroma was almost overpowering. It was exotic, a mixture of familiar herbal preparations with their astringent undertones, meat cooking on a spit near a nutman selling roasted chestnuts.

My mouth watered as the meat and nuts reminded me it had been some time since our last meal, but a waft of something reminiscent of fertilizer quickly doused that. A soft squish under my shoe announced I'd found the culprit. I scraped off the dung I'd stepped in, glancing to see if anyone had noticed.

The brilliant golden glass buildings I'd dreamt of when I thought of Sunglen shone in the sunlight, taking my attention away from the mess on my shoe. We were surrounded by smaller buildings similar to the ones in the Low Forest village, but it was those buildings of legend we wanted to reach.

The streets narrowed the further we penetrated into the city, and soon we found ourselves in a rabbit warren of alleys and streets. I was certain we were hopelessly lost but even as I began to worry, Gwen crouched down to say something to Swift. They stared at each other for a moment, then Swift took off, turning left down an alley and disappearing.

I turned to her, curious about what was happening, but she merely held up a finger and gave me a cryptic smile. When Swift returned a few minutes later, she crouched down again. They repeated the process a few times before Gwen stood and gave both Sel and me a confident smile.

"Swift says we're only an hour away from Abrecem Secer. If we follow him, he can take us there."

I flicked a glance to Sel, but he just shrugged, so I looked

SOUL GOBLET

at Gwen again. I bit my lip, finally asking the question on my mind. "Are you sure this is the right way?" I couldn't disguise the tremor in my voice. I wasn't comfortable in the alley we'd ended up in, and my uneasiness with our surroundings made it hard to sound calm. The hair on my neck felt like it was standing up and I had to wipe my suddenly clammy hands on my pants.

"It's not what you expected, is it?" She gave me a smile. "I know. I was only here once, a few years ago, but a city is made up of all kinds."

Gwen was doing her best to look unconcerned, but her shoulders were tighter than they'd been when we first arrived and her gaze was fixed at a point just beyond my shoulder. My uneasiness multiplied in the form of sweat trickling down my back when I turned around to find a shifty-looking human dressed in rags, watching us with glinting eyes.

I quickly turned back to Gwen, my eyes wide. "I trust you. Let's keep moving."

"That's always the best idea in places like this," she agreed. "Keep your friends close, and your money belt closer." Her voice dropped. There was a tone of amusement, but her words were meant to be taken seriously.

I drew my belongings closer.

Trusting Swift was correct, we practically bolted from the dark, narrow alleyway we'd found ourselves in. My heart rate slowed when the road widened again and the beautiful decorations we'd seen from a distance became more prominent. I cast a final look at the dingy back road. My illusions about the glory of life in the big city had been thoroughly shattered by the reality. Disappointed, but hopefully wiser, I took a deep breath and turned the corner.

Shock halted my feet. I stared, mouth falling open as my eyes traveled all the way up the massive edifice before me. The building I'd dreamt of seeing since the first moment I'd heard

CHAPTER 8

of it. The Library. The most valuable building in the known world, at least in my estimation.

It was fashioned from the same golden material I'd seen from the distance, with large, arched windows topped by fierce gargoyle statues. It was enormous up close, expanding to fill the entire block and I couldn't decide where to look first, as every nook and crevice seemed to have another statue, carving, or decoration to draw my eye.

Blinking back tears, I smiled. Within this gilded building, I hoped to discover the answers to stop the darkness from spreading and destroying my entire world.

CHAPTER 9

The longer I stared at the Library, the more I felt like an imposter. What if I wasn't allowed in? After all, what training did I have? The Library was important, and I was no one. Gwen seemed completely unconcerned, but I was mollified to observe a similarly stunned expression on Sel's face. At least someone else was overwhelmed.

"Rhin? Are you going to be okay?"

"Yeah, I'll be fine. I ... well, it's beautiful. I was expecting it to be beautiful, but I wasn't expecting it to be ... this." I gestured helplessly with my hand as her eyes twinkled.

"*You* may not have expected your reaction, but I did. When you're done staring, we should go inside, where the actual books are."

She paused, nudging Sel.

He jumped, smiling back sheepishly. "Sorry. I've never seen anything like it."

"Good, because you may need to catch her when she faints. If the outside of the building can bring her to the brink of tears, I'm worried about the strength of her heart once she sees the actual books."

CHAPTER 9

He snorted, looking down quickly when I glared first at him, then Gwen.

"I'll be just fine." I enunciated my words carefully, crossing my arms for emphasis.

She held her hands up in front of her as if to ward off my anger. "Sure. In that case, let's go." She turned without a backward glance, walking toward the massive front entrance.

The stairs went straight up at least two floors. I didn't attempt to count them as we climbed. They were wide and made of white marble laced with veins of gold which caught the setting sun as it shone down. My blood thrummed in my ears when I stepped on the first one. It was like I was walking into a magical kingdom, a place I desperately wanted to belong, but wasn't sure I would be allowed. I thought of the dung I'd stepped in and my heart sank at the thought of dirtying the beautiful staircase.

I tried to focus on reality, not on what I was creating in my head, but it was hard. I reminded myself the items inside were what gave this building its power, not the outward appearance, but each step closer made me giddy despite my attempts.

A wide archway with elves and humans coming and going rested at the top of the platform, some with their noses in books, others with their noses firmly in the air while servants carried their books and followed behind. For the first time in my life, I felt at home. Sure, the building wasn't homey in the traditional sense, but I was amongst my people: the tribe of scholars.

I stepped over the threshold, unable to stop my eyes from opening wide as I tried to drink in the details of the ceiling in front of me. It was intricately painted, a masterpiece itself. It depicted ancient stories I'd read before, but never seen. I recognized the cliffs, the Low Forest, and what I thought were the mountains near the Dragon Dominion. Before I could get past the first few pictures though, an imperious voice interrupted, jerking me to what was happening in front of me.

"I'm sorry, but animals are not allowed."

I turned, seeing an elderly elf dressed in dark blue robes. He was standing beside Gwen with his arms crossed, his problem evident. Wolf-walkers weren't respected among elves, most elves considering wolves as nothing more than wild animals. I opened my mouth to argue with the old man, but Gwen stopped me, placing a gentle hand on my arm.

"I understand."

She bowed, taking a step back as she looked at Swift. Without a word, the wolves stood and trotted back to the steps, waiting just outside the entryway. She turned to me, biting her lip, then gestured for me to come closer.

I looked at the elf. He was standing silently with his arms crossed like he was guarding the entrance. I moved Gwen a few feet away.

"Why won't you let me say anything?"

"We both know it won't make any difference. The Librarian is unlikely to change the no animal policy, so the only thing you'll do is ruin your own chance for entry. I'll find a place to stay nearby that will allow my wolves. I want you to be extremely cautious. This place is more than it appears. I've heard stories of its power, and rumors the cities are somehow connected through Abrecem Secer. Most importantly, I want you to remember not everyone who helps you can be trusted."

"I'll be careful, but I'm more worried about you being out there by yourself."

She pointed at her wolves. "I'm not alone. As long as I have Swift, Kiya, and Daimyo, I'll never be by myself."

"Fine. I'm not alone either. I have Sel." I pointed to the boy, who was still gawking at the ceiling. "I'll be back soon," I promised.

She glared at the old elf who was still watching her with cold eyes. "If you're not back in a few hours, I'll come and find you. *With* the wolves."

She raised her voice loud enough for the Librarian to hear.

CHAPTER 9

"I'll find someone to help me start searching. You get lodgings and I'll join you as soon as possible. If you can leave a message with someone, we'll meet you when I'm finished here."

Gwen winked and ruffled Sel's hair quickly before getting out of range of retribution. He looked surprised and I had to bite back a laugh. They got along well, but Sel wasn't used to being teased. It was cute and I was reminded of my relationship with my siblings when we were younger.

We watched Gwen and the wolves run down the stairs with an easy grace, and a strange feeling of loss passed through me. Her warning stuck with me though, and I reminded myself to be cautious. Slowly I turned back to the old elf.

"Thank you for allowing us entry, even if we are disappointed about our other friends." I kept my tone respectful but couldn't help commenting on the lack of welcome for Gwen and her wolves. "My name is Rhiniya of the Cliff Elves, daughter of Elsinore and Arwan. I've come to find a specific book from Abrecem Secer. Any assistance you can provide me would be most appreciated."

I bowed, keeping my voice formal and polite, and watched as his arms slowly relaxed. He uncrossed them. He stared at me with half-lidded eyes and paused long enough that tension rose in my shoulders, then finally responded.

"My name is Luban, and I am the Head Librarian here. I will assign you a Librarian apprentice while you are here. The Library contains many wonders, but it would be wise if you stick with him and do exactly what he tells you. People have become lost, and sometimes, the lost are never recovered."

I shivered, remembering Gwen's misgivings about the Library, and reminded myself to always remain on my guard. "That would be much appreciated. Thank you, Sir Luban."

Luban cut me off. "Just Luban. The Librarian I am assigning you is one of our newer, younger ones. Please let me know if he fails to live up to the high standards we expect from our bookkeepers."

Hopefully, the Librarian he was assigning me would prove up to the challenge. He seemed like the kind of taskmaster who would punish minor infractions. A young man about my age or slightly younger appeared at Luban's side as if summoned by magic.

"Yes, Luban?"

The young man remained bowed, looking up with a darting gaze before staring at his shoes. Luban narrowed his eyes and examined him from top to bottom. The plain brown robes he wore were neat, as was his short, chestnut-colored hair, but somehow, Luban seemed disappointed in him. Eventually, he grunted an answer.

"Jarid, I think you are the best choice for the patron in front of us. Please ensure you watch yourself and do not overstep. I would like you to assist Ms. Rhiniya to retrieve the books she's searching for. Any questions?" Luban looked down, one eyebrow arched imperiously.

Jarid bobbed his head. "No, sir. I shall do my utmost to provide exemplary service. Is there anywhere you wish for us to avoid today?"

Luban narrowed his eyes, turning to me, his cold gaze burrowing into me. But just as with Jarid, whatever he saw within me seemed to reassure him, if not impress the stern man. He turned back to Jarid.

"She may be allowed full range of any of our books. But it will be important to keep this guest safe from getting lost."

The way he intoned *this guest* left a funny sensation in the pit of my stomach. Was it not always important to keep patrons of the Library safe? Did people really go missing? Before I could question him, Luban gave a shooing motion and I realized we were being summarily dismissed.

"Please, follow me. We'll get started in the information room for me to better assist you with your search."

I followed Jarid through the foyer, hardly noticing the decor now, my mind full of questions. After a few steps I real-

CHAPTER 9

ized Luban was nowhere to be seen. Strange. How he had been there at just the right time to turn Gwen away, but the moment I was set up with a helper he vanished? I hadn't seen him leave, and there was nowhere I could see where he could have gone. The combination of Gwen's warnings coupled with the mysterious Librarian filled me with a sudden truth—the Library *was* far more than met the eye.

Jarid reminded me of Sel. A little older and taller, but he had the same pleasant, easy-going, open face and gangliness which made him appear eager to please. I could instantly tell he was a fellow lover of books. His commentary was informative and interesting as we walked through the empty halls.

"This part of the Library is the oldest. It was built to convey the impressive might of the elven kingdoms and the wisdom of the world at the same time. But the Library itself is more than just a building, with many facets which can be more dangerous than anywhere else one could visit on our planet."

I stopped, looking at Jarid. "What do you mean? Am I supposed to be worried about something in particular?"

"No. As long as you stay close to me and pay attention, you should be fine. The reason they assign a Librarian to every guest is because of the potential of taking a wrong turn and losing your way, as much as is it is to assist with book selection."

I wasn't sure I believed him, especially when he gave me such a blandly polite smile and when I raised my eyebrows, he recited what sounded like another carefully scripted sentence.

"Please ensure you do not open any doors I haven't designated as safe or opened first, and ask before you remove any books from the shelves. For your own safety, of course." He bowed his head respectfully. "The first place we are going to stop is the archives."

I was suspicious of Jarid's tantalizingly polite doublespeak, but not afraid. I knew there were secrets he wasn't sharing, but I was hopeful if I spent more time with him, I'd get the answers I sought. Only now, in addition to my questions about the Dark War and the ritual Onen Suun had used to trap Dag'draath, perhaps I would find out the mysteries of the Library they seemed to be hiding.

At the atrium, Jarid steered me to a set of overstuffed chairs across from each other with a small table between them. He grabbed a book from the shelf directly beside the table, then sat and opened it while gesturing for me to sit in the remaining chair.

I wrinkled my nose at the unimpressive volume but sat, sinking into the velvety surface. It was surprisingly comfortable, but as I tried to peer over the table at the book, I had to stretch further than the chair would allow and ended up half-standing, half-leaning over the table. Even so, I couldn't quite make out what it said from where I was. Reading upside-down handwriting in an archaic text clearly was something I needed to practice.

Finally, his finger stopped in the center of one of the pages and he looked up. "Here. The appendix says we need to go to the west wing for the books you require."

"I didn't tell you what I was looking for. Did I?"

Jarid smiled at me for the first time, the same wicked smile of amusement my brother would get pulling a prank on me. For the first time, I saw a hint of personality behind the bland brown robes and quiet responses.

"You may not have told me," he drawled slowly, pointing at the book. "But the book knows all."

"I'm assuming this is what Luban meant when he mentioned the Library had magic?"

The smile faded, and his voice became hushed. "It is. However, this is a more ... pleasant aspect of the Library's magic. The Library has far more to offer than just books, even if many of the other aspects are less helpful than this."

If even the people who worked at the Library seemed

frightened of the magic, I could only guess what was truly hidden within the walls.

"Shall we?"

He stood, tucking the book underneath his arm, and I followed his lead.

"Yes, thank you."

We left the open atrium, which had been filled with natural light, and entered into a winding hallway. The walls were covered in shelves of books which reached as high as I could see. It struck me as odd, because from the outside the building only seemed a few stories high. From here, they stretched beyond what they should have. Another mystery.

My heart sang as I walked through the hall, with the dark wood of the shelves and books smelling of parchment and time filling my senses. I'd never seen anything so wonderful. Every twenty feet or so there was a door in the same dark wood of the shelves which absorbed the light, provided by torches on sconces on the walls every few feet. I followed him silently, doing my best to keep my hands to myself without asking why we never opened any of the doors we passed.

At one point I was distracted by a bookshelf made of a glossy cherry-colored wood. I veered slightly to the right, compelled by its luster to trail one hand along the shelf. I felt tingles from the contact shoot up my hand, but didn't pull away. When the shelf ended abruptly, a doorway was right in front of my hand. I reached out to grab the handle without thinking, but just before I touched it, Jarid realized I wasn't beside him.

"Rhiniya."

I pulled my hand back at his sharp tone, surprised to find how close I'd been to opening a door I hadn't even intended to. I glared at it, surprised and disappointed it had been about to do something I was certain would have gotten me in trouble. I tucked it into my pants pocket, scurrying to catch up.

Before long, we'd arrived at the room the volume had

directed us to. He double-checked the book before snapping it closed with confidence. He directed me to a long table with benches on either side. Although less comfortable in appearance than the atrium, it also was more practical for research and I sat down at the table, folding my hands in my lap as I waited for direction.

"This is where we are to start. Now, please, before you or your manservant take anything off the shelves, run it by me. I'll be happy to hand you anything you require."

He shot a warning look at Sel, who'd been a silent shadow until now, but he merely moved to stand behind my seat at the table quietly, in his usual attendant fashion. To my surprise, Jarid assumed an almost matching position on my other side. I blinked, not sure what to do with my unexpected foot soldiers.

"What I would like to look at first are some volumes I'd found mention of in my library, about the Dark War. Can you find those for me?"

I smiled slightly when he jerked his head at Sel. As their eyes met above my head, Sel dipped his chin slightly before they walked together to a large bookshelf on the back wall of the room. It stretched at least two stories tall but had an end, unlike the ones in the hallway. From somewhere behind me, Jarid procured a rolling staircase which he moved into position and climbed quickly.

He began passing books down to Sel, then once he'd passed a half dozen or so, he climbed down and took half. They returned together, placing them on the table in front of me.

"This should be enough for today. Please, respect the age of the texts and be gentle, and above all else, do not write in them."

"I would never deface a book in such a crass manner." I huffed with indignation, unable to believe anyone would suggest such a thing. I was sure it was a standard warning, but

CHAPTER 9 107

the idea of defacing such old and valuable sources of information felt like a personal insult.

I pulled one volume toward me, and quickly forgot any irritation as I fell into research mode. Within a few pages there was nothing else in the world except the book I was reading. The next time I looked up, it was because my back was sore, and I needed to crack it. Sighing once that had been accomplished, my stomach rumbled and I was stunned to see how much I'd already read. We'd likely already been in the room for several hours. When I looked up at Jarid, he bowed and came over.

"You have a question?"

"How long have we been here?"

A ghost of a smile passed over his face. "It is, in fact, nearing full dark. So perhaps it would be best to return to the books tomorrow? I'm sure your friend will be expecting you soon."

I blinked, not realizing he was aware there was another member of our party. He smiled again, the same mischievous smile from earlier.

"I was waiting nearby when Luban told your friends they weren't welcome. As much as he's a good teacher and Librarian, he is rather old and set in his ways, which unfortunately includes prejudice against others who are not up to his standards."

"I wanted to protest, but she felt it wouldn't be worth it."

"Your friend was correct. He's not the most demonstrative of elves, but he would have caused problems had your friend entered, which your friend likely surmised would have impacted your welcome here as well."

"No matter. This way, Gwen was hopefully able to procure lodgings for tonight. I doubt the Library is her favorite place to be, anyway. She's much more of an outdoors kind of girl."

"I assume from the presence of the wolves you're correct in this case. Come, let me get you back to her. You must leave all of the books here, but this room can be set aside for you so you can leave them on the table."

"That would be much appreciated, thank you." I stood up, my muscles confused and protesting the change from activity to being sedentary again.

He tucked the small book under his arm he'd used to lead us there and walked a few feet ahead.

As we traveled the same hallways in the direction we'd come, the same ornate door I'd almost touched earlier was there, but this time to my left. Once again, my hand went toward the handle against my will and turned the knob, as if controlled by an external force.

I was plunged into night. I rubbed my eyes, bewildered at the change. Where only a moment earlier I'd been in the Library, now I was deep inside a rocky chamber, lit by only the dimmest flickering blue lamplight. I panicked, stepping back a few times before whirling around to find Jarid standing in the doorway which had been invisible a moment earlier.

He held out a hand and I grabbed on to it like a lifeline. He pulled me back into the hallway before shutting the door with a snap and shaking his head, a look of fear on his face which he hid almost immediately.

"I told you to stick with me. The Library can be tricky, remember? That's not the right door."

He gave a weak laugh as he shooed me to walk in front of him. "I'm going to have to watch you more carefully, or you'll end up lost. Now, this time stay with me." He cast a warning look at Sel as I walked past. "Keep an eye on her."

He turned his gaze back to me. "I never would've thought of you as someone who'd break the rules, but it seems curiosity may be your driving force."

I shrugged, unable to disagree with his statement but perplexed by the strange motivation which had caused me to turn the handle. It hadn't been my curiosity in control. I wasn't sure I could accept responsibility for my actions for once, and

CHAPTER 9

looked at the doors in the hall uneasily after that moment, worried it would happen again.

After we'd traveled through the same twisting and turning hallways, he brought me back to the first doorway we'd taken.

"From now on, make sure you only use this one and next time, stay close. The other doorways are not ones you're supposed to be using. If you do chance them, only Suun knows where you'll end up."

I meekly looked down at my scuffed and dirty shoes as I bobbed my head without replying. My pulse was still racing from my brief foray into the darkness I'd plunged into unexpectedly. I had no idea where it was, but I was certain I hadn't been in the Library, or even Sunglen. If I hadn't known better, I would've thought we were in the Deep Fell.

But surely, that was impossible.

CHAPTER 10

Jarid steered us through the door and to my surprise, we entered the accepting hall at the entryway. I'm sure I looked confused because Jarid chuckled.

"Surprised? Don't be. Remember this place has a magic of its own. Doorways don't always work the way you think they should when you're in the Library. No matter, we've arrived at the beginning, as it were. Did you need help finding anything? Your friend perhaps, and her wolves?"

I raised my chin slightly, trying to hide my insecurity. I may not know where to go, but Sel was still with me. My gaze flicked to him. Throughout everything I'd experienced since arriving at the Library, he'd been silent, watching with an impassive face. His eyes would widen at times, but overall he was doing extremely well for his age. I couldn't help feeling a niggle of self-consciousness telling me he was doing better than I was.

"Thank you. But I have my manservant, and I'm sure Gwen is close by. She was heading to secure lodgings when we came in. How long have we been here, anyway?"

Jarid shrugged. "A few hours." He looked around the Library, squinting at the arched roof that had been lit by the suns when we'd arrived. "I'd say it's close to suppertime. You should go find your friend. The light will be gone soon." He gave me an uneasy smile, adding, "As beautiful as it is here in Sunglen, it's best not to be out after dark. There are unsavory people in the neighborhood near the Library once the other businesses shut down for the night."

I remembered the creepy man who'd stared at us earlier when we'd gotten turned around in a back alley. If it hadn't been for Gwen and her wolves, I was sure he would've done more than just stare. I forced a smile to my face.

"Thank you for your assistance today. I want to come back tomorrow. Shall I look for you again, or will I be assigned another apprentice?"

Jarid pointed to a small room behind a shelf of books near the entrance.

I hadn't noticed it before, neatly tucked away behind the ostentatious statues and away from the ceiling which had captured me earlier. Inside the room were several young men and women, dressed in dull grey or brown robes similar to what Jarid wore. Their heads were bent studiously, over books I assumed, even though I couldn't see them from behind the window. A young woman lifted her head and met my eyes. I blinked and looked back at Jarid.

"What's in there?"

"It's a waiting room, of sorts," Jarid shrugged. I noticed his face remained carefully blank. For the second time, it made me wonder how harsh a taskmaster Luban was. "We do most of our work in rooms such as that. There are several scattered throughout the Library. This is where we look for information for the richer and more prestigious guests who do not wish to waste their time in the actual Library themselves."

His eyes widened and he looked at me with horror. I bit back a smile as redness spread across his face. "I mean you … I mean, you aren't less than prestigious, I mean…"

He appeared panicked as he rushed to explain, and I realized despite his gangly and scholarly appearance, he was relatively attractive. Too bad he was human, and I'd likely never see him again once I left the Library. I took pity on his discomfort and changed the subject.

"In that case, I shall look for you in the morning." My eyes searched the room for Luban and when I didn't see him, I leaned closer and whispered barely loud enough for Jarid to hear. "Is Gwen allowed in tomorrow if she doesn't bring her wolves?"

Jarid paused for a moment. "I believe so. It's just the Head Librarian feels animals would ruin the books and the atmosphere." He gave me another apologetic look. "Unfortunately for the older Librarians such as Luban, centaurs and other hybrids also count as animals. While I may not agree, I have very little say. I would love it if centaurs were allowed in the Library, as they are the wisest creatures I've ever encountered."

I'd been missing Loglan's wisdom since he'd returned home. "I agree. Unfortunately, as much as I wish I could change minds and hearts everywhere I went, I'm old enough to know just from my own dealings at home such a thing is almost always impossible without an open mind."

I pressed my lips together, allowing the disappointment of the failure I wasn't even sure was mine to leak out. As I shared a look with both of them, I hoped that regardless of what they may think of elves, they could see I harbored no ill will toward them and with time, Jarid would see that I viewed humans as equal to elves, as individuals, even if we may have different abilities.

I turned to Sel. "We should find Gwen before it gets much later."

He bowed to Jarid before opening the front door to allow me to go first, just as the girl who I'd noticed look at me rushed over, whispered something in Jarid's ear, and departed. I paused, curious and perplexed on the steps outside. Jarid

CHAPTER 10

surreptitiously glanced around then joined us outside, emanating worry as he shifted his weight from side to side.

"That was a message for you, Rhiniya."

"Rhin," I corrected.

"Rhin." Jarid winced.

I'd been encouraging him to call me by the name Gwen and Sel did, but I could see he was having a tough time with the informality.

"What is it?" I prompted when he paused.

"Oh! Sorry. Gwen is waiting one block down the street, to the right at a tavern run by Marthe Wentir."

"Thank you, Jarid. That's helpful."

Jarid waved an awkward goodbye and jogged back inside.

I took one last look at the beauty around me. In the sunset, the marble stairs were darker than they'd been earlier, while the fading sunlight made the veins of light sparkle. Inside the Library, more golden light spilled down the stairs to meet the fading sun until the massive wood doors swung shut behind us. I sighed, beginning the long journey down the stairs.

WE HADN'T GONE a full block when the sound of a commotion erupted outside a large building to our right. Sel assumed a defensive posture in front of me which made it difficult to see past him. For the first time I realized he was slight but quite a bit taller than I was. Had he grown since we'd left the castle?

A shout from the heart of the crowd brought me back to the matter at hand. I pushed Sel to the side and peered around him. The woman in the center was furious, and the wolves beside her had their teeth bared as they stood protectively around her. Swift stood in front, crouched with his head over his front legs. Each wolf was ready to spring at something in front of her.

"Gwen!"

Sel cast a warning look at me as I shouted, but I brushed him aside and pushed my way through the crowd.

"Is everything okay?"

I surveyed the group of about twenty people who were milling around, forming a loose circle around them. Most seemed average, men and women carrying food or other articles, watching with curious expressions. One man stood out in stark contrast from what could have been a normal market scene.

He leaned carelessly against the wall as if unaware of anyone around him with the exception of Gwen and her wolves, who he watched with a glowering intensity. He was human from what I could tell, but massive. He was easily double my size, making Gwen seem positively diminutive in comparison. His face was pockmarked with old scars, one which dragged the corner of his eye down to meet his lip, giving him an evil sneer as he watched her with a glittering intensity which she seemed to be ignoring. His arms crossed across his chest were the size of my head. I was scared enough for the both of us.

She looked at me, raising her chin in acknowledgement. "Guys. I was just returning from taking the wolves for fresh air after exploring the neighborhood. Did you get my message?"

Clearing my throat, I uneasily looked at the crowd around us. "Um, yes. You gave it to the girl at the Library?" I was rambling, but I couldn't think of anything smarter to say, feeling the demonic man still staring at us.

She pointed at the large three-story building behind her. "Got a room for all of us. Are you hungry?"

At her continued nonchalance, the crowd seemed to lose interest and began to disperse. I didn't relax though, because the one observer who terrified me didn't move.

"Oh, good." I was certain I sounded stilted, knowing there was far more than a simple walk in the fresh air going on at the moment. Her eyes were bright and her cheeks were flushed

CHAPTER 10

with a tinge of pink as she looked everywhere but directly at the man beside the wall. I wasn't sure if I felt better or worse at her alertness.

I did feel worse when the crowd's dispersal left the stranger a clear path to watch us. I straightened to my full height and threw my shoulders back while I glared at him. Without thinking out my actions, I began to walk forward. I felt the startled eyes of Gwen and Sel on my back as I left them, but before I could take more than a few steps, a hand gripped my arm.

I looked down, prepared to tell Sel to let me go, but the hand on my arm wasn't his. It wasn't even hers. My eyes followed the broad hand up a dark blue arm. It was a uniform, I realized, when I saw patches on the shoulder and a sword in a hilt around the waist. I looked up to see a young man about my age, with a sweep of dirty blond hair that carelessly flopped over one dark blue eye, hiding half of his face. For a moment I panicked, thinking I was about to be arrested, until I recognized the look on his face was one of caution.

"Don't." He'd spoken so quietly that his words were almost inaudible.

I blinked, and he added a second, stronger warning.

"That man is dangerous." He flicked his eyes to the man I'd been about to approach.

My bravado instantly deflated. What had I been thinking? My shoulders slumped under the weight of my stupid attempt to be the hero and protect Gwen. How could I have thought for even a second I was a match for that gigantic man?

"I don't like the way he's watching my friend. He looks like he wants to steal her, or worse."

The young man pressed his lips together, shaking his head. "No, he doesn't want your friend. I'm almost certain he wants her wolves."

"What?" I pulled my arm away, rubbing it absently as I tried to process his words. "Why would anybody want the wolves? They're beautiful, but without her they aren't able to communicate with anyone."

He looked at her, then at the wolves. "He's a slaver. Wolves like the ones your friend has are rare, but if they can be trained to have a connection with a human or elf, that connection can also be broken if you know how. In that case, they can be made to re-bond with someone else, which is highly prized in some circles, and makes them extremely valuable."

I looked at Gwen and her wolves again, my fear changing its focus. "But how and why?"

"I'm not up on the details of how it works. But I know it does, and I know him by reputation. It's best to stay as far away from him as you can. Believe me when I say he's done it before, and he'll try to do it again. There's a lot of money to be made with those animals." He spoke calmly, but his brows were still knit together in concern.

"So, what should we do?"

"Best bet? Take your friend and her animals inside. Let her know he's dangerous. Oh, by the way, my name's Will."

I smiled absently in acknowledgement. I turned my gaze toward Gwen. She was staring unflinchingly at the remaining crowd, arms loose at her sides. If I hadn't known her, I would have thought she was completely indifferent to their regard. But her eyes gave her away. Tight lines beside her eyes and a clenched jaw in a face a shade paler than normal showed me she was faking her lack of concern. I touched her arm and she turned stubborn eyes toward me.

"Gwen, let's go inside. I was just given a warning, but I want to talk somewhere quieter." I tugged gently on her arm and she looked at the wolves before heading toward the hotel door.

"Okay. I'll show you where we're staying."

She looked for Sel, but he was already at my side. We followed her inside and I shot one last uncertain glance at the dangerous slaver Will had warned me away from.

CHAPTER 10

The entire time he hadn't appeared other than mildly interested in the proceedings. But now as we passed, his eyes tracked our movements. I suppressed a shiver of fear and disgust and moved closer to her, blocking her from his view as much as I could. When I glanced over my shoulder as we entered, I was surprised to see Will take up a position just behind us, his hand resting loosely on the hilt of his sword. The crowd was gone, but the slaver continued to watch us until we were inside.

As I looked around the room, some of my tension eased. The smell of fresh bread filled the air and belied the bar in the center of the room. We'd entered a comfortable square main room, with tables and chairs clustered around the center bar. Quiet conversation could be heard, but most of the patrons seemed to be focused on the plates or bowls in front of them and were eating instead of speaking.

The people closest to me were eating a stew of some sort, with thick doorstopper sized pieces of bread. The smell of the meat and cooked vegetables overpowered the bread's smell now, tickling my nostrils and causing me to salivate. I looked at Sel, catching a look of longing on his face I was sure matched the one on mine.

Gwen smirked. "Don't worry, meals are included with our lodgings. I just need to let the proprietor know the rest of my group has arrived."

She pointed her chin toward the bar, where a stout, matronly looking woman vigorously wiped a glass. She wore a plain green dress with a white apron, and her hair was pinned up in a no-nonsense bun. It was more grey than red, and she had lines beside her eyes and mouth that suggested she wasn't someone to be trifled with, but when she caught sight Gwen, she smiled and put the glass down, pointing to an empty table. Gwen inclined her head in response.

"Come on. Marthe knows you're here now. She'll bring us each a plate of food. But a word of warning: she's quite motherly and her cooking is good, but if you insult her, I wager she's also a woman capable of making your life a living hell."

"Good to know," I said, looking at the hostess in a different light. I didn't know nearly as much about people as Gwen did. She seemed to have a knack I lacked. Or perhaps it was because she'd had more bad experiences than I'd had. She'd told me multiple times she was horrible at reading people, but I was finding the opposite was true.

Either way, when Marthe came over and plunked three glasses of water down, I made sure to give her the brightest smile I could.

"Hello there." She gave both Sel and me a thorough once-over. "My name is Marthe, and this is my establishment. What can I bring you to eat?"

I smiled again, feeling my composure tremble a little now that we were safe. "Hi, Marthe, my name is Rhin. And if there's enough to go around, I'd love a bowl of whatever they are eating, and some of the bread, of course." I smiled again, adding, "It smells amazing and I'm starving."

Marthe nodded briskly. "What about you, Miss Gwen? And you, boy—what would you like?"

"I'll have the same," he responded.

Marthe tilted her head at Gwen, who agreed. "Me three. She's right, it smells amazing."

Marthe looked at the wolves. "Did you need something for your animals?"

Gwen looked at the wolves waiting patiently by her feet. They followed Marthe with large, hopeful eyes, tongues lolling out as they watched her every move. Gwen smiled, and I couldn't help but be amused at the pleading on their furry faces.

"If you have some meat I could purchase for them, it would be appreciated. But they'll be fine if you don't."

Marthe brushed away her respectful answer with a sniff. "The butcher gave me a bad cut of meat yesterday. It's not fit

CHAPTER 10 119

for people and I've already complained and had it replaced. He left me the extra for the fact it wasn't worth him taking back. I just threw it out in the alley an hour ago. It's yours if you want to take your wolves around back to eat it, and they can stay in your room as long as they're trained not to leave messes."

"Thank you."

I could tell by the shy smile she gave the tavern keeper that she was surprised and touched by the woman's generosity. I was a little surprised myself, after the way everyone else had been acting when it came to her wolves. So far, Sunglen was different than I had expected. Not sure if I should be disappointed or intrigued, my thoughts quickly turned to food when Marthe returned hardly five minutes later with three steaming hot bowls of the same stew the other patrons were enjoying.

As I ate the stew, my senses were overwhelmed by its fragrant rich meatiness. It was simple but filling, the gravy perfectly complementing the carrots and potatoes accompanying the venison.

After my stomach stopped complaining, I leaned back in my chair and sighed, perusing the room with a lazy satisfaction. I almost missed Will's lanky form, tucked into the far corner. With his hat tipped over his eyes, he gave off the impression of being asleep until I spotted one dark blue eye surveying the room from underneath the brim.

His uniform was disheveled, as though he'd slept in it already, or was deliberately trying to look unthreatening. His hair curled in dark waves that were tousled, hiding a firm jaw which made him look dashing and stubborn.

I sat up and glared, but his only response was to tilt his hat lower and put his boots up on a nearby chair.

Shaking off the feeling Will was guarding us, I looked at my friends.

Sel was already scraping the bottom of the bowl with his bread, which was every bit as delicious as it had smelled, and

Gwen, eating at a more sedate pace, also appeared to be enjoying the cooking Marthe had brought us.

Sighing inwardly, not wanting to bother them with my suspicions, I tried to focus on my food. Yet no matter how hard I tried, my gaze kept returning to the strange man who'd warned me about the slaver and followed us in. Was it possible he was there to make sure he didn't come after us? I didn't know, but his continued presence kept my nerves on alert.

CHAPTER 11

The next morning, I rolled over to see four sets of eyes regarding me calmly. I blinked, sitting up abruptly in the bed. It groaned under my weight and I responded by gasping. There was something so unnerving about waking up and being the focus of other living creatures' attention. I cast a glance at Gwen but found her still sleeping in the other narrow bed in the room. Sel was on the pallet on the floor near where the wolves had bedded down, and it was their intent gazes, which had woken me.

Marthe was more lenient than other places would have been. Not only were the wolves allowed in the eating area, but she had no problem allowing them to stay in the large family room we'd rented.

"Even if they piddle on the floor, they'll still be tidier than other guests I've had," she'd laughed, before leaving us to our lodgings.

"Have you been awake long?" I turned to Sel.

"Just a few minutes. When I woke up, these guys were all sitting by the door and their hackles were up. I cracked the door to see if anyone was in the hallway, but there was nothing there." He kept his voice low, which I imagined was due to the fact that Gwen was still sleeping, but his words bothered me.

"You think someone was watching us?"

He looked awkward as he unfolded from the floor, his long legs sticking out at right angles as he pushed himself up. "It's hard to say. The wolves might be on alert because we're in a strange place and they're protecting her, but either way, I think it's important to stay on guard. It's a large city." A hint of unease crept into his eyes.

A yawn caught me by surprise and I covered my mouth. "I didn't say anything yesterday, but I think the soldier I spoke with outside the hotel may have followed us."

His eyes narrowed. "Do you think he's who the wolves were watching?"

"I'm not sure. He didn't seem dangerous, but I think he's the reason the large creepy slaver didn't follow us inside. He sat in the corner the entire time we ate and didn't leave until we came upstairs."

"Interesting. You may be on to something. Well, once she wakes up, we can head down and get breakfast. I imagine you'll want to head back to the Library right away?"

"Yes, we should find Jarid again. I'm hoping he can take me back to where we left everything yesterday. His reference book was highly convenient. It will certainly cut down on my search time if I can continue to use it."

"I'll join you for breakfast, but I'll leave you two to your own devices in the Library." Gwen's sleepy voice cut through our conversation.

Surprised she was awake, I turned to see her leaning on her elbow in bed, watching us talk with half-closed eyes.

"Are you sure?" I wasn't comfortable with the idea of her being left alone after what we'd returned to the day before.

"I'm sure. Besides, there're things I need to do while we're here." She swung her legs over the side of the bed, brushing the wrinkles out of the clothes she'd slept in as she moved.

CHAPTER 11

123

We'd all traveled so light, the clothes we'd been wearing when we arrived in the city were the cleanest things we owned. The sight of her wrinkled and travel-stained clothing reminded me of the condition of my own, and I looked down and sniffed. Yup, I needed to either get new clothes or find out where I could clean my change of clothing, which was currently bloodstained, torn, and crumpled in my travel bag.

A chuckle from her brought my attention back from my current clothing situation, and she said the one thing guaranteed to keep me from arguing with her about joining us at Abrecem Secer.

"Why don't I find somewhere to clean our clothing?"

Gwen included Sel in her question and his eyes widened before he looked at me. He waited silently for me to decide. Finally, I rolled my eyes, knowing she had me beat.

"Fine, but I want you to be careful. That soldier I talked to yesterday, Will, told me that large guy watching your wolves was a slaver. It sounded like he was interested in taking them from you somehow and selling them."

She got up, snorting as she pulled her other set of clothing out of her bag. She sniffed the shirt and made a face. "I'd like to see him try. The connection I have with my wolves isn't easily broken."

"I know. That's why I'm worried. He didn't seem like the kind of man to be stopped by a little bit of difficulty. He also looked like the kind of person who wouldn't mind killing to get his way." I sat on the side of my bed, looking at her seriously. Relief rushed through me when her lips tightened.

"I'll be careful," she promised, all her earlier bravado replaced. "I'll stick to the hotel or other populated areas and main thoroughfares. Will that help you feel better?"

Getting out of bed, I considered her question. I had no idea what would help. I'd only just realized how much I had to learn about people and civilization. More and more, it was clear to me that none of the books I'd read over the years could capture the true nature of creatures—human, elves, and others—and they continued to surprise me. I just wasn't sure if it was good or bad so far. I did know the idea of her being injured filled me with dread.

I turned to the door, deciding not to dwell on the what ifs or change into my dirtier items. I could wash up later. Maybe Marthe had laundry facilities in the building. "We may as well get food now, since we're all awake. Soonest begun, soonest done," I quipped.

The others joined me without changing and we didn't speak on the way to the common area. I was trapped in my own thoughts, and they seemed equally stuck in theirs, or maybe we weren't yet fully awake. The wolves took point, with Swift in front and the other two behind us without a word from her. I had the feeling they were guarding us, but from who or what? The memory of the slaver's scarred, evil face flashed through my mind and I shivered.

When we arrived where we'd eaten the night before, it was empty apart from a familiar figure. I narrowed my eyes. To the casual eye, he looked like he'd been there all night, and then I noticed the pants he was wearing. If it hadn't been for the fact I'd seen his boots on the table the evening before, I probably wouldn't have seen it. Yesterday, they had been patched near the ankle, but today they were not.

I strode over to the table where he was pretending to be asleep, slamming my hand down hard enough the mug in front of him rocked, spilling some amber fluid. He jumped to his feet, hand falling to the pommel of his sword so fast I flinched and stepped back. But I was determined to get answers and stopped when I remembered my irritation.

"Why are you following us?" I glared, crossing my arms as I waited for a believable answer.

He took his hat off, placing it on the table before he stretched lazily and stood to face me. I realized for the first time he was quite a bit larger than I was. In the confusion and

CHAPTER 11

noise of the crowd yesterday, somehow his size had escaped me. I glared harder, willing him to see my anger.

He continued to watch me with an impassive expression. Now that he was up and saw who'd confronted him, his hand had fallen away from his sword and he'd crossed his arms behind his back.

"I'm not." He pressed his lips together, offering nothing else.

I exhaled, frustrated at his non-answer. Something in my expression must have made him reconsider his response.

He rolled his eyes and elaborated. "Fine, maybe I was. But it was just to make sure you and your friends were safe. The slaver you saw last night is bad news, and I didn't want you or your friends to be another victim of his mercenary greed."

Some of the tension from my shoulders eased, but not all of it. I believed his words, but there was more to it than that. Something in his eyes told me more was going on here than he had divulged.

"Everything okay here?"

An arm draped over my shoulder as Gwen joined me, staring distrustfully at Will. I patted her hand, shooting her a brief smile as Sel and the wolves joined us. By the look on Will's face, any chance of exploring why he'd followed us was lost for now.

He arched an eyebrow, turning his attention to my friends. "Good morning. I trust you all slept well? Marthe has a lovely facility here. Reasonably priced, *clean*," he emphasized, raising both eyebrows briefly, "and best of all, the food is filling and delicious."

To my surprise, she smiled at him easily, offering him her other hand in greeting.

"Hi, thanks for worrying about us last night."

I looked at her and blinked. Surely I'd somehow misheard her easy thanks? But the corner of her lips turned up when she caught my expression.

"Come on, surely you realize he was who the wolves sensed outside our door last night?"

"Now I know you're all alive and well, I must be about my duties." He took his hat off the table and placed it back on his head, tipped the corner, walking out the door without a backward glance.

I watched him go, shaking my head at the entire interaction. "You can't tell me that wasn't strange."

Sel was more focused on the kitchen than my words. Based on the way his eyes kept darting toward the kitchen, I gave him up as a lost cause until he'd eaten. When I looked at her, she watched me with narrowed eyes, as if she was assessing my reaction and I'd surprised her.

"Do you think I'm overreacting?" I didn't like thinking I'd disappointed her and was becoming uncomfortable under her steady gaze.

"I don't know why he felt the need to protect us, but if he was worried about the slaver, I'm glad he stayed. As we didn't come to harm while we slept, you have nothing to be upset about." Gwen's voice was mild and her words were reasonable.

I wasn't sure what bothered me the most. The fact that he'd stayed, or that I was upset and didn't know why. I wrinkled my nose.

"Something about him just strikes me as off. You know? Like he's doing one thing with the right hand while slipping something behind his back with the other."

Gwen sighed. "Things in Sunglen are different than what we're used to in the Low Forest. If he was worried enough to watch us, without causing us harm, I think saying 'thank you' is a safe enough gesture."

I was still suspicious, but conceded her point. "For last night, of course. But I'm not sure if he's someone we can trust to watch our backs, or if we need to worry about having him behind us."

"Anything is possible," she agreed. "But for now, let's eat so

CHAPTER 11 127

you can return to the Library and find whatever it is you're looking for."

I pressed my lips together, giving a grudging nod.

We sat down at the nearest long table and waited less than a minute for Marthe to appear. She wore a dark red dress with a clean apron, which she used to wipe her hands before greeting us.

"Good sleep?" She waited for our agreement, then briskly announced, "the house breakfast is included. It'll be extra if you want something off the menu."

"Sounds fine, Marthe. Thank you," I smiled. "Do you by chance have facilities for washing?"

The corner of her lips tugged up as she looked at my face, hair, and clothing. She smiled wider at my discomfort before taking pity. "Aye, that we do. Second floor has the baths, laundry in the basement."

Before I could begin to express my gratitude, she'd whirled away in a dark red swirl of skirt, returning immediately with three piping hot bowls of greens and berries which we fell into with hungry anticipation.

We parted ways with Gwen after breakfast. After promising me she'd stay near the safety of the hotel as much as possible, we headed back to the Library. We'd taken the same route as the night before, through narrow cobblestone streets with shuttered houses. It was still early, and tradespeople were just beginning to go about their duties as the street sweepers worked furiously to clear away the garbage of the day before.

We rounded the corner and the mundane was wiped away and replaced by the indescribable beauty which appeared in front of us. The sun shone down on the golden spires, trumpeting to the world the Library was a glorious marvel of creation. It seemed larger in the early morning air, the marble steps veined in gold appearing to ascend to the place where the gods themselves lived.

At that moment, I was in the presence of a living, breathing work of art. The whimsical thought brought me back to my mission. To find how Onen Suun had trapped Dag'draath and see if there was a way to recreate the spell.

Upon entry, once I'd finally climbed the beautiful but intense staircase, I stopped to catch my breath and allowed myself time to absorb the details of the main entrance. It was a large oval, with creamy yellow walls interrupted by cherry-wood beams that went all the way around. There must have been at least twenty-four, likely more, but I couldn't see them in the corner, as they were blocked by the room Jarid had pointed out yesterday.

It was early yet, but I could see him standing behind the glass. He looked up at that exact moment and startled, then closed the text he'd been looking at and came toward me, the same nondescript reference book I remembered from the day before under his arm. I waited as he walked across the plush carpeting that muffled the sound of footsteps and stopped before me.

"Ready for another day?" The thin volume almost blended into the plain brown robes, like an extension of his body.

"Yes, and I was hoping we could start where we left off yesterday."

"Absolutely. If you would kindly follow me." He turned around, hesitating, before giving me a warning look. "Please ensure you stay closer than yesterday. We don't want you having any more unpleasant experiences."

"Of course."

A faint idea had begun to stir in my mind. The door I'd accidentally gone through yesterday had been enlightening. It had been frightening to end up in a strange place when I wasn't expecting to, but it had led me to thinking about just how big the Library was and what other secrets it held. As a scholar, I found it nigh impossible to let the thought go.

This time, I paid close attention to the winding path I was led down. From the main entrance with its thick carpets and

CHAPTER 11

grand appearance, the hall quickly narrowed down, branching out into several smaller spokes. The carpet thinned out, then became a dark hardwood. Our steps echoed now and the contrast raised goosebumps on my skin. If I did get separated from Jarid, I wanted to be able to find my way back.

We took the second spoke to the right, which I noted was marked by a sad statue of a unicorn looking into the distance. Each hall had a different statue, which I carefully examined in as much detail as I could before I saw I was falling behind. As I jogged to catch up, I was happy to see the hallway we'd taken was familiar. It seemed much more likely I'd be able to find my way if I did become separated from Jarid.

The hall continued on quite some distance, descending as it looped around, the large shelves I remembered from the day before the same. I counted the turns in my head, marking certain shelves with unique ornamentation as guideposts. It was time to use my memory for more than just recalling the things I'd read in a book.

Once we were in the room, I sat with my elbows on the table and rested my chin on my templed fingers, bouncing it up and down slightly. How could I best word my request to get the information I needed from the reference book?

Sel took up his familiar position at the doorway and I bit my lip, letting my eyes rest on the book in question. By now, I was certain the thin reference volume Jarid was cradling had magic of a sort I'd never seen before. I looked at it, a longing to have something so magnificent in my own library at home filling me before I pushed the thought aside.

"Do you have the volume written by Geōrgios of the Dragon Dominion?"

Jarid's eyes widened as I stopped. I had no idea where my request had come from, as I hadn't even thought of that book in years. Wait—had I read about him yesterday? For some reason, it seemed important now.

"Geōrgios? Isn't that one of the lost texts?"

"I'm not sure. But I think I read something about it yesterday. Wasn't he one of the famous dragon scholars from—"

"The time when Onen Suun disappeared."

"Yeah, him."

No one knew exactly what had happened, but the more I read, the more the pieces seemed to be forming a whole picture for me. "Yes, several High Dragons went missing at the same time as Onen Suun and Dag'draath. I know there was some sort of ritual, but not what it encompassed. If I can find accounts of what others thought happened during the time it happened, I might be able to fit together a timeline of events. And if I can do that..."

I allowed my words to trail off when Jarid leaned toward me with his eyes wide.

"You might be able to discover how he did it?" he blurted.

"Exactly. If I can find out how or when Suun trapped Dag'draath, maybe I can figure out how to put him away for good."

Jarid exhaled, his breath leaving on a low whistle. "That's a pretty big task. I'm not sure the Library will give you the answers you seek."

He looked around, shifting his eyes from side to side as if afraid someone was watching us. I had the sense not only that he wasn't sure how much he could say, but also that he was looking to the walls for permission to speak. After a long moment of this odd, silent communion with the room while we waited, Jarid gave one sharp nod and seemed to shake himself.

"The answers are here, somewhere, but I may not be the best guide for you after all."

I searched his face, looking for any sign he knew something. He seemed to believe what he was saying, but I sensed there was more to his words than what was on the surface. I could see Jarid wanted to help, but now I was suspicious he may not be able to bring me anything I desired, unlike Luban had led me to believe. Interesting.

CHAPTER 11   131

"Well, are you allowed to bring me the book written by Geōrgios?" I returned to the matter at hand. Surely his reaction would tell me something.

Now that he'd shown hesitation, this particular volume was even more important than it had been when I'd unexpectedly mentioned it the first time. Why *had* I mentioned it? I narrowed my eyes and looked at the walls, waiting for them to talk to me the way they seemed to talk to Jarid, but only silence met my attempts. I brushed the ridiculous idea aside as he returned a moment later, setting the book down as he touched it almost reverently.

He pressed his lips together and gave me a look full of caution.

"The reference book showed me where it was, but I'm not sure I'm supposed to let you read it. So please, read quickly. Assistants have been removed from their duties for less."

I narrowed my eyes at the word *removed*. From what I understood so far, that could literally mean they were removed from the Library—or worse. Could they lose their lives as well as their livelihood?

"I'll be careful and as fast as possible."

My hands caressed the elegantly bound volume. It was the deep purple reserved only for royalty, but the material was unlike any I'd seen—thick yet soft, luminous, with words inscribed in ornate gold leafing and jewels adorning the front. It was completely different in nature from the black volumes I'd found in my own library, but something about it reminded me of those texts and my excitement rose. There were answers in here.

I dove into it, a fluttery feeling in my stomach with the certainty this book would be important pushing me on. Every now and then I glanced over at Jarid because of the noise he made. Otherwise the room was silent.

He was squirming in his chair and startled frequently, which in turn caused me to look up. Sel wore a smirk as he stood ready, likely at the skittish apprentice, but I was less amused. The Library was his domain. If he was nervous about my access to this book, chances were there was something to be nervous about.

As I flipped through the pages, I quickly discovered everything was written from the perspective of the dragons. Three chapters in, I discovered a small, almost imperceptible figure on the corner of one of the pages. I was scouring the book for every little detail I could find, and I still had to squint before I could make out the small trident for what it was. Interesting. Why would a trident be in a book about dragon history? I read further, coming to a passage in the book where Geōrgios went from speculation to fact. My eyes widened.

Mermaids? Why were mermaids mentioned? To the best of my knowledge, mermaids and dragons had little in common and even less to do with each other. Mermaids inhabited the deep oceans, while the dragons lived completely different lives on the highest mountain islands, in a completely different region of our world.

By now, I'd completely forgotten Jarid and Sel were there as I devoured the book. It soon became apparent the mermaid-dragon connection was important, even though the specifics were vague. I leaned back in my chair and closed my eyes, allowing what I'd read to settle into my mind.

When I opened my eyes, feeling none the wiser, my gaze fell upon the door lintel of the room. My vision sharpened as my brain connected what I was seeing with and what I had just read. Pressed into the wood, in such a subtle way it almost appeared to be part of the grain, was a small trident, no bigger than my thumb.

Casting my mind back to the winding route we'd followed from the lobby to the reference room, I began to connect the dots. I'd seen other tridents in the Library. In fact, there was one just outside our reading room. Was it possible they led somewhere important? To another room or book that could

CHAPTER 11

explain what had happened on the long-ago day when Dag'-draath had been locked away? If it was the case, then maybe I could put Dag'draath away forever by recreating the spell.

Even as my excitement grew, I glanced at Jarid from beneath half-lowered eyelids. His head was bent over a book as he sat across the table, some of his earlier anxiety diminished by the sheer monotony of waiting. I didn't want to involve him in what I was considering. I was certain he wouldn't be able to play a part in the next leg of my journey.

Luban struck me as a strict master with crystal-clear rules for the apprentices at the Library. Jarid's reaction to my request for the book in the first place had told me everything I needed to know. Luban would certainly punish Jarid if he helped with anything I discovered from this forbidden text.

I stretched, faking a yawn which quickly became real. I wasn't sure how long we'd been sitting there, only that I'd managed to read almost the entire book in front of me. I stood from the table, startling both of them.

"May I help you with something?" Jarid cocked his head. My conscience read suspicion in his eyes and I smiled, trying my best not to look as guilty as I felt.

"I need to use the facilities. To relieve myself," I added, causing Jarid to flush and Sel to roll his eyes.

Jarid cleared his throat as he pointed at the door. "There is a chamber just across the hall from here." He looked at me, hesitating before adding, "Make sure you stay close by, and only take the door labeled for such things. Please come right back, or I will have to ensure you are safe."

I filed the information away for later. The more I learned about the Library, the more mysterious it became. Doorways that led to other worlds, perhaps? Was there real danger awaiting, other than losing my way if I took a different door? I didn't pause long though, too eager to test my theory about the small symbol from the book. When Sel moved, I held up a hand.

"I'll be back in a minute. Stay here. I won't require any help."

I raised my eyebrows and he looked away, but not quickly enough to hide an embarrassed flush of his own. I held back a smirk, their reactions confirming the little I knew about men, both human and elf. According to my younger sister, the best way to escape boring conversation or unwanted attention was to excuse yourself by mentioning the ladies' room.

I walked out, gently closing the door behind me to avoid any extra attention. I made note of the door across the hall, clearly labeled with the figure of a female. Instead of opening it, I turned right and walked down the hall and further into the Library.

CHAPTER 12

The hallways were winding but well lit, and it was easy to see where I was going. It was less ornate on this level compared to the first hallway, but it was still decorated with sturdy, practical materials I approved of. The shelves were sturdier, made out of rock instead of wood, and the doorways were a dark oak which reflected the light, making them seem almost alive. This odd luminescence allowed me to spot the symbol I'd thought I'd seen earlier. A trident. Smiling with satisfaction, I headed closer to get a better look. It was a trident for sure, but to my surprise, there was the figure of a small dragon on the other end of the lintel, as if they were bookending the door. The trident seemed to be angled to the left, almost like an arrow, so I continued in that direction.

Walking faster, almost jogging with the certainty I was on the right track, I glanced over my shoulder. Exhaling with relief I hadn't been followed, I turned my attention to the top of the doors I passed by. With nothing other than a gut feeling to go on, I expected the symbols would all be at or above eye level.

When I spotted another one around the corner and several doors down, my hunch was vindicated. I moved toward it.

Now I could see a trident, a dragon, and a sword on the lintel. Three symbols! I was definitely on to something, even if I wasn't yet sure what. But this time, the symbol wasn't on the door, but in the hall near the same height. This time I was sure it was acting as an arrow, so I kept moving. The sword seemed to be pointing around a corner.

I had almost given up hope when I hadn't seen another symbol after passing several doorways, thinking I'd missed my turn when I abruptly came to a dead end. A large, black archway surrounded a door far grander than any of the others I had passed, and more ornate than anything I'd seen on this level.

Was this the right door? Looking down the hall, I first ensured I was still alone. When I turned back to the door, my eyes shot right to the top of the archway, where I again noted the symbols I'd been following, except this time there were four.

I had already seen the dragon, the trident, and the sword, but in addition, this door had one more—a sun. I exhaled shakily, holding my hand out. I was sure if I stood on my toes, I would be able to touch it, if I just stretched a little farther...

My heart raced as the bubble of adrenaline coursed through my body. The door was gorgeous, dark, and mysterious. How could this not be an answer to what I sought? Everything about it screamed mystery and answers, wrapped in one onyx frame. I noticed with some surprise my hand was shaking as it reached for the door handle, and then I faltered, my hand curling in on itself, capturing my fingers as reality intruded.

What if it was another door like the one I'd felt compelled to open yesterday? What if the door I was attracted to for its dark and mysterious appearance was just dark and dangerous? What if whatever was behind this door led to my doom, not the answers and solution to Dag'draath I wanted? As my heart rate kicked up, I narrowed my eyes, berating myself.

CHAPTER 12

Stop being such a child. You've already come this far. You've fought ur'gels, killed a deer, and carried it back to a campfire you built yourself. You're tougher than this. I gritted my teeth, and this time my hand reached for the handle, as firm and steady as my resolve.

Once again, my hand was stopped. But this time by an external force. My eyes widened at the touch of a pale white hand gently pushing mine down and away. With a sinking heart I spun around to see Jarid with Sel standing just behind him. Both watched me with reproving and disappointed expressions.

"What?" I did my best to keep my voice innocent. "I got distracted after I went to the bathroom," I mumbled. Regardless of my weak explanation, I could tell immediately neither believed me based on their crossed arms and raised eyebrows. "Fine." I sighed, closing my eyes as I searched for a way to explain myself. Maybe I could emulate my sister. Whenever she got caught, she deflected. It seemed to work well for her, so maybe it would work for me.

"There was a symbol in the book I was reading. I didn't want to get you in trouble, Jarid, so I decided to try to find it without you." I shot an apologetic glance to Sel. "And you know I would've taken you, except…"

Sel's face smoothed out immediately. "Of course, it's not like you owe me an explanation. I just can't do my job and protect you if I don't know where you are."

Heat stained my cheeks. There was nothing accusatory about his words, yet I still felt as if I had betrayed him in some way. Jarid, I'd expected to feel less guilt over, because I really had slipped away in order to protect him, but his dejected frown hurt nearly as much.

"That door isn't one I've seen before." Jarid spoke, his voice tentative as he changed the subject. It sounded as though he was making a peace offering. While grateful for the chance to talk about something else, I was also perplexed.

"What do you mean? It wasn't there before?"

138 SOUL GOBLET

Jarid crossed his left arm over his chest and tapped his right index finger thoughtfully on his chin. "I was down this hallway a week ago, and I don't recall seeing this door. The ones on either side leading here were there. But this one is not a door I'm familiar with, and it's hard to miss."

He narrowed his eyes, causing me to turn back to the door, trying to see if I'd missed something on my initial survey, but it looked the same.

"If you've never seen it before, how can it be here now?"

For moment, Jarid looked uncomfortable. He wore the same conflicted expression he'd had earlier when he'd appeared to be trying to decide what to tell me. Finally, his shoulders slumped as he bit the inside of his cheek and responded. "The Library is not a normal building. I know I warned you with the barest of details I could give about the doors. But, for lack of a better way of explaining it, well, it may be almost like a living entity." He flinched, as though he expected me to burst out laughing, but it made sense to me.

"So, the door *was* here before."

From behind me, I could hear Sel groan quietly. And knew he was already regretting following Jarid to find me.

My interest was piqued, and I wasn't about to leave until I figured out what was behind the onyx door, especially after Jarid had given me such a fascinating bit of news. All my earlier apprehension forgotten, now only the mystery remained. I turned to Jarid and his eyes widened at the look on my face. I wasn't even trying to hide my excitement.

"I found a symbol in the book and something told me I should follow it. The symbol kept repeating in the hallway, except every now and then, another symbol would be added to it. First, it was a trident, exactly like the symbol in the book I was reading by Geōrgios. The next symbol was a dragon next to the trident, followed by a sword. Now this door has the symbol of the sun as well."

I looked between the two of them, both watching me with

confusion. I exhaled, frustrated at having to explain my thought process, but hardly surprised. My brain didn't seem to work the way anyone else's did. This was the part I hated the most. Explaining how to get from A to B.

"Don't you see? From what I've read, all the symbols involve groups present at the time Dag'draath was locked away. I think behind this door are some of the answers we need to find, maybe about the original ceremony, hopefully about how to trap him again and end the wars for good."

"Are you sure?"

Jarid blinked, taking in a quick breath. He looked at the door again, this time with a bright-eyed look of excitement.

I turned back to the door, feeling breathless myself as I considered the possibilities. "I just want to try to open it and see if I'm right." When neither made a move to stop me, I again reached out my hand. This was it, the moment where I'd find answers. I turned the handle ... but nothing happened. Confused, I jiggled it again. It didn't feel locked, but the handle just spun and spun and spun without opening. I frowned, looking at Jarid.

"Does it need a key or something?"

Jarid cocked his head, holding his hand out hesitantly. "May I?"

I stepped aside for him to try. He repeated the same thing I had, with the same results.

"That's strange," he muttered.

"I don't understand. Does this happen often?"

Jarid jiggled the handle again before looking at me with a grimace.

"No. Never. Either the door opens, or it's locked. Maybe the handle is broken." His voice trailed off as he leaned over to peer at it in detail.

I could tell he was trying to figure out how to get it to work, so I waited silently. I was becoming increasingly frustrated as he toiled away before he finally quit in frustration himself.

"I don't know what's wrong."

I took a deep breath and tried to re-center myself. What did I know for sure? Well, I'd discovered a book about dragon history with small trident symbols on it. It was written just after the time when Onen Suun had trapped Dag'draath, before he'd disappeared himself. I also knew the High Dragons had something to do with making the prison.

And as I had walked through the Library, which I was becoming more and more convinced was a living entity, the trident symbol had been joined by symbols of other groups. Which meant they were connected. I just didn't know how. Maybe in order to open the door I had to discover what the link was. My eyes widened as a bolt of enlightenment shot through the darkness.

"What if it's a puzzle?"

I watched Jarid's face change from frowning to wide-eyed.

"Maybe." Jarid's eyes darted around, then he leaned in closer and dropped his voice to a whisper. "I'm probably not supposed to tell you this, but some of the other apprentices and I think the Library tests people. There have been whispers of older rituals, but we aren't privy to information about what they entail."

I hummed as I considered his words, but instead of answering him I turned to the door. This time I wasn't looking for the symbols, but clues to the connection between them. I carefully examined every inch of the black surface. The lintel on the top of the door had the four symbols in a place of prominence, with the picture of the sun in the middle. But for the first time, I also noticed engravings along the sides of the doorway.

"What if it's a pictogram?"

I was half speaking to myself, half to them if they were still listening, and to my surprise, it was Sel who responded.

CHAPTER 12

"It could be." He stepped closer and squinted at the door. "If you look here, on the left, and over there, to the right, it kind of looks like the door was built in a series of blocks."

I blinked, surprised to find he was correct. It had initially looked like a single, uniform panel to me, but now he'd pointed it out, it was easy to see the pictures repeated all the way along both sides from the top to the bottom.

I did a quick count. Both sides of the archway had thirty plates which made up the solid appearance of the wood. I nibbled absently on my thumbnail as I considered them. The same as the symbols at the top had signified the different groups present at the time of Dag'draath's imprisonment to me, each of these plates showed scenes from several different cultures.

I saw the mountains bordering Cliffside, the Desert Lands sand, the cloud cities of what I assumed were for the dragons, and the depths of the ocean. Some of the figures were clearly meant to represent mermaids, elves, humans, and dragons. But others were more difficult to determine exactly what they were about. Those ones seemed almost abstract, and yet somehow not at the same time.

"Jarid, what are these?"

I pointed to one of the symbols depicted on a block I couldn't make out. He leaned so close his nose was almost touched the plate, remaining there for several long moments while I waited impatiently. He finally pulled back, shaking his head. "I've got no idea. I've never seen it before. But looks like a tree of some sort, like a huge oak tree, except it's dead."

He looked at me, brows pulled together, and it was evident he was as bothered by it as I had been.

I pointed at another one. "How about this one? What does this look like to you?"

"That looks like a battle, only after it's already been lost." Sel's quiet voice answered from behind my left shoulder.

142   SOUL GOBLET

"And what about this one?" I pointed at another that was unusual.

Jarid squinted at the block, turning to me with a gasp. "That looks like a pod of mermaids encircling the sun."

"That one?" I pointed to another one to the right of the lintel.

"That one looks like dragons, and lots of them," Sel replied, adding as an afterthought, "they look disappointed, if it's possible for a dragon's face to look disappointed."

Sel's interpretation confirmed what I had begun to suspect.

"What if we need to find the correct chronological order of these pieces?" I turned, biting my lip. "Like a locking mechanism. If we touch the panels in the correct order, maybe the door will open."

Jarid looked doubtful. "That seems fairly easy. How can you be sure?"

"It's not like you have any better ideas, unless you do, in which case I'm all ears." I touched the points of my ears to emphasize my point. Sel bit back a laugh, but Jarid was less amused.

"Fine, you could be right. But how do we know which order to press them?"

"We don't. I assume it's part of the challenge. If we knew the right order, it would hardly be a test."

"What if we get the wrong order?" Sel's question interrupted my attempt at convincing Jarid I was right.

I looked at him, raising my eyebrows. "What do you mean?"

Sel looked uneasy. I realized that during the entire time I'd been focused on the door, he'd been pacing back and forth. Now, his eyes darted around the hall, peering at the walls and even at the ceiling, as if looking for something before he responded. "What if we get the wrong order? If the door is guarded, perhaps something will happen to us if we choose incorrectly."

CHAPTER 12

143

I hadn't even thought about the possibility of a consequence for being wrong in my desire to find out what was behind the mysterious door. I caught Jarid's wince as he stepped back from the door he'd previously almost been touching with his nose from examining it so closely, and I suspected Sel might be correct. If a strange new door didn't open easily in the Library, which had surprised even Jarid, it was equally likely it was protected by magical or physical means to get rid of undeserving intruders who failed the test.

I took another look at the door and tried to make sense of everything I'd seen. So far, four symbols had repeated, leading us to this mysterious, non-opening door, which I was certain, was what I'd been looking for. Down the side, the same four groups were depicted in varying scenes. There were ones with dragons, with mermaids, one of a battle, which I had to assume was the sword symbol, and in addition to those there was also a dead tree. In fact, the only thing missing was any mention of my people, the elves.

I looked at the lintel again. There needed to be at least one more picture, whether elves were part of it, or not. As I searched, one figure caught my attention. It floated in the air, surrounded by bodies, and seemed completely unrelated to the others. I couldn't tell what the bodies were, but there seemed to be thousands. Next to the darkness covering the floating figure was the figure of the sun. Together they cast a shadow over everything else in the picture.

I drew closer, catching my breath when I realized this plate, unlike all the other plates, seemed to be alive and moving in front of me. Before I could think better of it, I reached my hand out to touch it, wondering if it was as warm as it appeared.

"Rhin! Are you sure?"

Jarid's sharp voice interrupted my trance, but it was too late. I'd already pressed it. I winced, shooting them an apologetic look. Sel was already too busy looking around with wide,

144 SOUL GOBLET

frightened eyes to notice. At the same moment, a chunk of ceiling gave way just to the left of where he was standing, and he yelped and jumped closer to me.

"Sorry, sorry. On the positive side, it looks like your theory was right." I laughed nervously. It wasn't ideal, but it did confirm I was on the right path.

"Okay. So, we have a war, or battle. Mermaids around the sun. Dragons. A dark figure with the sun, which we now know is definitely not the one to push first."

"You've been looking for the ritual, right?" Sel began hesitantly.

"Go on."

Sel pointed at the individual panels, careful not to touch them. "I'm guessing from common history the picture you touched probably comes last. Now we have to figure out which comes first."

"What if we went with the battles as the first picture? After all, it was Dag'draath's continued war efforts which drove Onen Suun to search for a way to lock him up in the first place."

I began to get excited again. "Okay. If the battles are first, and the dark guy is last, we need to figure out where the mermaids, dragons, and one more panel goes. I'm thinking the one with the tree is important, but I'm not sure why."

Why weren't the elves mentioned yet? With the memory of my conversation with Uncle Jorel at the banquet replaying in my head, I looked at the panels again. My eyes widened. In addition to the tree, which I was certain needed to be part of the sequence, I could now see another plate, interwoven amongst other panels of a ghastly image which corresponded to what I'd heard about the Dead Clan. But now I was left with six panels.

"Most of the other panels don't look important enough, but now I'm concerned I have one too many."

CHAPTER 12   145

"What do you mean?" Jarid looked at me, his eyes narrowed in thought.

I pointed to the new panel I'd found. "Look. Here's one depicting the Dead Clan, the tribe of elves who fought on the side of Onen Suun and almost completely perished as a result. It was an important part of elven history, so it must be involved somehow. But now we have six panels to place."

"What about the tree?" Jarid pointed at it again. "What makes you think that one is important enough to be part of the sequence?"

I looked at the tree again, shaking my head. "I'm not sure. There's something about it."

He snapped his fingers, causing me to raise my eyebrows. "I just remembered something. You know how I told you the Library is kind of a living thing?" When I inclined my head, he continued, voice animated now. "One of the whispers I've heard is that, right before he disappeared, Onen Suun came to the Library for answers on how to defeat Dag'draath."

"He did? So, the tree comes second." Bone-deep certainty filled me.

"That sounds right. First came the battles, followed by Suun and his desire to stop them. What next?" Sel leaned closer to the door, then turning to look at me.

I shrugged, staring at the door. "That's three. Two at the beginning and one at the end." I examined the panel of the elves again. "The other symbols on the lintel depict four groups. I'm wondering if this one of the elves is meant to lead me astray. I don't believe they had any major role in stopping Dag'draath. If I discard it, I'm left with the dragons looking betrayed and the mermaids crowded around the sun."

I continued to nibble at my thumbnail, but stopped when I tasted the tang of copper. I frowned at the blood welling from the ragged side of my nail, wiping it away as Sel spoke.

"The one at the end, with the darkness and the sun behind

it. Do the bodies on the ground look a little like dragons to you?"

I leaned forward, giving him a giant smile as I looked between the panel and him. "Sel, you're brilliant. They do look like dragons! Which if I'm right means the panel with the dragons looking betrayed should come immediately before."

"Putting the mermaids in the middle." Jarid's voice was clear. We shared the smile of scholars who'd come to the same conclusion, and I repeated the sequence for clarity before touching them.

"I'm going to press on the panel with the battle first, followed by the dead tree, the mermaids, dragon betrayal, and lastly, the plate with the dark figure and the sun. If I'm wrong, I'm betting something worse than a chunk of ceiling falling beside us will be the result. Sound good?" My voice cracked on the last word and for one uneasy moment, we stood still, staring at each other.

Finally, Jarid replied. "We're as sure as we're going to be. Go ahead."

Sel added a nod of his own.

I took a deep breath and pushed.

CHAPTER 13

My hand touched the metal doorknob. It was warm, like it was a living object or had been heated by the sun and turned easily in my hand. I almost stopped, surprised my theory had worked. After everything else, it almost seemed too easy. With them close behind me, I opened the door and held my breath. Anticipation bubbled through my veins and I carefully pushed the large black door open, only to be disappointed. Another dark, dimly lit hallway stretched in front of me. My shoulders slumped.

"That's it?"

Jarid was unperturbed. "If the Library is hiding something big, chances are it wants to make sure you are a worthy contender for the information. I'm pretty sure the door is only the first part of the challenge. There are likely more puzzles to come."

I groaned. "Is it possible the Library knows how impatient I am? I mean, I love a good puzzle as much as the next person, but I just want some answers already!"

My petulant tone rang through the hallway, rebounding and becoming louder as if amplified by an unseen volume enhancer, changing as it multiplied to the point where the noise

148   SOUL GOBLET

caused actual pain. When it crested, I winced and covered my
ears. But even still, it was all I could do not to cry and to keep
a single thought in my head until the reverberation began to
fade away, returning to normal levels after what felt like
forever.

"What was that?" I kept my voice low, almost whispering. I
was afraid to set off another deafening, whiny echo like the one
before and I feared that a second episode would kill me, or at
least render me permanently deaf.

Jarid looked pale and sweaty, slowly lowering his hands
from his head. Clearly, the sound had been painful for him as
well. "I'm not sure. Maybe it's another challenge."

My heart sank as I looked down the hallway. It was boring
and seemed to stretch endlessly onward. I saw a torch flicker
on the wall. The light moved sinuously, like long grass in the
wind and as I stared, a reflection of the three of us appeared
across from where we stood. But the reflection was wrong,
broken in a way I couldn't quite explain.

Sel stepped further into the hallway. Behind him, the door
swung shut loudly, once again causing the noise to echo deaf-
eningly in the small space. We waited, hands over our ears for
several minutes before it finally faded away to bearable levels.
Obviously, this hallway was enchanted to accentuate noise, if
nothing else.

Something about the mirrored wall bothered me.
Cautiously, I regarded my appearance in the mirrored hallway,
trying to convince myself things were normal, and when I
looked the way I imagined I usually looked, I turned away.
Maybe I'd imagined it.

"Let's keep walking. There must be another doorway at the
end somewhere."

I kept my voice low, hoping to avoid a replay of the loud
echo. I was successful and the guys followed behind me as I
crept forward in lieu of an audible response. Sel cast frequent
glances over his shoulder while we looked to either side and

CHAPTER 13

149

ahead. It wasn't until we were halfway down the hall the same oddness in our reflection caught my attention again. But unlike what I'd seen the first time, this unexpected vision caused my heart to pause before picking up speed.

Over my left shoulder, like a silvery image in water, was another me. Only this one had eyes that glittered malevolently as it turned to look me full in the face. My mouth dropped open in shock and the other me opened its mouth as well. With an evil smile swimming in the other's eyes, it let out a shrill scream.

The sound emitting from it was far more painful than the door slamming, or even my earlier complaint. This noise pierced my eardrums. I was certain it was blood pouring down my face at first due to the intensity of it, like knives were being inserted over and over into my ears. How could it be anything else? But as I wiped it away, clear fluid glistened on my hand and I realized it was a cold sweat pouring from my head. My heartbeat slowed, and coldness spread down my arms and legs.

I panicked. My throat clenched, terror freezing me solid as my brain frantically raced through the vaults of my memory for help. I recalled reading something years ago when I'd still been a child. A doppelgänger. Its cry could be fatal to the original, but there was a way to stop it. What was the secret? How?

My brain was numb now, sluggish, and I didn't have much time. Somehow, I'd ended up crouched on the floor covering my ears while Jarid and Sel shouted at me in distant, muffled words I couldn't make out.

Sel was kneeling next to me now, shaking my shoulders as I covered my ears. I could feel sweat streaming down my numb cheeks as though rain was falling on window panes. Digging deep, I cast my lure as far as I could to retrieve the information I needed.

I was back in my library, back in the book. It was a small, light blue book of myths and legends. My hair was tickling my face and I almost shut the book to push it back before the simple image had caught my attention. It was a picture of a beautiful mirror, but the look on the face of the person staring into it was one of striking horror as the likeness stood behind his left shoulder. In the image, the doppelgänger was screaming, trying to take the life force of the original so it could replace the spirit with its own and walk in the world beyond the mirror. But how could I stop it?

In a flash, it returned. One small line. Such a simple task, until now, when I could hardly move my body. My energy was nearly gone as I struggled, reaching for the small knife I carried in my belt, the knife Gwen had given me. I fumbled, dropping it. Despair filled me. I would have wept had I the energy, or any control over my body.

I struggled to look up, to look away from the mirror, away from the glittering eyes which had expanded to fill the face, mesmerizing me. They bored into mine. The pain intensified as they probed deeper into my mind.

"My knife." Croaking inaudibly against the deafening noise, I knew Sel hadn't understood when he stepped in front of the image, trying to support me as I fought to stand up. It broke the hold of the doppelgänger long enough for me to gasp one more word.

"Mirror."

Sel's worried eyes searched my face, and I wanted to scream.

"Sel! Break the mirror! Use the knife to break it, now!"

Was that Jarid? I could hardly understand anything now.

Without delay, he left me there, picking up the knife and slamming it, hilt first, into the mirror directly beside my face. Right where the doppelgänger was reaching for me. The shriek it had been sending directly into my soul faded almost immediately. The doppelgänger became paler, the enormous black eyes shrinking down until they were nothing more than pebbles.

As if it had never existed, only the reflection I could see

was Sel with his arms around my shoulders, lightly shaking me.

"Are you okay? Can I do anything?" He whispered, careful not to set off the echo in the room, placing the back of his hand on my forehead as if checking for a fever.

"Thanks, but you've already done a lot. What you just did, breaking the mirror? Thankfully it broke the hold she had on me. You probably saved my life."

His eyes widened and he turned to look at the wall again. The hallway was still reflective, but no longer the mirror-like surface it had been a moment earlier.

Jarid leaned over, examining it himself before standing up, his worried expression a perfect match to Sel's. "Are you sure?"

I attempted to stand. My knees held, but just barely. I was still shaky from what had almost happened, but I could already feel my energy returning. I tried to give them a reassuring smile.

"Yes. That was a doppelgänger. I've read about them before, but didn't think they were real. It's sometimes called a double-goer. Basically, if you see one who has your appearance in a mirror and it manages to lock eyes with you, it can travel from the mirror world and take over your life. Unless you're able to break their hold, which usually involves breaking the mirror, like you did."

Sel's eyebrows were almost in his hairline and Jarid looked even paler than before.

"There was a doppelgänger in the mirror?"

I grimly agreed, unable to believe how close it had come to killing me. "We should probably move faster. Make sure we don't spend any time looking at the surfaces of the walls again. If there was one here, there could be more."

Both boys swallowed. Without argument, we continued ahead, not looking to either side or speaking. The hallway, which had stretched on forever before my narrow escape, now abruptly ended after a few more steps. A doorway waited innocently in front of us. I looked back, a short hallway with the onyx doorway now easily visible and knew it had been another task.

Shaking my head, I examined the door we'd arrived at and wondered if we'd come to the wrong place. Unlike the last one, it was plain oak, without any decoration or archway. Even the size made it seem unimportant. It was hardly large enough for an average-sized human to pass through, but seeing no other option, I gritted my teeth and turned the handle. This time, the doorknob turned easily in my hand. It only reinforced my feeling something was wrong. I shot a look at both boys, reassured to find them close behind, and stepped through into...

A forest. Strange. As I looked around, Sel passed through the door and it instantly slammed shut. The moment it did, there was no sign of a door anywhere. Somehow, the Library looked just like the Low Forest.

"Oh dear," Jarid muttered.

When I turned to him, he attempted to curl his lip into a smile. It ended up looking more like a grimace, which made sense once he explained himself. "I don't think we're in the main Library anymore."

I looked around, once again seeing only forest. I couldn't see it, but the warmth of the summer sun beat down on us. Wherever we were was quite lovely and hardly threatening. But it also didn't look like the Library, as Jarid had so rightly pointed out.

"What did you tell me about the Library? The doors go to different places?"

Jarid surveyed his environment with trepidation. "Yeah. But I've never seen this door either, and I have no idea where we are right now. For all I know we could be back in the Low Forest for real."

"It does look the same. Perhaps it's another test?"

CHAPTER 13

"It looks like home. But also, somehow different." Sel scratched his head, a frown etching deep lines in his cheeks.

So, the Library meant to test me. But why? Was it simply what it did to any who came seeking answers, or was there something about the particular question I wanted an answer for? Was it more important and therefore needed protection? I remembered the way the books in my library had been so frustratingly vague and decided it was the question.

"Maybe we should start walking?" Jarid interrupted my internal debate.

"Sure." I glanced briefly at Jarid before beginning down the path ahead. "We may as well assume this is like another hallway. Perhaps it will lead us to the next doorway, or maybe even to the answer itself."

"Slim chance," Sel mumbled.

I didn't reply but couldn't help fearing he was right. At least the path was lovely, and the weather was comfortable for the walk. In fact, I was enjoying myself far more than I had when we'd traveled through the Low Forest. I wasn't weighed down by all our supplies, and I felt somewhat more confident in my hiking abilities. At least, I was enjoying myself, until the first flicker of movement came through the trees.

Before I even had time to scream, an ur'gel leapt into the center of the path. I reached for the small knife Sel had used to break the mirror, gripping it tightly. The knife was hardly as big as my hand, and I wouldn't last long against any opponent with only it as protection, even against one of the smaller ur'gels like the ones we'd fought before.

This creature had teeth the size of the knife I held and I crouched low, the way I remembered Gwen doing in our last fight. I reviewed everything I'd learned about fighting and fought to slow my racing heart. I felt strangely calm as I analyzed my opponent, and wondered if having just faced death had blunted my reaction.

Whatever the case, I used it to my advantage. The ur'gel

was grotesque, about the size of a large dog but misshapen and a sickly grey-green. Other than the obvious teeth, it had three sharp claws longer than my knife and obsidian eyes that were fixed on my throat.

A shriek came from behind me. I spun around, watching as another ur'gel landed on Jarid. Sel knocked it off with a branch he found beside the path before I could react, and I whirled to face the threat in front of me just as it leapt, claws grasping and scraping at my shoulders.

I winced as it tore at the same place I'd been bitten by the last ur'gel. Suddenly furious, I slashed at the monster without hesitation, causing it to whine and back up, its claws outstretched and teeth still bared. It was wary now, hesitating as it waited for an opening. I had gone from an easy target to an unknown.

What would Gwen do?

I brought my arms in front of my face, curling my right hand around my knife with a white-knuckled death grip. My left hand formed the best fist I could muster, and kept it high near my ear as I remembered my brother yelling 'keep your guard up" when we'd sparred as children.

The sound of fighting came from behind, but I couldn't spare a glance to see how my friends were doing as my own assailant attacked again, its hot breath stinking like rotten meat as it lunged at my face. This time, I was ready.

As it sprang, I ducked low, sliding through its forelegs, and came up under its soft underbelly. Without thinking or hesitating, I plunged my knife in as deep as I could before spinning away from the creature.

At first, nothing happened and I had no idea if I'd hit anything important. My knife was still in my hand, and I readied myself to stab again. The creature wobbled, walked a few steps, then slumped onto the path and lay there. I waited, not ready to declare success. I kept my knife, now dripping with dark blue gore, outstretched in case it approached. It made a few weak efforts to get back to its feet, but as the eyes glazed over and the creature went still, I knew I'd won.

Only now remembering the second ur'gel, I brushed my astonishment aside and turned, but Sel, or possibly Jarid, had managed to dispatch the other one. As I blinked, wondering what had just happened, the bodies of both ur'gels melted, bubbling into a sticky blue tar and fading into the path as though they'd never been.

I knelt, touching the earth with my fingertips, and rubbed the dirt together. No sign of the blue blood I'd let from the ur'gels. I looked at my knife, surprised to find it, too, was in pristine condition, as though our fight and opponents had never existed.

"Are you guys okay? What just happened?"

"Pretty sure the Library threw us another test." Sel looked around warily.

I turned to make sure there weren't more ur'gels lurking.

"I agree. The only question is whether we passed or failed." Jarid had a surprisingly gloomy tone considering we were still alive.

"What do you mean? You think we failed?"

Jarid shrugged, kicking at a piece of rubble on the ground beside him. "The Library tests everyone differently. Sometimes what it's looking for might not be the same thing we think it wants."

"Huh."

Maybe why I felt so guilty I'd killed the ur'gel was related. Part of me thought it wasn't the right solution, but I hadn't known what else to do. There was no way to know what the answer was— at least, not until we found a way out of the forest.

"Well, we may as well keep walking. Either we passed or we failed, or there's another test we have to complete before we're allowed back into the Library. Whether I get my answers today remains to be seen, but we should keep moving."

When neither objected, I continued in the direction we'd been traveling. Just as the last time, around the next corner the doorway was miraculously waiting. The route which had been beautiful but winding had ended abruptly after we'd been attacked, just like in the last hallway.

This door was again different from the others. It wasn't onyx and ornate like the first door, but neither was it plain like the second. Instead, this one appeared to have been carved from the hard, grey stones of the Deep Fell itself.

While not as richly engraved as the onyx door, when I looked closer, I could see there was writing. It was difficult to make out from the wear pattern and the old writing, but what I could make out was written in Elvish. I leaned closer, with the intent of brushing aside some of the dirt obscuring the words, until I remembered what had happened the last time I'd touched first. Perhaps I should just look.

This door had no pictograms, only writing. Elvish should have been easier for me to read than other languages, but the strange dialect and small, cramped writing made it difficult to understand. I couldn't help wondering how someone had managed to write on the rock in the first place, but there it was, clear as mud.

"What does it say?"

Sel leaned forward, but I waved my hand and he fell silent. Jarid didn't say anything. I searched for something that was clear, but it was as if someone had smudged the words right after they'd written them. Just when I'd almost given up, I stumbled upon a simple poem. It was written in Elvish, but in a stronger hand which had etched the words deeper into the stone.

THE ANSWERS WAIT within this room.
    So, take a chance,
    forsake the tomb.

CHAPTER 13

All that you seek,
glitters not.
Open your senses,
use your thought.
Guarded by elves,
not for humankind.
One only can enter,
seek and ye shall find.

I TURNED TO FACE THEM. My face must have given me away because Sel looked resigned as Jarid slowly shook his head.

"You can't go in there alone. What if—"

"Look, I need you guys to guard my back. You have to let me know if anyone is coming. Plus, the rhyme is specific. Only one person can go in, and I think, based on the writing, it needs to be an elf."

"Be careful." Sel gave me a nervous smile.

"Jarid? Stay with Sel? Please?"

A frustrated growl escaped him, but finally he relented. "Fine. But if I see or hear anything, I'm coming in after you."

"Of course. I'll be as quick as I can."

I took a deep breath, placed my hand on the smooth metal handle, and pushed.

CHAPTER 14

The door swung open as though it had been waiting for me. I would have expected such a heavy door to take far more effort. Instead, it swung open just enough for me to walk through, then shut immediately afterward. My last look at them in the forest left me feeling as if I'd set off for battle without my best friends.

This room held the secrets I needed to discover. Remembering I was supposed to be cautious of my surroundings, especially given the ur'gel attack a few minutes earlier, I gave the room a careful once-over. It was huge, larger than any of the rooms I'd seen in the Library, aside from the entrance. It was every single one of my dreams about what the Library at Abrecem Secer would look like before I'd gotten here.

Books reached up to the ceiling, which towered several stories above me. The room was almost circular, seemingly without a beginning or end except for the door I'd just come through. I whipped around to verify the door was there, my heart sinking when I realized it was gone. While I was happy to be in the room where the knowledge I sought would assuredly be found, I was *not* happy there was no sign of an exit.

CHAPTER 14

159

I closed my eyes, taking a deep breath through my nose and exhaling from my mouth as I worked to calm my heart rate, which had picked up the second I noticed the door was missing. *This is just like everything else so far. I'm being tested by the Library.* I logically understood this was yet another test, but my efforts didn't work in the slightest to control my heart, which was beating too fast for me to be comfortable.

I ignored it, since it didn't seem to be something I *could* control and focused on taking in every detail of the room I was trapped within. I returned to the room, trying to examine it critically despite my concern. It was laid out in a circle, more of an oval shape, really. Books lined every surface except for the one wall where tablets were, which created an interesting *V* effect and gave the room a semblance of a beginning and end.

The stone tablets on the wall lit up as I approached and I was instantly intrigued. I'd never seen anything like it. The first held an interesting legend about the time Onen Suun defeated a kraken, but didn't seem related to what I was looking for.

When I reached the end of the tablet and was about to move further into the room, the one beside it lit up. Fascinated at how the tablets seemed to be responding to me, I continued, wondering what kind of magic could do this. Stopping, I forced myself to keep looking around. I needed to make sure I was safe first.

In the center of the room, placed as though to achieve maximum light, was a set of stairs which led to a stone pedestal. It appeared to have been hewn out of Khasa granite. While the pedestal itself was luminescent, it was the book laying on top which captured my full attention.

It was open, with a rich velvety place-marker laid at the center, as though left moments earlier by an unknown reader. But the smell of dust in the air of the chamber was stifling, and I knew I was the first living soul to enter this chamber in years, if not centuries. I was tempted by the pedestal and book,

SOUL GOBLET

finding myself drawn closer, but I forced myself to look around further, reluctant to be drawn in again the way the tablets had until I'd seen everything the room contained.

The shelving appeared to be made of the same grey stone the door to the room had been. Some of the shelves contained rolled pieces of parchment as well as texts, and I wanted to read everything all at once, but something about the stone tablets called to me. After first ensuring there were no other objects in the room, I turned back to them.

The first story had been interesting, but didn't seem important, which made me curious why it had lit up upon my entry. Perhaps it was worth taking a moment to continue it and find out more.

I read to the end when Suun defeated the kraken and once again, another tablet lit up. This one was higher, to the right of the previous one, and appeared to start a completely new story about someone named Beru. I stopped, the name sparking a chord of recognition. Hadn't Beru Halsted been Onen Suun's first lieutenant? I vaguely recalled a history of the gods mentioning him.

It was beginning to come back to me now. He'd been sent by Suun to find some stone tablet long lost to history, but had instead turned traitor and defected to Dag'draath's side. After that happened, Suun had made the alternative arrangements for the ritual using the nine High Dragons, trapping Dag'-draath and his lieutenants, instead of the way he'd initially planned.

The further I read, the more the tablets continued to light the way until I reached the end of Beru's journey to the Blasted Lands. Gasping, I reread the passage:

"AND SO BERU had achieved his goal and found the stone long thought lost for the ages. But as he was returning, he was trapped within the cave

CHAPTER 14

161

by Dag'draath and his top lieutenants. Having already seen them approaching on the horizon, Beru had known what fate was about to befall him. Before the dark army could reach him, Beru hid the stone again. When he met at last with Dag'draath, it was him and him alone, his armies slaughtered outside by the overwhelming masses of ur'gels.

"He fought with such skill, a warrior amongst warriors. It was more than any mere mortal could have accomplished. But Dag'draath and his forces were too much. Their inexorable advances proved so devastating during the time they fought that Suun received word Beru, too, had been lost to his enemy. Even though Beru held his own, Suun, now having lost his beloved and his most trusted ally despaired and went ahead with a new plan which did not require the stone, fearing for good reason that all had been lost to Dag'draath."

STUMBLING, I nearly overbalanced. During my reading, each tablet had become higher and higher until I was standing on my tiptoes, stretching as far as I could read them. There was one more tablet, but it was too high.

I could see it glowing, taunting me, yet not within my reach. I stretched my cramped toes, thinking about what I'd had read.

Onen Suun's top lieutenant had not betrayed him. He'd been caught, his army slaughtered, but through it all he had remained loyal and he *had* found the stone. It existed! Suun's original plan to trap Dag'draath had not been the one he used.

Something bothered me.

If there had been another *plan* involving a stone I'd always thought to be just another myth, maybe there was a way to trap Dag'draath other than how Suun had trapped him.

I scanned the room again, wondering how someone could reach the books near the ceiling. Surely there must be a ladder or lift of some sort. But nothing obvious presented itself and a small growl of frustration escaped me. How much could I read

162   SOUL GOBLET

and understand by jumping up and down? Then I remembered my satchel.

I wrinkled my nose, grabbing two books off the shelf. I looked them over carefully. They appeared to be elementary primers for young students, which was perfect for what I needed. I opened my satchel, which currently contained my notebook and writing implements, and stacked them inside with it. Together, they would add several inches, and hopefully it would be all I'd need.

Placing it underneath the tablet, still glowing as if it was waiting for me, I stepped up. I still needed to stretch slightly, but now I could at least read the text.

"WITH THE TABLET and his most loyal subject lost, Suun's original plan to kill the lieutenants and send Dag'draath to another planet was impossible. But not impossible was putting him into a stasis sleep, until the time when the stone or another plan could be found. As the gods are immortal, Onen knew even with his enormous powers it would be impossible to end Dag'draath's life on his own."

I SLOWLY FELL BACK on my heels, done. The original plan had been to send Dag'draath to another planet, removing him from ours completely. It would have been far better than what had happened, and the prison wouldn't now be breaking. Assuming, of course, he was unable to ever return. I looked at the wall, expecting to see another tablet light up, but there was nothing. Apparently, the story the Library wanted me to read was finished.

What had I gleaned? Several new, important facts. Firstly, no matter what the stories said about Beru, the tablets were evidence he'd likely never faltered in his devotion to his lord. Secondly, Suun had trapped Dag'draath in stasis only to buy time, not to remove him for good. The solution he'd found required the stone Beru Halsted had found and re-hidden when Dag'draath's army confronted him.

Was that why things were failing now? Not because Suun had done something wrong, but because it was only supposed to be a temporizing measure until he had the stone?

CHAPTER 15

I stepped off my bag and put the books back on the shelf, luckily no worse for the wear. I had no reason to believe the Library could talk, but still had the sensation of being watched.

"Thank you for showing me about Beru," I spoke aloud to the room, turning slowly on the off chance an answer would come, and wanting to see where it originated if so. "So, Onen wanted the stone. Is it still possible to send Dag'draath away, somewhere else, and end this if I find it?"

The room remained silent and I exhaled. I was ridiculous, talking to myself and pretending I was talking to the room. And yet. The sensation of being watched and potentially judged wouldn't leave me. I swung my bag back across my shoulder, tucking it behind me, and looked around the room again.

The deep grinding sound of a heavy stone caused me to turn around. The door had reappeared and along with it, Jarid. He raced in, looking panicked and short of breath, like someone was chasing him. He leaned over, bracing himself on his knees as he desperately gulped the stale air inside the room.

CHAPTER 15

In between his efforts to breathe, he looked up at me with wide eyes.

"Luban is coming," he panted.

I came closer, tentatively touching his back, which was unpleasantly sticky.

"Are you all right? Where's Sel?"

Jarid waved his hand behind him toward the door, which thankfully hadn't disappeared yet. "Yes. Fine. Sel's outside. Nothing. Except Luban. Sel. Holding off. We must go. He's. Furious."

It took me a moment to interpret Jarid's one- and two-word sentences. When I did, I crossed my arms and scowled.

"What do I care if Luban is coming? Wasn't he the one who told you to show me whatever I wished to see?"

Jarid's eyes remained wide and fearful.

"We weren't supposed to be here. I wasn't even supposed to show you the book on dragon history."

Less breathless now, it became easier to understand him. But it didn't change how I felt.

"I don't care. If the Library showed it to me, I was meant to see it." I punctuated my sentence with one emphatic head nod.

Jarid looked down, lips pressed together.

It was clear that no matter what I said, he didn't agree with me.

I didn't care.

We'd passed the tests to get here and find the room in the first place, which he hadn't even known existed. If the Library really was alive the way he made it seem, obviously I had just as much right to be here as Luban or anyone else.

Instead of arguing with me, he stopped, looking around with wonder. His breathing had returned to normal levels and he was obviously as impressed by the room as I'd been when I'd entered. Unlike me, though, he gravitated toward the pedestal.

I turned to the closest bookshelf, figuring I may as well find what I could while I had the chance. If the Head Librarian was going to arrive and yell at me, I didn't have much time.

Leaving Jarid to the pedestal, I scanned the row next to my bag. If Jarid's suspicions about Luban were correct, it was unlikely I was going to get a chance to do any extensive research in the room.

What would be worth spending my final few minutes on?

I'd already determined Suun had an entirely different plan involving a stone tablet from legend to send Dag'draath to another planet.

What could I read that could provide any information in the time I had left?

Then something caught my attention.

Sitting beside the two books I'd replaced after boosting myself was a small, red velvet-bound book, even smaller than my notebook. It shouldn't have seemed unusual. It was a small red book, tucked between ordinary reference texts. I wouldn't have noticed it, but something about it glowed, as if the red of the velvet hid a fire within its depths.

I found myself reaching out, picking it off the shelf cautiously. It felt like a normal book in size and shape, but it almost thrummed in my hand, as if it was emitting heat or had a heartbeat. I pulled it in, cradling it against my body, then another book caught my eye. It, too, was small, but, unlike the first book, was bound in dark blue. If it seemed the red velvet book gave off heat and light, then this one appeared to absorb it.

The moment my hand touched it, the unmistakable sound of Sel shouting just outside the door interrupted my trance and I made a split-second decision. I didn't have time to read the red book now, which was written in a language I wasn't familiar with, so I tossed it in my satchel inside my notebook. It was the perfect size to hide between the pages.

I snatched the blue one, glancing at the door, and flipped to the first page. It was enough to tell me what I'd hoped as the name Onen Suun jumped out at me from the first line.

The scrape of stone grinding against stone echoed through the room and I shoved this book into my tunic. I didn't know what kind of man Luban was, and while my bag may be searched, I was hoping my person wouldn't be. Hopefully, I'd succeed in sneaking at least one of the books out.

I stood, moving from the wall where I'd been to stand beside Jarid, who was moving just as rapidly away from the book on the pedestal. We stood together, defiantly waiting to see if the noises originating from the other side of the door were who we expected.

"I'm sorry. I held him off as long as I could."

An apologetic Sel bowed his head as the door swung open, revealing the angriest Librarian I'd ever seen.

"It's okay. He's the Head Librarian after all. He has every right to be here. Luban." I greeted him respectfully, hoping if I played dumb it would defuse his ire. But Luban was having none of it. His face was so red it was almost purple, and I was sure it wasn't healthy for anyone to have veins pulsing so prominently on their temple.

Did Librarians have veins burst?

"What in the name of the Lost Tombs of the Sisters do you think you're doing in here?"

Luban glared at me, but swiftly turned his fury toward Jarid when he saw him cowering next to me.

He dropped to one knee, bowing his head as he apologized. "I'm sorry, sir, but the reference text..."

Before he could get the whole sentence out, Luban had snarled and strode across the room, slapping him on the back of the head. The crack rang through the otherwise silent room and I winced, knowing the blow must have hurt.

Jarid crouched at the Librarian's feet, flinching as he covered the side of his head which had been hit. His shoulders were rounded as he cringed, glanced up as he apologized. "I'm sorry, sir. I didn't know. You told me to show her everything she required. I used the reference text as I've been taught, that's all…"

Luban cuffed Jarid on the opposite side of his head, and his other hand went up to shield his head.

I couldn't watch any more of the abuse and tried to intercede.

"Sir! How were we to know this was unacceptable? When we last spoke, I told you what I was looking for. Am I to assume you didn't mean what you'd said about Jarid helping me find whatever I needed? What type of hospitality is this, in the greatest Library in the world? Your young scribe here has been most helpful. The books I have found for reference have not found me the answers I sought yet, but I believe I'm close. Surely, if I passed the tests to get where we are now it means I'm supposed to have the information, does it not? Or am I to believe the Library does not have a say in what happens here?"

I raised an eyebrow, channeling my mother as accurately as I could. If all my friends called me a princess, surely, I could use my upbringing and her haughtiness for something.

The moment the words left my mouth, I could tell I had misjudged Luban. A flicker in his eyes gave him away when I mentioned the Library had allowed me.

Maybe I wasn't supposed to know?

Luban turned his ire toward me. He looked me up and down, sneering as he did.

"You told me simply that you were looking for a book, not that you were about to stir up something you have no business getting yourself involved in. You are a stupid, foolish elf." His words dripped with icy anger. "Go back to where you came from. Back to the cliffs where the *low elves* live. You are too stupid and foolish to understand what it is you are messing with. Go home and get married."

CHAPTER 16

I blinked, realizing I'd never been spoken to in such a dismissive manner. I was used to my family ruling me out as attractive marriage material while simultaneously attempting to marry me off, but I'd never been written off as a foolish girl before.

It stung.

Perhaps because my brain was the feature I valued most about myself.

"That's not very polite." I trailed off lamely, stunned not only by his hostility, but at having a stranger tell me what I'd been hearing for years from my family.

Luban looked close to physically attacking me, and it was obvious I wasn't the only one who thought so because before I could say anything else, Sel and Jarid flanked me.

"Get out! Get out, now."

Luban's face was now a vicious mask. I opened my mouth, then thought better of it at the frightened way Jarid hunched forward, avoiding eye contact with him.

I ducked my head as well, heading for the door while giving Luban a wide berth in case he made good on my concerns about a physical threat. While I'd learned how to fight somewhat during my travels, I wasn't eager to challenge someone so furious, especially on their own turf when I still needed access to the Library.

I pushed the door, fully expecting to enter the forest, but to my shock, the door swung open to the same hallway I remembered from earlier, when I'd first begun my search for the symbols outside the reading room.

Jarid avoided my questioning eyes, walking at a brisk pace down the hall.

I had to jog to keep up.

Sel and his longer legs had no such problem.

"What just happened?" I whispered to Jarid, but he didn't answer.

He seemed to be trying to place as much distance between us and Luban as possible. Had I ruined everything for him? I hoped not. He'd seemed to understand from the moment he'd given me that book this was a possible outcome but had helped anyway. He was braver than I might have been in the same situation, especially when I didn't understand the workings of the Library in as much detail as he did.

We were almost at the lobby when I put my hand on his arm and stopped him.

"Jarid, I just wanted to say thank you. You took a big chance today, and it means a lot."

His lips quirked in a half-smile, but he looked down, brushing aside my appreciation. "Don't worry about it. I'm sure he'll calm down in a while."

His eyes slid away from me and from the way he looked nervously toward where we'd last seen Luban, he didn't seem sure at all.

I left the Library with my faithful shadow Sel a few feet behind. I was strangely humiliated by what had happened. It was uncomfortable, like I'd been caught defacing an important monument. I hardly saw the streets or felt the cobblestone under my feet as I sifted through my uncomfortable emotions.

CHAPTER 16

But what I saw in front of the hotel caused my heart to stop, yanking me out of my head more completely than anything else could have done. A small circle of onlookers was in front of the hotel, almost an exact repeat of the day before, except for the fear gripping me by the throat.

In the center of the circle, the focus of all the bystanders, was the slaver.

And Gwen was pinned beneath him.

I leapt forward, only to halt when I noticed she wasn't alone.

Will had returned at some point during the day and moved to intercede just as she slipped out of the slaver's grasp. She twisted in a way that looked almost magical, squirming into a position behind him which allowed her to kick out hard with her legs. She sent the slaver sprawling into the dirt, almost knocking over one of the onlookers on his way to the ground, where a puff of dirt made a small cloud on impact.

"Let me help you!"

Will yelled at her, but she waved him away, her face tight with anger.

"You have to let the wolves go. They're basically gone already. The minute he wants something, he won't stop until he gets it."

"No!" she snapped.

To my shock, she hauled off, pulling back her arm before letting it fly, her fist neatly connecting with his nose.

As though she'd pressed a button, blood spewed from his face, all over the front of his uniform tunic as I covered my mouth.

I had to intervene.

If I didn't, someone was going to get hurt, or worse. I just wasn't sure if it would be him, her, or the slaver.

After her impressive punch, I was a little less worried about her than I was for Will.

I weaved my way through the crowd until a tug on my arm

stopped me. I turned, irritated, but came to a standstill when Jarid appeared behind me.

"Jarid? Why aren't you at the Library?"

He looked around furtively before extending his hand.

Perplexed, I put my hand out to accept what was in his palm. When I felt the crinkle of paper, I became even more confused.

"What is this? Where did you get it?"

A blush spread rapidly across his face and he looked away. After a moment, he met my eyes with difficulty. "I was supposed to. Well, I had to." He shrugged, blush firmly intact. "I know it was a big day, so I'm not sure how much you believe, but it was almost like the book told me to."

I accepted the paper dumbly, not understanding a single thing that was happening, but before I could open it, a yelp came from the center of the crowd. This time, it sounded like Swift. Without looking at the paper, I opened my bag and stuffed it in with my notebook and the other books and headed for the center where the action was.

"You son of the spawn of Neira…"

Gwen practically spat the epithet, but didn't get a chance to finish her sentence because the slaver backhanded her violently across the mouth. I winced when she spat blood at him, but she didn't appear upset at all.

Will had backed off and was now standing at the side of the loose crowd, holding his nose while he glared at her. He clearly wasn't going to help her now.

I didn't wait to see what was going to happen next. I could tell by the fact that the slaver was raising his hand again he wasn't about to let her go without creating as much damage as he could.

I looked at Will and Jarid then threw my bag at him. His startled hands grabbed for it as I slid my small knife out of my waistband, taking a second for a quick prayer to whichever

CHAPTER 16

god looked after elves with more courage than brains, and jumped between her and her adversary.

The slaver blinked, a cruel smile spreading across his face as he began to laugh. It was a deep sound, and amused, but it held no warmth.

"Look, another little girl. How many of you must I kill to get the wolves?" He didn't expect or wait for a response. "I don't mind, of course. There's nothing makes a man feel more alive than killing someone before supper."

He chuckled again, but uneasy mutterings rose from the crowd.

It appeared they hadn't signed up to watch him injure more than one person.

However, it was as though his words unleashed a beast in me.

Fight scenes I'd read, watched, and other things I had no way of knowing flashed through my head.

He threw a meaty fist directly at my head, but I ducked, feeling only a whisper of air from the movement as he missed by a wide margin.

His eyes went wide and he blinked, then narrowed them, his lip curling in a sneer.

"Oh, you're going to run, are you? Not a fighter like your friends, hmmm?"

I pulled my lips back, baring my teeth the way I'd seen Gwen do as I flashed the knife.

"Why don't you try me?"

He leapt toward me, with both arms outstretched to grab my throat. His arms up close were even more like tree trunks, his hands the size of dinner plates. It made it easy for me to slip inside his guard.

I threw my knife to the side as I grabbed his wrist with both hands. I moved, twisting as I spun around and used his own weight as leverage. With surprising ease, I flipped him over my back in one smooth movement that took a fraction of a second.

He landed flat on his backside for the second time, a stunned look on his face as the air rushed out of him. Unfortunately, he quickly got back up, springing to his feet in a cat-like fashion I hadn't expected from someone so large.

Any advantage I'd gained was lost as his amusement at my size and his surprise at my initial rally gave way to rage.

Instead of fear, exhilaration filled me. I let loose with a flurry of movement, bobbing, ducking, and kicking, adding in punches and a few elbows for good measure.

He had size, but couldn't keep up. I moved around, dodging each punch he threw, avoiding the knife that he'd pulled from his waistband at one point and kicking it out of his hand, sending it spinning into the crowd.

I hardly felt my knuckles contact his face as a spray of blood flew from his nose,

Even as I attacked, beating him down with a strength I hadn't known I possessed, part of me wondered how I was managing to fight with movements I'd never performed before.

Before I could process what had happened, the slaver was laid out on the ground beside a startled Gwen as Sel stood protectively next to the wolves.

My breath came in short gasps, but I had done it.

Somehow, I had knocked out the slaver.

CHAPTER 17

I stared at the massive slaver now laying spread out on the ground at my feet, numbly bending to pick up my knife and put it back into its sheath at my waist, not once taking my eyes off my fallen foe.

Once she'd reassured herself the wolves were okay, Gwen approached me hesitantly.

I didn't blame her.

I looked down at my hands, turning them over and flexing them. My knuckles were bruised and bloodied from hitting the slaver, but they didn't hurt as much as they should have.

I looked at my legs, bending them slightly. They didn't hurt at all.

Somehow, miraculously, I wasn't injured. And my fighting. It was as though I'd been doing it for years, not just fumbling my way through the basic self-defense moves Loglan and Gwen had walked me through after our fight with the ur'gels.

It was as though I'd suddenly become a warrior.

But surely that was impossible. Wasn't it?

"Rhin…" Gwen paused, looking me over.

Her beautiful eyes sparkled, and she was regarding me as if

she'd never seen me before. "What was that? How did you learn to fight?"

"I have no idea. It was like the information was suddenly there. My body just knew." Even as I spoke, a thought dawned.

Was it possible?

I searched for Jarid in the dwindling crowd. Once the slaver had been laid out and no further entertainment was forthcoming, most of the crowd scattered, leaving only a few stragglers behind.

Thankfully, he was still standing there, waiting with my satchel. I walked toward him, looking over my shoulder as I answered her.

"I'm wondering if it was something I learned at the Library. Maybe some of those books are responsible."

I held my hand out for my bag, his wide eyes confirming my suspicion as he handed it over. As I slung it into the comfortable carrying position, his hesitant voice interrupted.

"You mean, you've never been able to fight before?"

I sighed, looking between them.

"If you ask any of my friends, they'll tell you I'm a bit of a princess. So, no. When I jumped into the ring with the slaver, the best I can say is I was a perfect example of sheer stupidity in action. I got lucky. Somewhere between yesterday and today, I apparently learned how to fight, which I didn't know when I took him on."

Jarid bit his lip as he looked at my bag, causing me to abruptly remember the piece of parchment he'd given me. I fished it out, holding it up.

"What is this? Where did you get it?"

He looked down, kicking the ground with his shoe. "From the book on the pedestal. I told you about it, just before you jumped into the fight. I felt like I had to give it to you. Who knows, maybe it'll come in handy."

I remembered the large, hairy man on the ground, looking

CHAPTER 17

at him nervously. "Well, thanks, I guess. I don't know about you guys, but I think we need to leave. We can't stay here if he's after your wolves, especially not after fighting in the middle of the street. We have to get to one of the other seven cities and lie low for a bit."

"Sounds good to me." A resolute expression on her face, she turned to her wolves.

The faintest flicker of movement from the ground caught my eye. Our time was running out.

"I'll be much happier when my wolves are away from this excuse for garbage human."

I looked at Sel, who'd been standing back with Swift.

"Is it okay with you if we leave?"

He dipped his head deferentially, but didn't speak.

I turned to Jarid. "What about you? Are you going to be safe here?"

Jarid shrugged and smiled in what I was sure was meant to be a reassuring fashion.

"Yes, most likely I'll be confined to one of those offices where you found me this morning for a while. I technically wasn't doing anything other than what he'd requested, so there isn't anything he can punish me for. What we saw back there was his anger at being, well, outsmarted by a girl." He winced. "I'm sorry, but Luban can be somewhat archaic in his beliefs."

Gwen snorted. "Yeah, the nice dude in the Library I met the first day? He seemed lovely. I'm not surprised he feels he's better than you if he wouldn't let my wolves inside."

I couldn't help but agree with her assessment, but I was still worried about his reaction and the repercussions for Jarid. "You don't think you're going to be in any danger going back to the Library? Because if you are, you should come with us."

He smiled, looking more certain now. "No, I'll be fine. Like I said, I'll likely be relegated to filing for the next year or two, but I'm not going to be beaten, killed, or let go. Besides, it's far better than where I grew up. It beats the heck out of living on

178 SOUL GOBLET

the street. At least in the Library I never have to fight anyone for scraps of bread."

A look of camaraderie passed between them, causing an odd twinge of jealousy to lance through my chest.

"Great. So, if you're sure you're safe at the Library, are you able to stay there? It may help to have someone on the inside. I'm sure we'll need information from the Library again, but I don't want you getting hurt just for me."

He tilted his head. "I wouldn't be doing it for you. I'm doing it for my home, for the Library, for all of Lynia. Your mission is one I'm comfortable sacrificing myself for. If there's any way to stop all the death and destruction we fear is coming, I'll do everything I can."

"Okay. Go back to the Library and we'll contact you if we can find a way."

He gave an awkward half-bow and took off.

I hoped I wasn't sending him back to an awful fate.

With Jarid gone, we returned to the room and packed our meager belongings. Luckily, Gwen had already cleaned our belongings before she'd been caught in the middle of a fight with the slaver, so we had something fresh to wear.

I briefly debated the merits of wearing the clothes we were in versus the clean items, reluctantly putting them in my bag instead of changing. If we were traveling again right now, I may as well keep the dirty ones on until we got wherever we were going. No point in having both sets filthy again.

Gwen stopped me as I went to open the door.

I looked at her with surprise. "What is it?"

"What happened to you in the Library? How were you able to fight so well? I mean, I've had a lot more experience fighting, and he was tough." She rubbed her jaw and winced.

I could see a bruise already blooming on the side of her normally smooth, porcelain-colored cheek, but had no answers for her. I was confused as she was.

CHAPTER 17

"I'm not sure. I mean, it was like I'd always known how to do it. I'm sure it's nothing like what you're thinking."

Her eyes narrowed and a warning tone crept into her voice. "What am I thinking?"

I sighed, certain I'd insulted her. "I didn't mean it like that. I just meant I didn't read anything specific about fighting. I'm not sure how to explain it, other than maybe it's because of a book I found in the Library. I wasn't supposed to read it apparently, based on Luban's reaction when he found us."

I rolled my eyes, and she snickered.

"It led me through a set of doorways where we were tested. Well, *I* was tested."

I wondered why I was the only one tested, but I figured it was probably because Jarid and Sel were only along at my bidding. I *had* been the reason everything had been set in motion.

"We went through three doorways into a room with a whole bunch of books."

"As much as I love listening to you talk about books, maybe skip ahead?"

"Sorry. It's probably like you talking about wolves."

Gwen shrugged.

"I found an amazing room at the end with tablets on one wall which lit up. As I read, I discovered something about Beru, Onen Suun's first lieutenant. He was after a stone tablet but got trapped with Dag'draath's firsts after his army was slaughtered. Suun thought he'd turned traitor, but I don't think he did. He managed to hide the stone before he was cornered by the Dark Army. The last thing I read ended with him fighting everyone off."

Her eyes widened.

"The tablets!" We spoke in unison.

I lightly tapped my palm on my forehead. "Of course! Beru was the best fighter in history, according to legend. Maybe somehow reading about him allowed me to channel his fighting ability?"

"I don't know, but if everything else you did today had nothing to do with fighting, I'd wager good money something about that room was the cause for your new skills."

"That Library was so awe-inspiring, and it gave me an idea. I think I know how to get to the other cities. I took two books and Jarid gave me this piece of parchment in the square out front. I think I need to look for more symbols, like what led me to the room in the Library. I'm hoping we can get out of Sunglen with this. See? It looks a little like a map."

I held up the paper from Jarid and after squinting at it briefly, she pursed her lips.

"I trust you. Now, let's go. I want to get my wolves as far from the slaver as I can before he wakes up. We should probably go out the back."

We left the room and headed down the hall. We were almost to the door where she'd been feeding the wolves, thanks to Marthe and her high-quality meat castoffs, when Will reappeared.

"What are you doing here?" She sneered, looking him up and down. Her arms were crossed and she glared at him with distrust.

He took a deep breath, touching his nose and wincing before he responded. "You need another sword. And it just so happens I have one. It's not safe here. I'm coming with you."

She opened her mouth for what I was sure would be a blistering rebuttal, but I stopped her, putting my hand on her shoulder.

"No. He's right. I may have randomly developed the ability to fight like a warrior, but we're up against the darkest forces of evil. If he has an extra sword to spare, unfortunately, I think he's got a fair point. We're going to need all the help we can get."

She gritted her teeth, looking at him with a pinched expres-

CHAPTER 17   181

sion before grudgingly agreeing. "Fine. But remember this—
those wolves are every bit as important to me as books are to
Rhin, or Rhin is to Sel. You get between me and the wolves,
we're going to have a problem."

He put two fingers to his brow and gave her a jaunty
salute. "Yes, ma'am. If we're agreed, let's take off. A minute
ago, the slaver was at the front desk yelling at Marthe, trying
to get her to tell him what room you're in."

I gasped, wondering if he would hurt the landlady.

Will gave me a half-smile. "Don't worry, Marthe can handle
him. But we don't have much time."

I took one last look around and entered the alley. Things were
starting to get interesting.

CHAPTER 18

A commotion erupted as we rounded the corner of the alley. We couldn't be certain, but based on the noise level and the sound of large objects hitting the wall, the slaver sounded like he'd just entered the alley we'd exited.

It was time to pull out my plan and hope it worked.

Remembering how the symbols had shown me the way in the Library, and based on something I'd read on the parchment Jarid had stolen from the room with the tablets, I was certain a similar method would work in the city of Sunglen itself. Surely, with the Library being as magical as it was with doorways coming and going, the seven cities could be accessed in a similar way.

I looked at the folded paper Jarid had shoved in my hand and used it as my map. Of course, it wouldn't have looked like a map to anyone else, but I was looking for something specific. A small trident, the same as what I'd found in the dragon book that started the entire adventure in the first place. I'd seen the same symbol on the ripped-out page he'd been compelled to take. I mourned the destruction of the book, but the Library had clearly wanted me to use the paper for something important.

CHAPTER 18

We moved through the alleys, the wolves taking point with Swift in the lead and the other two flanking Gwen. She moved as gracefully as they did, her smooth, long stride making me feel awkward and stiff in comparison until I realized I was also moving in a more agile fashion than I'd ever moved, and I wasn't even out of breath. Maybe reading about Beru *had* given me some of his abilities.

I stopped, looking down at the page again. I couldn't quite decipher the geometric figures and blew out my breath, dropping the page against my leg. I looked at our surroundings, and at that exact moment the sun split through one of the tall golden spires in the distance, refracting onto a statue into the open square we'd entered.

As the statue glowed with light, one of the figures on the page lit up. I blinked, wondering if I was seeing it correctly.

"Huh." I didn't know what to tell them, so I pointed at the square. It wasn't glowing anymore, but it had been. It had to mean something. "Okay, I think the statue and this symbol go together. Any ideas?"

I left out the fact I'd seen it glow. I didn't want them to think I was crazy. Sel squinted at the page before looking away with a shrug, but Gwen looked at it more closely.

Pursing her lips, she stared at the symbol I was pointing at, then the statue in the center. It depicted elves frolicking in the forest. The two appeared to have nothing in common.

"Could it be a doorway?"

I looked at the symbol again. It was a rectangle with an X inside. It seemed to be taunting me, so I turned to examine the statue instead. Her idea sounded plausible, and we needed to keep moving.

As far as I knew, we were still being followed.

I glanced at Will, but he wasn't paying attention. Instead he was doing what I was sure he did best: watching our backs, hand resting loosely but competently on the pommel of his sword.

"Maybe. But we have to get closer."

Gwen looked around, then headed closer to check it out.

Sel followed as we approached the statue.

Will seemed to simultaneously keep watch on our backs while staying with us.

It wasn't like there were many people around. The sun was tucked safely behind the buildings and out of our eyes.

Approaching the statue with what I hoped was the normal amount of curiosity of a traveler, I walked all the way around it. Nothing appeared extraordinary until I returned to the spot I'd begun my search and took a step back. This time, I took the statue as a whole and for the first time noticed the elves standing in between two large oak trees.

The branches of the oak trees formed the outline of a rectangle at the top, joining in the middle in a way that was too straight to be natural, or accidental. The way the elves stood together, I could just make out the shape of an X in the alignment of their bodies as they stood with one arm around the other's waist, each extending an arm and a leg out in joyful celebration.

"That's it!" I pointed to the elves.

Gwen and Will squinted, trying to see what I had seen, while Sel scratched his head. To my surprise, it was Will who agreed with me.

"Yup, it looks exactly like your picture. Now what?"

"I'm not sure. If this is the gateway or doorway, how would one normally access it?"

Gwen and Sel gave me blank looks.

Will flashed a cheeky smile. "Easy."

When she glared at him, he wiggled his eyebrows, walking right up to the elves without a backward glance. He pushed hard with both hands dead center in the middle of the X.

The sound of stone grating along stone echoed loudly in the quiet courtyard.

I had the overwhelming feeling we were still being

CHAPTER 18

followed, but every time I looked, no one was there. There was, however, a doorway where Will had just pushed, where a moment ago there hadn't been.

I paused, uncertain I wanted to enter blindly, but Will had already forged ahead without waiting for us. Gwen and Sel had similar expressions of surprise on their faces, staring blanking where he'd entered.

I hurried to follow, unsure if it would be the same as it had been in the Library, where once the door was open, it closed swiftly behind.

It was three short steps down into the entrance, and as I'd feared, once we were inside, the door shut. Even as my heart clenched, another door opened in front of us when Will put his hand on the handle and pushed.

It was another three stairs up and we emerged into a place familiar to me.

Will turned, giving me a wink. "Recognize it?"

When I slowly nodded, he pointed down the street.

"If you go two blocks to the left, the Library is right there."

I looked uneasily in the direction he was pointing. "I'm not so sure this is a good place for us to stay. We need to get further away, maybe find another gate to a different part of the city, or even somewhere other than Sunglen."

"If you don't mind letting me guide, I may know a few other doorways. I know you've got your magic paper there," he eyed my hand, "but I have a few tricks up my sleeve. You see, this city can be an interesting place. If you know where to look, it becomes a lot easier to get around."

I looked at Gwen, wondering what she thought of all of this.

She was still eyeing him with a look of suspicion which hadn't softened since he'd suggested she leave her wolves behind, but she didn't seem inclined to disagree with him now.

Sighing, I turned over my shaky leadership. "Fine. If you know a better place to hide, take us there."

Full dark had fallen by now. Any residual light from the suns was long gone, and there were no more flashes of light on golden spires pointing the way. The streets were only lit by the faint glow of the eerie green street lamps which bounced softly off the cobblestones and hid the dark and dingy corners of the alleys.

I wasn't sure what they used in the lamps, as we didn't have anything like them in the Cliffs, but they reminded me of tiny captured fires. They flickered even though there was no wind, almost alive and even dancing. How could they last an entire night? Were they replenished daily, or was there some spell to keep them burning?

Will was already walking, thankfully in the opposite direction from the Library. The feeling we were being watched hadn't left me, so by the time he arrived at another doorway my nerves were on end.

He stopped. "This should be the way to the marketplace. I've used it multiple times when I wanted to slip away from the barracks for a bite of non-ration food."

Gwen, who'd been silent until now, interjected. "Are you sure the marketplace is the best place to hide if someone's after us? Won't we be more obvious there?"

"Nope. I find it easier to hide in a crowd than within an empty room. Besides, I'm not sure about you three, but I'm hungry. I know a few late-night vendors who stay open to serve people on their way home from work. I'll take you to my favorite guy."

Sel's stomach rumbled audibly.

I raised my eyebrows.

He just smiled, looking down at his midsection and patting it. "What? He mentioned food. My stomach heard him, loud and clear."

Gwen and I chuckled as Will smirked, then began walking.

We ended up in front of a corner which looked nothing at all how I expected a doorway to look. At least with the other

CHAPTER 18   187

entrance, there had been a statue to hide it. This was just an empty bench on a corner. Hardly something anyone would recognize as a doorway between places.

Will caught my skeptical look and winked again. "You'll see."

He sat on the bench, crossed his legs, and leaned back. Within seconds a hole opened beside the bench. He immediately sprang to his feet and sauntered through.

The sound of his footsteps scampering down a flight of stairs echoed as the others quickly followed. I sighed, entering another dark, mysterious passage followed by the wolves and heard the snick of the door sliding shut behind me.

"Oh man," Sel moaned, turning his head and sniffing loudly. "It smells so good here."

Will mumbled around the food in his mouth. "I know. It's my favorite place in the world."

Gwen and I ate, but I continued to scan the crowd. The doorway had brought us to the marketplace, and Will had been right about the food. He'd also been correct about hiding in plain sight. I didn't have the same feeling we were being watched, but I wasn't confident we'd lost whoever had been following us.

It seemed too easy.

If he knew a way to hop around the city, surely others did as well. When I'd finished eating and my stomach was content, my mood was a little brighter. Turning to my friends and Will, who I wasn't sure how to characterize yet, I decided it was time to get going.

"I don't think were safe in Sunglen. Will, do you know of any gates to other cities? Surely if we can move between places in Sunglen, there must be ways to move to the other cities as well."

He swallowed his food before taking a swig from his flask. I wasn't sure what he kept in it, but he hadn't offered to share, and I wasn't about to ask. I did notice Gwen's face soften when he slipped Swift a piece of venison as he answered.

"Sure, I know a gate to Greenwick. It isn't exciting, but it's where my parents live. We could hide there for a while if you don't think Sunglen is safe."

I looked at her. "What do you think?"

"As long as his parents are fine with wolves, it's fine with me. I think it's best to get out of Sunglen." She glared at Will. "But don't try to get me to leave my wolves behind, because it's not happening."

He raised both hands in front of him before he placed one over his heart. "I promise. In fact, they have a little farm so there's plenty of room for them. If you make them promise not to eat any of the livestock, it should be safe for all of us there."

She looked at her wolves for a moment and I could tell she was silently communicating with them. When she looked at him again, some of her frostiness had faded. "Fine. We're in agreement."

He stood, brushing his hands off on his pants. "Let's be on our way. This one takes us through a less-than-decent neighborhood, but I think you'll appreciate the gateway a little more this time, Rhin."

It was my turn to look at him suspiciously, but he'd already turned.

We followed him through increasingly narrow and dirty winding back alleys. The sensation of being followed returned as a creeping prickle on the back of my neck. I could tell I wasn't the only one who felt it, based on the way our footsteps hastened. So, while I was happy when he stopped in front of a tree, the lonely looking dead-end made me uneasy. What had he meant by, "I'd like this one"?

It looked horrible, half-dead and hanging on to life by a few straggly leaves. How could such a poor excuse for a tree serve as a gate to anywhere?

He smirked, leaning on the poor thing.

CHAPTER 18   189

"Appearances can be deceiving. I believed you of all people would understand." He stared steadily at me.

I flushed, feeling somehow as if I'd been judged and found wanting.

He was right.

I hated it when people called me princess and how others thought of Gwen and Sel, but I'd never let their opinions stop me before. Now here *I* was, judging a half-dead tree and finding it lacking.

The image of the tree on the plaque in the door at the Library flashed through my mind. It had been large with roots that extended to the bottom and bare branches to the top of the plaque, but without any leaves. Had it been half-dead, or had it been all the way dead?

A tingle crept across my neck as I considered the symmetry. I was barely catching the edges of something here. Filing the thought away for later, I followed Will down another dark rabbit hole with stairs.

CHAPTER 19

I tried to fake it, but I caught myself flinching at any unexpected sound. This tunnel was longer than the others and when we finally arrived on the other side, I had an overwhelming sense of relief.

Will had glanced back to make sure we were still behind him a few times, but otherwise continued to whistle a jaunty, irritating tune until we left the tunnel. The only good thing I could appreciate so far was that the nagging sense of being followed had abated. I wasn't sure for how long, but I appreciated the vacation, especially considering Will wasn't even trying to be quiet now.

"How much farther is it?"

Gwen's tone had lightened, and she sounded curious instead of angry for the first time since she'd punched him in the nose.

She still watched him warily, but I thought she'd relaxed the farther from the market we'd come, not to mention that when he'd shared his meat with Swift, I'd seen her look confused, then soften. That simple step had likely gone further in winning her over than the fact he'd offered to help us escape in the first place.

CHAPTER 19

191

Will held a finger up to his lips and we fell silent. If he thought we shouldn't talk, there was likely a good reason. After another unending maze of streets and alleys, we arrived at a small house on the edge of the city.

Will flashed a mischievous smile and, with a rakish air, knocked loudly.

I wasn't sure what time it was, except it was long past nightfall by now. But before long, the sound of footsteps approaching the door grew louder.

A light came on, visible through a small window at the top of the door. The cheery yellow glow was a stark contrast to the darkness otherwise surrounding the house.

When the door opened, I almost expected an ur'gel or creature to leap out, but instead I saw an older woman. Her grey hair was tied neatly back with a leather strip, streaks of light brown the same color as Will's providing color against the white of a long nightdress. She only came up as high as his shoulder and seemed tired, as if we'd woken her from sleep. But the moment she saw who was at the door, her half-closed dark blue eyes opened wide, lighting up with vitality as small wrinkles at the corners creased with a smile.

A small cry of joy escaped as she opened her arms and embraced him while the rest of us stood back awkwardly and waited. "Oh, how I've missed you, son!"

She pulled back, wiped a few tears from her eyes, then held him out at arm's length to examine him thoroughly. "What are you doing here? I didn't think you had any time off for another fortnight."

His gaze shifted uneasily to me.

For the first time I realized maybe he wasn't supposed to be helping us. I raised an eyebrow, but he'd already turned back to his mother with an innocent smile.

"It's fine, Mother. I'm helping these travelers out. They're on a quest to save the world."

192   SOUL GOBLET

He'd been serious as he answered her, but it made me wince at how naïve we sounded.

"Oh? And how exactly is this ragtag group—do I see wolves?—going to achieve such a marvelous thing?"

"Not now, Mother. Can we come inside? I'll tell you everything, but it's been a long day and we could use some food, some rest—"

Before he could finish, his mother had sniffed us and wrinkled her nose. "And to wash up as well, I'd hope."

She sniffed again, gesturing us into the house with her head as she held the door open. One by one we filed in, including the wolves, who she watched with a look of subtle amusement on her face. Animals appeared to bother her as little as they had bothered Marthe.

Once inside, his mother was every bit as efficient as the tavernkeeper had been. It was obvious she hadn't been expecting company, but within moments of our arrival, she'd prepared a full spread. I watched with awe as she pulled a loaf of bread out, cutting thick slices off, then turning her attention to a block of cheese from a small icebox beside the door. She cut off several squares apiece, adding fruit and a dark brown spread to the plate, then took meat out of another container.

She placed the large plate in the center of the table along with smaller plates for serving, gave Will a look, and went back into the kitchen. He passed the plates out silently, taking a bit of everything for his plate before sitting down. We followed suit, and had just sat when she returned a moment later with hot cider in large mugs.

The apple-cinnamon smell wafted through the kitchen and I felt more at home than I did in my own room at the castle. I'd eaten only a few hours earlier at the market, but the rich warmth of the kitchen seemed to multiply my appetite and I was grateful to eat such a lovely assortment of food.

Will's mother waited until we were fed and watered, and

CHAPTER 19

193

once even Sel was leaning back in his chair, she crossed her arms, arching an eyebrow as she turned to Will.

"All right, young William. Details, if you please."

I sat up straighter in my chair.

Her words hadn't been directed at me, but she had the authority of a schoolteacher, or my father. She was clearly a woman used to people doing what she wanted. As I looked around the small kitchen, it crossed my mind for the first time that maybe leadership and strength had nothing to do with your possessions, your position in the world, or even your physical attributes.

I'd never considered that a woman of humble means would have the very quality required to lead an army, and yet instinctively, something told me this woman did. She sat calmly, not shouting or acting out, simply waiting with a solidness for her son to answer.

I watched as he composed his response carefully. Would he develop that air of command someday? He had the courage already, but he still seemed young and inexperienced. As I looked at her again, I hoped I would develop the backbone she had now.

"They came to Sunglen the day before yesterday. I happened to see them approach the guard post. Something about them made me curious, and yes, a little suspicious."

I caught surprise flash over Gwen's face as my eyebrows went up, but Sel listened calmly as if hearing last week's news.

"I spoke with my sergeant and requested permission to follow them. As a potential threat to the city."

My eyes went wide and a gasp escaped before I could stifle it.

Will shot me an apologetic smile.

"I was pretty sure you weren't dangerous, but when I noticed the slaver had an obsession with Gwen and her wolves, I decided it would be better to stick around." His eyes lingered on Gwen briefly.

194 SOUL GOBLET

I felt my hackles rise. I didn't like being tricked, even if it had been for a good reason, but tried to calm down. I realized he was speaking again, and turned my attention to his words.

"It was a good thing, too, because today he made his move. If I hadn't been there, he likely would have taken the wolves and killed Gwen."

"If it wasn't for you?"

Gwen's voice raised and she glared at him incredulously. "It was your fault he almost won in the first place. If it hadn't been for Rhin and her sudden unexpected fighting skills, we'd all be dead."

Gwen looked at me and I flushed.

I still thought it had been the passage about Beru I'd read in the Library which had somehow imbued me with his skills. Clearly, the Library had plans which required me to stay alive, at least for now.

"Anyway, after the fight, Rhin suggested taking off. I knew Gwen wouldn't be eager to have me along for the ride, since she'd punched me in the nose moments earlier." He paused to rub his slightly bruised nose.

His mother looked at Gwen, amusement twinkling in her eyes. "Continue. I think I like you, young lady. By the way, you can all call me Ethel. So, your friends decided to leave Sunglen?" She relaxed her shoulders, her lips still curved in a smile as she waited for Will.

"I grabbed my bag and doubled back. I'd already told my sergeant I was going to tail them, and *may* have mentioned the slaver." Will winked, proudly lifting his chin. "You'll be glad to know a few soldiers collected him shortly after we took off down the alley. They would've gotten him in front of the tavern before he woke up, but unfortunately, I got the message to them too late."

"Wait, what?" I drew my eyebrows together, confused when he'd done any of this.

Will smiled smugly. "While you and Sel were at the

CHAPTER 19

Library, I kept an eye on Gwen. When the slaver returned, I sent a message back to my regiment he was going to try something, and gave them the location of Wentir's tavern, but the barracks are just far enough away they didn't arrive until after you'd already knocked him out. The scuffle we heard in the alley was them ... detaining him."

"Wait, so if he is out of the way, why did it feel like someone was following us this whole time?"

"I don't know. But obviously, whatever it is you're looking for has stirred a lot of interest in Sunglen. Which is why I think it's best we spend the night here, out of Sunglen and out of the way."

I pressed my lips together. The idea of a person following us who wasn't the slaver was more bothersome than I'd expected. At least with him, we knew he wanted to steal the wolves and kill us. Being followed by an unknown person or persons when you didn't know their motivation was infinitely more frightening.

Before I could ask anything him if he knew where we should go next, a knock came at the door.

Will's mother looked at him, raising her eyebrows, but he held both hands up, obviously as surprised as she was. She narrowed her eyes, then moved to the doorway, gliding soundlessly to grab a large stick from behind the door before she peeked through the small window opening in the door.

Whoever she saw on the other end was someone she knew from the way she immediately put the stick down, throwing the door open with a broad smile.

"Jarid! Wonderful to see you. Come in."

She scooped him into a hug almost as big as the one she'd given Will, ushering him inside the house before shutting the door and locking it behind her. She paused with one hand on the last lock, raising an eyebrow as she looked at us in turn.

"Should I be expecting anyone else tonight? I've half a mind to put a spell on the door so nobody else can come in."

Gwen, Sel, and I shook our heads.

I blinked, suddenly making the connection with Ethel's reaction. "Wait, you two know each other?"

They exchanged glances.

"Yeah, of course."

Will smiled blandly, turning to Jarid, who echoed his statement.

"Yeah, the soldiers come by the Library fairly often. Sometimes they need information, other times it may or may not be to check out the—"

Will smacked Jarid across the abdomen, interrupting him.

"Anyway." Will's eyes narrowed warningly at him. "Jarid and I are friends." He looked at Jarid again, but this time tilted his head to the side. "But why are you here? The last time you..." His eyes widened. "Oh. Is everything okay at the Library? Are you in trouble?"

Jarid looked around and Will's mother obviously saw something in his face, because she quickly fixed him a plate and a drink, placing them on the table in front of an empty chair.

"Sit. Eat. This has been a most enlightening night so far."

A smile split her face, and I could see where Will got his mischievous good looks.

"First some travelers with my son, and now his friend who never leaves the Library. What's going on?" Her eyes still conveyed amusement, but her tone had sharpened with interest as she waited for him to answer.

Jarid sighed and ran his fingers through his hair. "Well, I wasn't lying, exactly, when I said I'd be safe going back to the Library. But things are a little more complicated. From what I've been able to pick up, you guys need to stay hidden. And you aren't exactly sneaky walking around Sunglen with three wolves. I think you need to get out of town, and stay out. It's a good start hiding here, which was what I was hoping had

CHAPTER 19   197

happened when I couldn't find Will. I don't think this is far enough away, though."

He sighed, taking a sip of the hot cider and closing his eyes appreciatively.

"Thank you, as always, for your hospitality, Ethel." He set the cup down and continued. "I think I kept the Librarians off your tail."

When my head jerked, he gave me a grim look. "Yes, Luban was so angry he's declared the Library off-limits for you. Not only are you not welcome back to the Library at Sunglen, but I'm certain he's got the other Librarians looking for you as well. I've never seen him so furious."

"Yeah, I don't think I've ever seen anyone that mad at me, either. What should we do?" I slumped lower in my chair, feeling defeated. "I still need information. I can't let them stop me just because someone is mad the Library let me into a secret room."

Will exhaled, and I turned to him, wondering what he'd say next.

"Jarid and I discussed this already."

"You have? When? Based on what we heard earlier, Will was following me the entire time you were with Rhin. How could you possibly have communicated without either of us seeing you?" Gwen's surprise was obvious.

Jarid bit his lip, but Will waved his hand at the young apprentice. "You may as well show them."

Jarid sighed, bringing out two small, plainly bound brown notebooks from his satchel. "Will had this with him until yesterday. He gave it back to me in front of the hotel. We thought as long as you stayed in Sunglen we'd be able to keep in touch, but if you're going where I think you'll be going, it will be impossible, unless you have this. If you keep this book with you, we can pass information to each other without anyone else knowing." He handed me the bland book.

I accepted it with delight. "Is it magic?"

"Yes, of a limited sort. Once you write in this one, I'll get the message in mine. But when we run out of pages, that's it. It doesn't disappear. So, make sure whatever you write is important. We have no idea how long we'll need it."

I understood completely, relief making me a little giddy. Even if he couldn't be with me, I'd still have the benefit of his knowledge.

"Thank you. I'll be very careful with it. Where is it you think we should go?"

"I'm not sure, but I think the Library has already given you the answers. I saw you slide a book into your bag, and as I was leaving, this one began to attack me." Jarid held another small volume up quickly, placing it on the table before I got a good look at it. "I couldn't understand why, but it seemed really important I take it." Jarid gave me an unexpectedly sneaky smile, similar to the one Will had displayed earlier. "I managed to get away without Luban noticing."

I was about to comment when he continued.

"Part of the reason you're in so much trouble is because the room won't lock now. Luban stationed guards all around it, but something's up. The Library isn't acting the way it usually does."

"Interesting. So, a strange elf shows up looking for answers to lock Dag'draath up for good, and in the process, wakes something up in the Library, and now all the Librarians are going crazy?" Will leaned back in his chair, looking amused.

"Exactly. And I'm pretty sure the answers to where you're supposed to go next are on the paper I gave you earlier, as well as in this book and the ones you took from the Library."

All traces of fatigue vanished as another mystery fell into my lap. I barely even noticed Gwen and Sel shoot each other a look.

Will's mother caught Gwen's yawn however, and stood up from the table. "How about while Jarid and Rhin take a look at the books, we get the rest of you cleaned up and sorted for

CHAPTER 19

the night? Once I have them taken care of, I'll come back for you. I know you're in the middle of a puzzle, but you'll still need your rest to solve it."

She smiled at me knowingly as I spread the books and paper out in front of me.

"Thank you, that's very kind," I said, touched. I hardly knew her and yet she'd been so accommodating, anticipating exactly what I wanted.

She continued to be wonderful, as within moments, she'd hustled the others away, leaving Jarid and me in silence to look through the books. One was in Elvish, which he apologized for not being able to read. The paper he'd given me had more symbols on it. Some I recognized already from the places they'd led me around Sunglen, but the idea others I hadn't seen before would lead to our next location struck me.

My head snapped up. "Jarid, could this be a map to the different cities?"

He squinted and looked at the symbols before shaking his head. "I don't know how to read it if it is."

I turned back to the book. It was obvious this page was important, but we could likely rule out the symbols we'd already used. I looked at the book Jarid had brought, this time noticing a faint watermark in the shape of a cloud, which I'd just seen in the one I'd borrowed. Opening it, I compared the two books. They were both in an ancient form of Elvish, but it was difficult to decipher and seemed jumbled.

"Wait a minute — what if it isn't a map, so much as a key?" Jarid's voice was full of excitement.

I looked up, tilting my head as I considered that possibility.

"What do you mean, a key?"

"These two are in Elvish, but you can't read the other one at all, correct?" When I agreed, he continued. "What if it isn't a language either of us knows, but instead, has been written in code? And the symbols on the page are the key to reading it?"

A smile spread across my face as an idea presented itself. "I want you to take the page and this book and see what you can figure out. I have an idea about these other two books which may or may not work."

He accepted the task while I looked at the dark blue and the luminous red books. I placed them beside each other and whenever a sentence didn't make sense, I read the sentence on the corresponding line in the other book. Immediately, the answer was clear.

"Of course!" I shouted.

"Already?" He looked down at his page, his pinched expression making me think he hadn't expected me to figure it out so quickly. To be honest, neither had I. It felt as if my brain was supercharged. Maybe it was another effect of the Library trying to help me find the answers? Was it possible it wanted Dag'draath out of the way as well?

"I think these two books are a set. Duality. I could read them in Elvish individually, but they didn't make sense. When I arranged them together, though..." I smoothed the pages out, showing him how I'd placed them. "The sentence is comprehensible if I finish it on this page, in the other book."

"That's amazing. I'm not sure I would have figured it out, especially since I can't read Elvish. What does it say?"

"It's strange. It seems to be a natural history of the dragons, nothing that would need to be written in code. Nothing I can see here looks secret at all."

He looked down at the page and the book I'd given to him.

"Sorry, but I'm not understanding my assignment. So far, the only thing I can figure out is the word for dragon on this page, which is hardly helpful."

Looking disappointed with himself his words stirred something in my memory. What was it?

I snapped my fingers. "You're a genius! All of this is leading us to the dragons. Maybe the next place we need to go to is the Dragon Dominion. The ritual Onen Suun performed

CHAPTER 19

201

used nine High Dragons. Maybe we need to find out more about the original spell and the dragons who were part of it."

Jarid's face paled. "But how are we supposed to get there? It floats."

I felt in my bones we were on the right path. "I don't know. I've never been there."

He sighed, but before we could make any plans, Will's mother returned.

"That's enough for tonight. Pack up your books for now. I'm sure you have a busy day ahead of you, and you'll need sleep." Her tone was brisk and no-nonsense.

I longed to do more reading, but she was right. If we hoped to find a way to get to the Dragon Dominion, it would be easier to plan with fresh minds in the morning.

CHAPTER 20

I slept like a rock. Will's mom was an even better hostess than Marthe had been. We had to bunk together due to space, with Gwen and I sharing the guest room, while Jarid, Sel, and Will shared his old bedroom.

With the wolves nestled around the bed, I couldn't remember ever feeling cozier. But from the minute my eyes snapped open, I was feverishly thinking about the Dragon Dominion and our trip.

I snuck out of bed when I found Gwen still asleep, but once in the kitchen I discovered everyone else was awake and eating the hearty breakfast that Ethel had prepared.

The guys grunted hello and continued eating, so I grabbed a plate and sat down, eating quietly until Gwen joined us. Once my stomach was full, I leaned back and sighed happily.

"So, does anyone know how to get to the Dragon Dominion?"

Sel continued to eat, but Will choked on his mug of cider.

"The Dragon Dominion?" Gwen cocked her head to the side. "Why would we need to go there?"

Jarid and I exchanged glances before he answered. "We

CHAPTER 20 203

found something in the books last night. Everything seems to point to finding the next clue with the dragons."

Gwen and Will looked at me blankly. I hadn't told them anything, but it was time. "The ritual Onen Suun used involved nine of the High Dragons. Everything I've read has led me toward the dragons and the role they played. While I'm confident the next step in our journey lies there, I don't know how to get there. I mean, it's not exactly next door."

Gwen agreed. "True. I've never been there, so I can't help. Will?"

"We could head to Starside—it's on the outermost rim of the Dominion," he added helpfully.

I bit the inside of my cheek. "Do you know how to actually get from Starside into the Dominion?"

I hoped Will had the practical answers I lacked. I fondly remembered the books tucked in my satchel, wishing I had more time to read them.

"Maybe. Do you have any contacts at the Starside Library?" Will deflected to Jarid, who looked surprised to be on the spot.

"It's possible. I'm not unwelcome at the Library, but Rhin might be. Luban has already spread word to all the other Librarians, I'm sure." He grimaced at the idea.

"I'm sorry. I never meant to ruin your life," I offered, feeling my apology was inadequate for the situation.

"This isn't your fault. In fact, I don't understand why Luban's so angry. He's the one who told me to help you, and we all know the Library only shows the worthy a resource above what's ordinarily available. In my opinion, I'm serving the Library in the most loyal way I can by helping you. But just knowing your mission is to stop Dag'draath so the wars end for good would have been enough for me, even without the Library's permission."

"Thank you for your support. I'm not sure I deserve it." I wished I didn't feel so guilty.

Gwen placed her hand on mine, the familiar warmth causing a small tingle to spread as she looked at me seriously.

"Rhin, we're all here for the same reason. We believe in you. We may not always agree on how to do things." She shot a pointed look at Will. "But we all know you're someone special. Stop apologizing. In fact, I'm impressed by how far you've come since we first started this journey."

It was nice to hear praise, but I didn't think I deserved it. At least, not until I found the answers I was looking for.

"All right, if everyone's ready, we should get moving." Will stood abruptly from the table. "Even with the gates, it's going to take us a few hours to get to Starside."

We cleaned our plates, packed our meager supplies, and quickly departed.

AFTER ANOTHER DIZZYING trip through alleys, streets, and gates, we finally arrived at Starside.

It was another place I'd only read about, but the reality was so much more than I'd imagined. I'd grown up on the side of the Cliffs, but the altitude here almost made me dizzy. Each time I looked out at the view, my breathing became more labored, but I wasn't sure if it was from the view or the height.

I felt close enough to touch the clouds, and almost regretted it was daytime when we'd arrived, because I would have loved to have seen the stars from the white cliffs as they jutted over the ocean below. But the suns showed the true beauty of the city. It was built on the side of the mountains, and most of the houses were square white blocks, like stairs leading toward the majesty in the center, the Library.

Jarid and Will had stayed in front and when we arrived, where they whispered something among themselves before Jarid looked at me with a pained expression.

"I have a contact here, Kramson. I'm not sure if he'll help us, but I've always found him to be fair, not to mention more even-tempered than Luban. He's the Starside Librarian in charge. I can't guarantee his reaction, but it's the only way I can think of to get to the Dragon Dominion from here."

"If you trust him, that's good enough for me. Gwen? Sel? What do you think?"

Sel nodded once, and after a moment, Gwen reluctantly nodded as well.

"I'll trust your decision. From what you've told us, we need more information from the Library anyway. Whether or not we can get to the Dragon Dominion from there remains to be seen."

I turned to Jarid, excitement taking over now that we were all in agreement.

"Let's find Kramson."

With Jarid in the lead, we climbed to a Library entrance even more awe-inspiring than the golden spires in Sunglen. It was built out of a dark stone that sparkled in the sun, reminding me strangely of the glory of the night sky. I wondered if the architect had intended such a thing with each step I took up the flight of stairs closer to the answers I hoped to find.

Breathing rapidly, I was relieved to reach the top after several minutes, finding a lobby almost the duplicate of the Library in Sunglen.

Gwen hesitated at the entryway.

"I'll wait here. I don't want to start things off on the wrong foot." She pointed to the wolves. "Go on, it's fine. Talk to Kramson, then come back and let me know what you find."

"I'll stay with you," Will offered, giving a gallant bow.

Gwen gave him a surprised smile, and Will blinked. A lazy smile crossed his face.

"Sel, why don't you stay with them too?"

Sel inclined his head. "Of course."

"True, it's probably best if it's just the two of us. The less people traipsing through the Library, the happier he'll be.

He's a little territorial when it comes to his books," Jarid chimed in.

I followed him inside, looking over my shoulder as the rest of the group sat down at the side of the entrance steps to wait. Gwen caught my eye, giving me a thumbs-up before she turned back to respond to something Will had asked her.

When I turned, Jarid was introducing a short human with a fringe of curly red hair and a plump face with laugh lines beside his mouth and deeply etched grooves between his eyebrows.

"Rhiniya of the Cliff Elves, this is Kramson, Head Librarian in Starside."

I turned, greeting him with the most elegant curtsy I'd ever performed.

"It's lovely to meet you, sir. Jarid has told me of your immense knowledge and I would be so grateful if you would share it with me."

Kramson answered politely, but his expression was wary. "It's nice to meet you as well, Rhiniya of the Cliff Elves. I've heard of you already."

"Please, sir, we need to get to the Dragon Dominion. Can we get there from here?" Jarid began pleading before I could speak, but it was no use.

Kramson pressed his lips together. "I cannot help you get to the Dragon Dominion. I am also quite reluctant to have you in the Library after what occurred in Sunglen."

I kept my eyes downcast to hide the frustration brewing within. "I understand. Do you mean you will not help at all?"

Kramson sighed. I looked up, surprised to see his face now appeared drawn and tired. His mouth worked for moment before he finally answered. "I don't agree with what is happening, but this morning I received word this was for you to keep."

Before I understood what he was doing, Kramson held out a small golden key on a chain.

"What is this?"

CHAPTER 20

I accepted it cautiously. It was beautiful, bold yet intricate. Small enough I could easily wear it around my neck and tuck it into my shirt. But I held it in front of me as I stared at him, not wanting to accept it until he told me what it was for.

"Apparently, the Library has decided this rightfully belongs to you."

His tone was clipped, betraying neither excitement nor approval, but his explanation didn't help.

"But what is it?"

Jarid answered. "It's a key to the Library."

His voice was soft, and he couldn't hide his awe as he stared at the key, stars shining in his eyes.

The key felt warm in my hand and for a moment I could only blink, stunned by the enormity of his simple statement as I watched it sparkle, the antique color glowing softly in the light. Or maybe it was my imagination.

"A key to the Library?" I looked at Kramson, disbelief making my voice squeak in an unbecoming fashion. "Does you mean I can come and go as I wish?"

Kramson snorted. "Hardly. The Library may, for reasons I don't fully understand, consider you the equivalent of a full Librarian, but you haven't proven your worth to the rest of us. *That* will be far more difficult."

CHAPTER 21

I regarded Kramson without speaking as his words echoed in my ears. The *Library* considered me a Librarian? If I hadn't been on a quest to find answers, that would have made my dreams come true.

A Librarian at the great Abrecem Secer?

My heart fluttered at the idea.

But even as I stared at the key, it was no longer enough for me. He was right. It was going to take a lot to impress the Librarians, and I had no idea how I'd accomplish that task.

Hadn't finding the secret book room been enough for them? Though come to think of it, I was probably less popular because of that, at least with Luban, if not the rest of them. The fact guards now stood outside the room also made me wonder just how much knowledge was kept locked away from those who sought it.

But instead of dwelling on the "what ifs", I gave Kramson another gracious curtsy and stood up proudly. "Thank you for the key and thank you for your honesty. I wish it were otherwise, but I can respect a man who tells me the truth, even when it isn't a truth I wish to hear. I shall guard this carefully."

CHAPTER 21   209

I held the key up before slipping it around my neck and tucking it beneath my tunic.

I turned to Jarid. "I believe it's time for us to go. We still need to acquire transportation to the Dragon Dominion."

"Thanks for the information." He bowed politely.

Kramson gave him a faint smile, lightly grabbing his arm and searching his face. "Be careful. You are choosing a difficult path. You may find when you return to the Library it could be a place which you no longer belong."

I couldn't be sure if it was a threat or warning, or if there was another, more cryptic meaning to his words.

Something I couldn't read passed between the two men.

Jarid stood up from his deferential posture, giving the Librarian one last dip of his head before turning toward me and the door.

I looked at him curiously, but he kept his face blank. As much as I wanted to ask, now wasn't the time. Kramson was watching us, almost as if he was ensuring we were leaving. *Good thing I have this now.* I put my hand on my neck where the key was, and smiled slightly.

As we approached the others, Will stood as Gwen and Sel regarded us with hopeful expressions.

"So?" Gwen's voice was soft and hesitant.

"No, we can't go through there."

"While you were inside, I remembered one way we can get there."

"Oh?" Jarid's ears perked up, his face open and his earlier solemnity replaced by interest.

"We can take one of the flying ships." Will's eyes twinkled, and although he was clearly in a good mood, I wasn't sure I liked his suggestion.

Jarid shook his head, giving me a sad smile. "I think I should stay here, do some penance. You go, and remember—you have the two-way book. I'll look at it as often as I can and answer right away. This way, I can still give you information when you need it. Be safe."

Disappointed, but knowing he should do what he could to mitigate the damage I'd caused to his role in the Library, I waved goodbye.

As it turned out, I was right to be concerned about the plan to take a flying ship. It was like nothing I'd ever seen before. A tall woman presented herself the moment we arrived at the docks, and I could tell from the way Will spoke to her this wasn't the first time they'd met.

"So, you'd like to go to the Dragon Dominion, would you? It's going to cost you." She crossed her arms and tilted her head in a jaunty fashion, throwing out a number and waiting, as if daring him to be shocked at the price.

To my surprise, Will agreed.

"Only if you can you be ready to depart within the hour." He threw back a challenge of his own, eyebrow cocked in a rakish fashion that made me want to smack him. More and more, he reminded me of my brother. Maybe it was the military aspect, or his behavior in general.

Sel appeared overwhelmed by excitement, and was unable to keep his eyes from flicking between flying ship to flying ship.

Gwen, on the other hand, was pale.

I searched her face and leaned over, nudging her with my shoulder.

"Are you all right?" I wasn't reassured when she gave me a smile that was more bared teeth than anything else.

"Yeah." She gulped as the sound of a bell went off and another flying ship took off two bays down. "I'm not sure I'm going to enjoy flying." Biting her lip, she looked at the wolves sitting beside her.

Kiya was whining softly as her hand reached down to gently weave through the strands of soft fur. She closed her eyes and leaned against the wolf.

CHAPTER 21

"Will the wolves be okay?"

"Likely as well as I'll be." She let a humorless chuckle escape. "I know I live in a treehouse, but I'm not fond of actual heights. The idea of being in something floating high above the ground, when I have no ability to get back down safely on my own, is a little nerve-racking."

She paused to look at an enormous flying ship that had just taken off. It was covered in a dark brown material, reminding me of a floating brown cloud as it majestically pushed off from the dock. When I looked back at her, she sighed, her face gloomy.

"At least if we fall from up there, the view will be nice. I really shouldn't worry because we likely won't survive long enough after we land to notice our fatal injuries."

"Oh, my Suun! There's no need to be so morbid. I'm sure we'll be just fine. The captain looks quite competent. Then again, I'm not sure if the fact Will knows her is a plus or minus," I added as an afterthought.

We waited as they wrapped up negotiations, giving a firm handshake to seal the deal before he returned, the captain close at hand.

"Guys, this is Captain Baeley. She's agreed to take us to the Dragon Dominion for a reasonable price." Will raised his hand, making a see-saw motion before he continued. "We'll be leaving shortly, so we can head onto the ship now."

I forced a smile I didn't feel, patting my satchel for reassurance, feeling the familiar weight of the books soothe me.

Gwen made no effort to appear happy. Her eyes were wide, and she kept her mouth pressed tightly shut.

Sel practically skipped his way onto the ship.

It looked exactly like the ships I'd seen in books, the ones that sailed the large bodies of water. Of course, I'd seen them from a distance in the past, but as the privileged daughter of the leader of Cliffside, and an aspiring Librarian, the docks where the airships were wasn't a place I'd ever been.

Up close, it was easy to see that the biggest external difference was on the underside of the ship, which I'd glimpsed prior to boarding. As it wasn't in water, it needed a way to lift and steer in the air, but I was impressed by the arrangement of propellers and wheels underneath. It was different up close compared to the books I'd read about them.

Captain Baeley was dashing back and forth, commanding her deckhands. People were racing back and forth at her bidding and when she pointed us toward the below decks, we followed her directions and placed our stuff in a roomy berth large enough for us all. As

Sel looked longingly upstairs, and Will took pity on him, slapping him on the back.

"I imagine you'd like to go above deck again to watch as we lift off?"

I smiled at Sel's exuberant head nod. I patted my satchel again to reassure myself the books I required were still within and stood up.

"I'd like to go to as well. I've never been on a flying ship before."

I was nervous but wanted to experience as much as I could. After all, if I succeeded in our mission and life went back to the way it was before, it was likely I would go back to my quiet life in the Cliffs and do what was expected. If we didn't succeed, I'd already resigned myself to the fact that I would probably die, not that I was eager for that to happen.

As excited as I was frightened, I turned to Gwen.

"Do you want to watch, too?"

By now, Gwen's face was an unpleasant shade of green.

"No. I think I'll stay here with the wolves."

When she looked at her friends, I felt even worse for her. The wolves were lying down, looking sadder than I'd ever seen an animal look. Kiya was whimpering softly, her head resting on Gwen's right foot, while Swift rested his chin on her other and Daimyo curled on the bench beside her.

CHAPTER 21

"All right. Would you like me to bring you some food?"

The look on her face told me all I needed to know, so I reached my hand out to gently squeeze her shoulder.

She exhaled, looking as dejected as the wolves. I pulled her close for a hug, feeling her grip me tightly, as if trying to absorb my strength. I stroked her hair gently, wishing I could make her feel better. She rested her head on my shoulder for a moment, and it was nice.

Sel was shifting impatiently in the background, and the noise reminded me we had an audience.

I pulled back with a smile. "I'll check on you as soon as liftoff is over," I promised. "I have some reading to do anyway, so if you want, I'll join you for a bit."

Gwen smiled and waved us out. I felt guilty leaving her alone, but I was too excited about watching the ship take flight to turn around.

In the end, it was almost anticlimactic.

After the initial hustle and bustle of the crew readying the ship for departure, we were away with only one small bump to rock the ship. The docks moved farther away from me and it was quieter than I'd expected, truly making me feel like we were floating into the clouds through some sort of magic.

I looked at the rigging, trying to figure out how the ship was able to maintain power, and Captain Baeley noticed me staring and came over.

"Trying to figure out how it works, are you?"

I gave her a sheepish smile. "I've never seen a flying ship up close before, let alone been on one. I've read about them in books, of course, but I don't remember learning about how they work." I waved my hand at the mast. "How does it run? I mean, how does it take off and stay in the air?"

She laughed, a surprisingly infectious sound given her tough appearance. "Well, with magic, of course." A dimple appeared in her cheek, then she winked and turned away to another duty that required her attention.

214   SOUL GOBLET

I understood now how Will and Captain Baeley knew each other. They seemed to share the same cockiness, courage, and mischievous streak. I smiled as she left, but was disappointed. I already knew airships ran by magic, but her answer added nothing to what I knew. Maybe if she wasn't as busy later, I would press her for further details.

As expected, once take off was complete things settled into a smooth ride. Will assured us it was a long flight, with plenty of time to catch up on sleep if we wanted. I checked on Gwen as promised, finding her curled up with all three of the wolves on top of her, fast asleep. I tiptoed out, not wanting to disturb them if they'd managed to find enough peace in the air to rest.

Once back above deck, I took out the book I'd been dying to read. I had a hard time focusing at first because I kept catching glimpses of the scenery passing by which distracted me. From Starside to the Dragon Dominion, we covered an amazing swath of land.

We went from the mountainside, over grassland, and up into the clouds. It was misty and cold then, and I couldn't see much past the ship. Finally, I was able to focus on the text and most of the trip from that point on was spent searching for our next destination in the book I'd stolen from the Library.

By following the symbols, as I had in the Library, I was able to find the clues hidden within the text. Once again, the texts were vague and didn't give an exact location, but it seemed from what I was reading we needed to head to Bomrega Island, where the nine High Dragons had resided before Onen Suun had used them to trap Dag'draath.

I didn't know very much about how dragon society was run, but even I knew Bomrega Island wasn't a safe place for most other creatures. Since the nine High Dragons had gone missing, other dragons had warred over the territory, passing it back and forth repeatedly between feuding clans.

Tucking my book back into my satchel, I looked over to where Will and Baeley were chatting next to the stern.

CHAPTER 21   215

Sel stood nearby, his upper body leaning almost all the way over the side as the wind ruffled his hair with his eyes closed.

Asking Baeley to take us to Bomrega Island was huge. Even though we were paying her well to take us to the Dragon Dominion, I wasn't certain she'd be able or willing to take us there. I stood up and walked over to where they were enjoying the view.

"Hi." I had to clear my throat as my voice betrayed my hesitancy. When they looked at me with curiosity on their faces, I dove right in.

"Is it possible to get to Bomrega Island from here?"

Will just blinked, but her head jerked back in surprise.

"Why do you want to get there? Of all the places in the Dragon Dominion, it's the most dangerous."

"I know, but I have reason to believe we need to get to the Temple of Light. I'm positive I'll find what I'm looking for there."

"If we live long enough," Will muttered.

When I shot him a glare, he looked off in the distance, pretending he hadn't spoken.

I looked at Captain Baeley, who was shaking her head. "I'll do what I can. It's easy enough getting there, no more difficult than anywhere else in the Dragon Dominion, but you'll only have a short period of time. They also may not let me remain docked, which could mean you'll have to find your own way back."

"That's a chance I'm willing to take. Do you think you can buy us some time?"

I tilted my head to the side, maintaining eye contact as she searched my face.

"What can I say? I love a challenge. I'll change course to land at Bomrega Island. I'll dock and try to buy us some time. But it may not be long enough for what you need. If I'm unable to stay until you complete your mission, I'll try to return to pick you up."

"That would be wonderful, thank you. How long will it take to get there?"

She looked out over the stern, and squinted off into the distance. "My best guess is about another hour or so of travel, then arguing with officials alone should buy us close to an hour once we dock, even if they don't buy my reason for landing."

"Hopefully it's enough. How far is the Temple of Light from where we land?"

She shrugged a shoulder. "Perhaps ten minutes or so. I've only flown over though, so I can't tell you how long it takes to get there by foot."

"More like twenty," Will interjected, his face serious. "I've been there. Once. We'll need to move fast, and it's best if the wolves don't come with us. They'll draw too much attention."

I sighed, but knew he was right. The wolves would draw too much attention. "Are you going to tell Gwen, or am I?"

He winced, looking toward the passenger berths. "If it's all right with you, maybe we could do it together."

Knowing we didn't have much chance of making my hunch work without a miracle or intervention from a god, it was time to come up with a plan.

"Captain Baeley, what kind of diversion do you think would buy us the most time?"

CHAPTER 22

We came up with a plan, of sorts. It wasn't as sophisticated as I would have preferred, but it was all we could come up with. We decided we'd let Captain Baeley beg for supplies while we snuck off of the boat and headed into the city to find the temple.

To make her plea more realistic, she had her first mate hide most of the food in a secret compartment in case they were searched. She freely admitted it was a flimsy excuse, but it was better than nothing. Hopefully, it could buy us at least an hour. The rest of the plan was shaky, us getting off the ship unseen and heading right to the temple.

She explained that in the Dragon Dominion, humans could be bonded to a dragon. The humans who were bonded basically functioned as servants, but there were benefits to both parties, unlike when elves kept humans as slaves. I'd felt a twinge of shame at that, but focused on her instructions, knowing I couldn't change centuries of culture by myself.

When we docked, she'd speak with the dragon-bonded dock-master and apply for permission to have a berth. This would be our one chance to escape, as it was rare a non-dragon owned airship was approved. We'd only have as much time as she was able to argue with him to accomplish our mission, which made the timeline tight indeed.

Gwen reluctantly left her wolves, agreeing it was for the best. The wolves whined when she explained it to them, but settled in the bunk to wait patiently, their sad eyes following her as we went above again.

We watched from deck as we approached the island. Similar to the ones on Starside, the docks here were larger, with wider gangways and boardwalks to accommodate several dragons walking abreast.

The smell of lush greenery was noticeable on deck even before we landed. Even though the clouds had been misty and cool, the air here was humid and warm, and a trickle of sweat tracked down my back as I considered everything which could go wrong.

Captain Baeley gave us the sign as we pulled closer. We followed her first mate to the side of the ship, waiting until the ship bumped to a halt before we moved. The sound of people talking was our signal, and with the assistance of two of the deckhands, we snuck out the back using the rope ladder the first mate had rolled out.

While she kept the official busy, I followed Gwen off the ship. Even with her concern about heights, she did better with the ropes than I. I discovered it was hard to climb down while my knees were shaking so hard, and almost lost my purchase and fell off ladder twice before we hit solid wood. Leaving everything behind except my satchel with the books and paper, we darted away from the ship and left the docks behind.

Moving deeper into the city and away from the port, I found, to my dismay, the city was nothing like what I'd expected. The descriptions I'd read were old, and nothing matched up with the pictures or explanations the way I'd hoped.

"Where do we go now?" Gwen looked around at the massive buildings, craning her neck.

CHAPTER 22

There was nothing shorter than several stories high, with even the single-family dwellings more closely resembling castles due to their larger size.

I flipped through the pages, looking at the pictures of the cityscape around me.

"I don't know. This book was written ages ago. Nothing looks the same. Will? You mentioned you'd been here once."

Will shrugged. "Yeah, once. I don't know where we are."

I blew out a frustrated breath. Surveying the street, I looked around for someone who may be able to tell us where the Temple was.

"What if we ask someone?"

I looked at Will and Gwen, both of whom shrugged.

To my surprise, Sel winked at me.

"Let me," he offered, looking eager with his head up and shoulders back.

"Are you sure?"

"I see a servant over there. I may have more luck than you. Give me a moment, and I'll be right back."

Sel approached a human girl who was sweeping off the steps of a nearby store. She appeared about his age, and while dressed plainly in a grey dress with an apron, she had rich brown hair and pretty blue eyes.

I was fascinated by the way his personality changed when he was talking to someone he considered his equal.

Instead of the quiet and deferential servant I was accustomed to, he smiled, joked, and perhaps even flirted with the pretty human girl with confidence I hadn't expected.

He came back a few minutes later, looking pleased with himself.

"What did she say?"

Sel glanced back at her with a smile. "Nothing. She didn't know about the Temple of Light. She was able to tell me the more important buildings are down that way, though. Maybe we'll find it there."

My shoulders slumped. I took out the paper from my bag again. It was full of symbols, but none appeared to match up with any of the scenery around me. I allowed my hands to fall to my sides, the paper hitting my leg.

"Let's go. We don't have much time before we need to return to the ship, so any direction is better than nothing."

He led the way, walking briskly. I wasn't sure if he actually knew where he was going, but seeing this new, confident side of him gave me some hope. The houses and buildings seemed double or triple the size of what they had been in Sunglen, or even Starside. At times I felt the light was blocked completely by the enormity of the buildings.

Suddenly, we emerged from the walls of buildings into a large clearing. My breath caught as I stared with wonder.

"Is that the Temple of Light? It looks like a dragon temple."

Gwen crossed her arms, one eyebrow raised and her nose wrinkled. Her doubt was obvious, and I couldn't blame her for it.

"It could be. The Temple of Light was supposed to be the place where the High Dragons held important summits. This one looks newer than the one depicted in the book, though. I wonder if this temple could be hiding the original?"

I noticed it had guards stationed all around it, with a clear entrance across from where we were standing. The doors were enormous and wide open, giant rectangular red slabs encrusted with jewels that opened outward, with three dragons standing with large swords at either side. Even with them there, the entryway looked large enough to fit at least two more dragons in between.

The building itself rose to a point which shone under the bright suns, having been tipped in gold. The rest of the triangular structure was built in a shimmering white stone, similar to the marble of the Library in Sunglen, right down to the gold veins through it. But otherwise, there were no statues or other

CHAPTER 22

decorations. It was a smooth, glowing monument to simplicity and beauty.

"Can you see another entrance?" Will squinted, tilting his head from side to side.

"No, just the main one."

I pursed my lips. Not only was it guarded, it was currently being actively used. I couldn't see any way we'd be able to slip inside without being observed.

"It looks like it's about time for Gwen and me to put on a little show. What do you think?"

She blinked, narrowing her eyes as she looked at Will. "Are you saying what I think you are?"

Her words came out slowly, but I could see her lips curl up with amusement.

"What are you saying, Will?"

"Well, I'm sure she'd like to get back at me for suggesting I leave her wolves behind. What better time to do it than while you search for the entrance to the temple?"

I looked between the two incredulously and was about to object when Sel piped up.

"If you two can keep the dragons at the front along with the dragon-bonded humans busy, I'll go around the back of the building with Rhin. If we get stopped, I'll create another distraction so you can continue searching."

"Oh, I don't know, guys. I don't like this plan's potential for disaster."

It sounded like my friends all planned to draw the fire of the dragons so I could find an entrance, which was a horrible idea.

Gwen placed her hand on my shoulder, giving me a confident smile. "You know as well as I do, you're the one who needs to get inside, not us. I highly doubt anything awful will happen if we start a fight in public other than being thrown off the island, which will happen if we get caught anyway."

"I don't want you guys taking the fall for me."

My protest was ignored. All three had crossed their arms and were looking at me as if I was a stubborn child.

"Okay, fine. But be careful. I want you to run instead of letting anyone get their hands on you." I waited with narrowed eyes for them to agree to my terms.

"Absolutely," Will agreed. "I have no intention of letting anyone catch me. But at least this way you might be able to find the way into the Temple of Light without a dragon guard catching you first."

With my heart in my throat, I walked away from the obvious front entrance while Will and Gwen headed straight toward it.

We'd almost made it around the building when the commotion erupted. People were shouting, and I heard the crash of something breakable. I moved faster.

Not sure how much time we had, I was beginning to despair we wouldn't find another entrance when I noticed a golden door behind one of the guards stationed on a smooth and otherwise boring corner of the temple. It called to me, and when I got closer, I saw the same dragon symbol from the Library front and center on the archway, shimmering in the light just above the dragon guard's head.

"I see a way in. But how do I get past the guard?"

Sel squinted. "It looks like I'm up."

He gave me a smile as I looked at him with a furrowed brow.

Taking a page out of Will's book, Sel winked. "Don't worry. One of the things I've learned as a servant is to be both invisible and fast. I'll be fine."

I watched, my heart in my throat as he darted toward the guard. I hesitated briefly, worried I could be unleashing something unstoppable if I opened the entrance, but knew I needed to move while he created the diversion.

My desire for answers and my need to stop the growing evil was stronger than my fear, and I acted. Slipping behind

CHAPTER 22

the guard once his attention was firmly fixed on Sel, I overheard him acting like a complete miscreant.

I was relieved to see a simple mechanism on the door when I sized it up. With the guard stationed so close, I needed it to be easy. But even as I prayed for it to be unlocked, my eyes fell upon a small engraving beside the entrance. Symbols, the same as the ones on the page in my bag. Without even pulling it out, I recognized a line corresponding exactly to three symbols on the page and pressed them.

Dragon. Sun. Dragon.

As I waited breathlessly, a small panel slid open beside the golden door. I walked into the darkness beside it, and into the ground below.

CHAPTER 23

The darkness inside the temple was overwhelming until I allowed my eyes to adjust, the way I'd been taught in the forest. I remembered I still had the notebook Jarid had given me. I hadn't used it yet, and while I hoped I didn't need to, it was nice knowing I had a Librarian who could help me in a pinch.

Slowly, the walls and the shape of the temple gradually took form in the dim grey light. I couldn't help remembering the mirrored walls in the Library with trepidation. Hopefully, nothing dangerous awaited me here, as I was completely on my own.

I patted my satchel, feeling the comforting weight of the books within. I paused, pulling out the paper. With barely enough light to see the paper in front of me, I blinked, rubbed my eyes, and looked again, certain I'd imagined it. In the dimness of the temple it appeared to me the symbols were rearranging themselves.

What had vaguely resembled a map in Sunglen had now rearranged itself into lines. It *was* a map, but not the way I'd thought it was. Squinting harder, my mouth dropped open as

CHAPTER 23

the dragon symbols began to line up. Nine symbols, to be exact.

Tracing them with my finger, I looked up. I needed to head to the right if I was understanding the symbolism correctly. A few short feet down the narrow hallway, I came to a door and I smiled. The main entrance had been ornately decorated with priceless gems, but this one was a stark contrast, appearing to have been etched into bare stone.

Hieroglyphs were arranged across the top and down the sides, traveling to the right and down before moving back up and across to the left in an ever-decreasing circle. Otherwise, the door was bare. No handle, no lever, nothing I could use to enter other than the symbols themselves.

I compared the paper to the doorway. The characters rearranged themselves again. Now the nine dragons were organized by size. I looked back at the door, realizing each dragon was slightly different. I held up the paper to compare them. What was the map trying to tell me? I looked at the narrow hallway behind me, realizing the temple, at least the part where I was currently, was too narrow for any dragon. Unless...

Suddenly, I understood. The hallway was only wide enough for a dragon who could shift into a human form, which meant only a High Dragon would be able to access the tunnel and this doorway. Or a dragon-bonded human or elf. This doorway was impassable to any of the dragons currently residing on Bomrega Island, which meant it *must* be part of the older temple.

Based on the amount of dust shrouding the halls, no one had been here since the High Dragons had disappeared.

I closed my eyes, thinking of everything I could use to help me open the doorway. I smiled, grabbing the book Jarid had given me and quickly jotted a note.

"What is the name of the last High Dragon king?"

I waited only a brief moment and watched with amazement as words appeared in response, along with the name in

Dragon. He'd explained it, but seeing it for the first time was still impressive. When I looked at the hieroglyphs on door again, I knew exactly which one to touch to open it.

"Thanks, Jarid," I whispered into the silence.

I didn't have to wait long. The wooden door slid sideways, revealing a well-lit room which almost blinded me after the dimness of the hallway. Something about it bothered me despite it being easier to see.

That was it—it felt too easy. I stopped in the entrance, carefully examining the room. If it was too easy, that could mean ... my heart sank. The floor appeared to be a plain and creamy marble, without cracks or color changes, but set into the decorative paintings around the room were tiny holes that almost blended into the wallpaper.

Holes which looked exactly like the motion-activated dart holes my brother had been learning to make this year.

Luckily, I had some knowledge of elven traps and how to avoid tripping them thanks to him letting me watch him work.

I closed my eyes, remembering the words to the spell I'd learned at my father's knee in childhood. This spell was useful with this particular style of trap. The air next to me began to shimmer as I chanted the quiet words. The spell was working! It had been a long time since I'd used it and I hadn't been sure I remembered it well enough to activate it.

I stepped forward, placing each foot cautiously after checking the floor, and focusing on the walls and ceilings.

Praying I was correct about the floor and the trap in the walls, I moved slowly, in case the spell didn't hold. I had no idea if it would last long enough to get me to the other end of the room.

Sweat trickled down my back as I moved with agonizing care to where the exit waited, tantalizingly close, yet so far away.

This door was a brilliant crimson red, but instead of reaching for it when I was close enough, I stopped.

CHAPTER 23

No, this wasn't right.

The first door to the outer temple had been golden and matched the surroundings. The second door had been plain, engraved stone. This door didn't match the room, even though it was gorgeous and seemed to be the proper door for a king to enter.

I turned to survey the room again for another way out and this time, my eyes were drawn to a small, ceramic urn resting just beside the crimson door. It was completely out of place compared to the rest of the room, which had been decorated to benefit someone of great wealth and style.

The plain brown jar, not even ornate enough to earn the title of vase, did not belong in this room.

Another test.

But as I leaned over to pick it up, I saw the shimmer around me vanish and I ducked, hitting the floor just as a silent whoosh passed my head, pulling a strand of my hair as it thudded directly into the wall next to where my face had been a second earlier.

I rolled, placing my hands on top of the jar, and was whisked into a tornado as the faint sound of darts missing their target echoed in my ear. The racing of my heart told me I was still alive, and against my better judgement I pried one eyelid open. I was in another room, still holding the jar. Clearly, I'd been right about the door.

This one was decorated in solid blue and filled with treasure as far as the eye could see. Gold objects filled every available surface—floors, chairs, tabletops. Even the chandelier glowed with diamonds and semi-precious gems. I couldn't see a light source, but the whole room was bright as day without the aid of lamp or candle.

I exhaled, still holding on to the brown jar. I was reluctant to put it down. It might be my only way out. My eyes were drawn to the center of the treasure room, where a single large emerald, as beautiful as Gwen's eyes, beckoned me.

"Rhin, Rhin. We're waiting for you. So lonely. Can you take us home? Show us the daylight. We would be ever so grateful."

Trying to clear the thoughts the gem was putting in my head, I tugged on my ears. How many times had I read about objects controlling someone's mind? If you didn't know how it was talking to you, it usually meant it was trying to kill you. The compulsion was almost overpowering to pick it up. I screwed my eyes shut again, bringing the urn closer and hugging it tightly.

I focused on the jar, noticing for the first time it wasn't a uniform color. Instead, it had hieroglyphs painted in a slightly darker brown than the background. Now that I'd detected them, I could see similarities between the hieroglyphs on the door and the paper I'd been using as a map.

I shifted the weight of the jar to my left arm, curling it into the crook of my elbow as I rummaged in my bag for the paper Jarid had ripped out for me.

Yes! It was the same symbols.

But when I examined the sheet further, I realized there was one symbol which wasn't on the page. Or anywhere else I'd been, for that matter. It was a goblet. I looked around the room, careful to avoid looking at the emerald I could hear now shouting my name in increasingly strident and nagging tones. In a strange way, it was starting to remind me of my mother's admonitions to be more ladylike. The bizarre idea made it easier to ignore, and I turned my attention back to the room.

When I'd first opened my eyes, I'd only seen the blue background and the riches around me before being transfixed by the emerald. Now I could see the blue was varying shades. The wallpaper had intricate circles layered on each other, the ceiling was a pale sky blue, and the floor a pale grey.

The goblet wasn't on any of the tables, but that didn't mean it wasn't in one of the many piles of items that covered the floor. Despite it not being anywhere obvious, I wondered if I needed to find it to get to the next room.

CHAPTER 23 229

There were no doors or windows now that I was here, and if the portal was another object like the jar, I didn't know what it could be. Nothing looked out of place, other than the jar I was already holding. Every other object was valuable and some sort of jewel or decoration. Except...

I turned around.

A simple fireplace was behind me, lit with a small but cheery glow. It was nestled in between two diamond-crusted armchairs and I'd already ruled it out on my primary survey of the room, but I realized it was because I'd been looking at the chairs.

The fireplace itself was plain grey marble, unadorned by any trim or priceless objects. Even the floor had veins of silver and gold through the marble, but the fireplace had nothing I could see to break the uniform stone appearance except for a tiny detail on the left corner.

I held on to the jar while placing the paper back in my satchel, stepping cautiously onto the plainest sections of floor I could see. I didn't know if the floor would move, but I was expecting at least one more trap, if not more, to be lying in wait for me.

Then the inevitable happened. I fumbled the jar. A yelp escaped me but I managed to catch the jar before it fell. As I did, I stepped on one of the gold marble veins in the floor. Just the tip of my shoe, barely a brush, but my foot felt heavy. Eyes wide with surprise and fear, I looked down to see gold on the toe of my shoe. Real, heavy gold, and the worst part was that I couldn't feel my pinky toe.

"Not good," I muttered.

To make matters worse, the floor next to me began to disintegrate. I moved faster, tiptoeing my way across the floor with as much speed as I could muster, while avoiding any other gold veins. I had to reach the fireplace before the floor vanished completely.

Great yawning holes opened in the floor. I rushed to fireplace and just as I reached the armchair, the floor crumbled beneath me.

I lunged. My left arm tightly gripped the jar as my right hand stretched for the symbol. For a moment, I was flying. Then, I was falling.

CHAPTER 24

I opened my eyes to a bright light.
I was still holding on to the jar, but somehow, I was in another room that was even more awe-inspiring than last. While the blue room had been full of every type of riches, the air in this one swirled with power, visible and invisible alike.

The entire room was lit with alluring turquoise energy waves. I realized I was sitting at the edge of the room while the energy swirled in front of me, and in the middle was a single, solitary ball acting as the origin of each of the crackling bolts dancing from side to side. It was an orb, with a pearlescent quality reminiscent of a semi-precious gem from the ocean. I tore my eyes away to look around the room, but there was nothing else there.

Nothing else was in the room. Except me and the orb. I realized, unlike the other rooms I'd seen in the temple, the walls in this one were clear.

Across the hall on the other side of the orb, waving frantically, were Gwen and Will.

I stood up, only now realizing I'd managed to hang on to the jar. I waved my free hand.

"Can you hear me?" I shouted at my friends.

232   SOUL GOBLET

She shouted something in return, but I couldn't hear her.

We could see each other, but the walls wouldn't let us interact.

I looked at the orb in the center and clenched my jar, my determination to solve this rising. I still had to get to the center of the room without assistance from either of them, even though I could see them there. I remembered the book and Jarid, and began rummaging in my bag with the other hand.

The book was still there, so I jotted a quick note. I hoped he'd heard or knew something about the energy orb crackling in front of me.

It took a few moments, but as the writing appeared on the pages I smiled.

Yes, but it's supposed to be in the Library, not on Bomrega.

Jarid, it turned out, had heard of a ball of energy before. But it was supposed to be in the Library?

"Interesting."

I glanced at Gwen and Will, who were still frantically searching for a way through. Maybe there was a door on their side, maybe not. Either way, they wouldn't make it inside before I acted.

I quickly scanned the rest of Jarid's entry.

"It's called the Eurosphere, and it was an item long thought to be lost in the deepest bowels of the mermaid kingdom."

I looked up, appreciating the glowing beauty. That would certainly explain the pearlescent nature.

"Rumor of its continued existence only reappeared in scholarly texts two hundred years ago. At one point, a Librarian at Starside thought he'd seen it in a mysterious room that appeared one night while he was cataloguing, but the room vanished before his report could be confirmed. He was written off as crazy. His account was recorded, but was the last report in the Library archives about it."

I jotted down one sentence.

"What does it do?"

CHAPTER 24

The response flew back.

"You need to brave the energy around it to get to the Eurosphere. However, if the energy traps you, it's unlikely you'll succeed. There's no record of what the energy will do, if it will kill you or drive you crazy. It's possible no one has ever lived long enough after seeing it to write down what happened."

I groaned, not at all reassured by Jarid's help. It was pretty much what I expected from the tasks the Library had set me so far. A chance of death if I failed. At least now I knew I needed to reach the ball in the center.

But how? Something told me my trick of semi-invisibility wouldn't work here. It had barely worked the last time I'd tried it and these energy waves would be much harder to confuse than a weak elven defense trap.

I remembered the key Kramson had given me. It had begun to feel strangely warm after I'd entered the room. I took it out of my shirt to look at it and inhaled sharply. Where it had been an ornate but simple bronze object last time I looked at it, it now glowed faintly, pulsing slightly as it warmed and cooled against my skin.

A tingle of premonition filled me.

I was obviously trapped in this room by myself until I figured out what to do. Jarid made it sound like the orb itself was out of the myths and legends section of the Library, lost to the records for hundreds of years, and the energy emitting from it had the potential to end my life.

On the other hand, I had a key from the Library that was doing something new and strange. It filled me with the certainty the Library itself wanted me to accomplish my task. I had the paper Jarid had given me, the book with Jarid available to answer questions, and lastly, the simple brown jar I hadn't wanted to put down in case I needed it again.

I looked at the book again, wondering if Jarid knew any specifics about what the orb did, but he'd written nothing else.

234   SOUL GOBLET

Either it was so ancient the information had been lost, or what it did depended on the seeker, and the nature of the orb changed as needed.

I couldn't know for sure, but the latter felt correct.

Placing the book and map back in my satchel, I swung it behind me, holding the jar with one hand and clasped the other around the key.

I held my breath and looked down. Praying I wasn't completely wrong, I touched the two objects together.

The moment they joined, the energy in the room went wild. If I'd thought energy was swirling before, now I was trapped in a tornado. I realized, even as I worried, that the energy was sparking out of control everywhere except where I stood.

I was the eye of the storm.

Taking a hesitant step forward, the area free of lightning moved with me. I glanced at Gwen and Will, wanting them to see my triumph, but as Gwen looked at me, her eyes full of terror I could tell the intensification of the energy had blocked their view of me and caused her to panic.

Not wanting to upset her further, I looked away and moved faster.

Within ten great strides, I'd reached the orb, still maintaining the key on the jar the entire time, but the second I stood in front of it I could feel a voice. Or was it voices?

They whispered I could put the jar down, that I'd reached my goal.

I paused, wondering if it was a trick or another test, but again came the certainty I was exactly where I needed to be. Allowing the key to fall back against my chest, I placed the jar carefully on the floor at the foot of the orb and stared into the swirling blue-green center of the universe.

Compelled to be closer, I placed both hands on top of it.

The moment I touched the orb an image of a goblet flashed in front of me. It was the same as the one on the fireplace, but much more beautiful. This was what my reward was, this was what I had come to the temple to find.

But I had barely caught a glimpse of the goblet before images of my life bombarded me.

My childhood, not fitting in. The other elves laughing at me.

"You're so strange and boring!"

"The spirit of an old man must have possessed you to waste so much time with books."

Running away crying, holding my books against my chest.

My mother's disappointment when I showed no interest or aptitude in ensnaring a husband like my sisters.

"Why can't you try harder to be like your sisters?"

"But Mother, I want to *learn*!"

"Then learn to be a lady. This obsession with being in the library has to stop."

My father turning his back while he trained my brother, even as I pleaded with him to let me learn the skills of a warrior.

"You need to listen to your mother. This is a man's job."

"But I can be just as fast and strong."

"Go away. Your duties are to marry well and create alliances, not die on a battlefield. You'll thank me later."

Faster and faster the images came, flooding me. I could feel the globe was learning everything it could about me as it probed my mind and memories.

Images of when the ur'gels had attacked us in the forest, the horrifying moment where the doppelgänger had almost stolen my life.

But I relived other moments as well.

Quiet moments, happy moments.

Smiles shared with Sel in the library, strange companions, and friends despite our circumstances.

Gwen and her wolves, my heart leaping with a warmth I wasn't familiar with, my first real female friend.

Loglan, his wisdom, kindness, and bravery in the short time I'd known him.

Jarid, his shy and bumbling determination to help, even at great personal expense.

Will's cocky smile and irritating demeanor, yet deep within was a solid core of goodness.

The incredible flying ship.

Images, both good and bad, memories I hadn't even remembered until they flashed in front of me once more. A sudden pause as they faded, leaving me one last image of myself in the room with the energies swirling around me.

It was as if a switch had been flipped, or an engine had wound down and I became aware we'd returned to the present. Then the images returned, but this time, of events I was sure hadn't yet occurred.

Gwen, fighting alone against ur'gels. One of the wolves lying still beside her, blood matted on its fur. In my mind's eye, I grabbed my knife readied myself to leap into the fray, but the image vanished before I could.

Now I was in the Library, in yet another maze with Jarid and Sel. Sel held a door open for me, but if I walked through it, I was certain he would be lost, and the door would slam shut on him. I would escape, but at the cost of his freedom.

I refused to take the easy way out. I pushed him through the opening to safety, while I took his place. I'd never let anyone die for me if I could save them instead.

The image changed again. This time, the slaver had found Will and had him pinned to the ground. Just as he was about to wrap his arms around Will's neck and twist, I lunged, a soundless scream echoing as I jumped onto the monstrous human's back.

Except I wasn't on the slaver. Instead, I rode Loglan, his smooth, muscular flanks rippling as we raced across the plains of the Low Forest. A darkness approached us, but I felt no fear

CHAPTER 24

as I held my knife in the air, a battle cry escaping me, as a strange joy swept over me.

Even as the scream left my lips, the crystal clarity there was no way to win flooded my mind. Dag'draath's army approached and I faced certain death. I realized then there may be no way to win, to trap Dag'draath or send him away where he couldn't do any further damage. But in the same moment of conviction, I understood it didn't matter.

With my friends, for my friends, for those I loved, and for my planet, I would fight to the death to protect everything I loved. One way or another, I would fight against Dag'draath with every last breath. If I couldn't succeed with my books, I would take down as many ur'gels with my knife as I could.

I blinked and the images vanished as though they'd never existed. The energy in the room quieted. And in the spot the orb had been during the indefinite amount of time it had taken to show me the truth, was the goblet.

This time, when I reached my hand out, the goblet came to me easily. I had been found worthy.

CHAPTER 25

I held the goblet, feeling its bronzed and ornately carved surface warm in a way metal shouldn't. The way the key from the Library had warmed when I'd entered the room. They were similar, both made from the same metal, acting in a way I'd never seen before.

As I held it, I realized I had in fact seen this goblet one other time in my reading, in the books in my library at home. The books which had caused me to seek out the Library at Abrecem Secer in the first place.

It was one of the objects I would need if there was a way to stop Dag'draath. But it was only one of the objects. There was still so much more for me to learn before that could come to pass. More books to read, more mysteries to unravel. But at least I'd found what I had come to the temple and to Bomrega Island for.

I remembered Gwen and her terrified attempts to get to me moments earlier, and looked over to see they were still waiting behind the invisible barrier to the room. Had they been able to see the images I had? What the orb had shown me felt personal, and I'm sure was why I'd had to do this part on my own. But that didn't matter. They were here, and I knew Sel

CHAPTER 25

239

was also fine, with a certainty I couldn't explain. But I was also positive we needed to leave immediately.

Staying on Bomrega Island any longer wasn't a good idea. The island was still in a state of anarchy unconducive to our continued health.

I bit my lip and looked around the room. The moment I'd taken the goblet off the pedestal the orb had sealed shut again. But now instead of the violent energies which made it so difficult to walk forward, and the images bombarding my mind earlier, I felt only soothing light emanating from it, as though the power within had simply gone to sleep.

Hopeful I wasn't being naïve, I walked directly toward Will and Gwen, leaving the brown jar at the foot of the globe, a subtle feeling telling me it was important it stayed in the room.

The key from the Library pulsed warmly against my chest as I stepped lightly to the wall where they waited. I touched my fingertips to the space between them and stepped through.

Gwen scooped me into her arms the second she was able to touch me. I felt the tears, warm and wet on my shoulder, as she squeezed me tightly. After a few moments of her desperate embrace I smiled, pulling back just far enough for her to wipe her face before I glanced at Will, only to see a matching look of relief on his face.

"Don't ever do that to me again, Rhin!" Gwen choked back a sob as she glared at me. "I was certain you were…"

Her words trailed off and I could see she'd stopped because it was too hard to voice her worries.

I understood exactly how she felt. I'd just felt the same earlier while watching her fight an ur'gel in an image the orb had given me. I leaned into her again, squeezing her as tightly as she'd squeezed me.

"I'm okay. We're both okay."

Our eyes met, searching. A smile passed between us before I blinked, and the moment passed.

"We do need to get out of here though. I'm positive the

goblet is something we don't want anyone to know we have. Not to mention the fact we snuck onto the island in the first place, which leads me to believe we should go, posthaste."

"Finally, something I agree with." Will's voice was harsh, but I could hear the emotion he was suppressing.

I let go of Gwen to give him a hug as well.

"Thanks for being there. Where did you guys come from anyway? How did you manage to get in here?"

Will shrugged, but the blush coloring Gwen's cheeks made me even more curious.

"We'll tell you back on the ship. It's a long story. I agree we need to get out of here."

Gwen looked around nervously and I realized this hallway was far better lit than the ones I'd come through.

"Are we in the…?" My voice trailed off, and my heart sank as I realized we had even less time than I'd anticipated.

"Yup. We're in the royal court. Luckily, we lost our pursuers, but I'm sure they won't take too long to find us. If we hadn't given them the slip, they likely would've gotten to us while we waited for you to play with the magic orb." He gave me a curious look.

I brushed his unspoken question aside, not yet ready to speak of it, certain we didn't have the time now anyway.

"Let's go. Did you see Sel?"

They both shook their heads and I sent out a prayer we found him before we got to the ship. "Any way for us to go out the back? I last saw him when I snuck in."

"Funny you should ask. As we were avoiding some irate dragon guards, I spotted a door which I think leads away from the front."

"Let's go. The sooner we get back to the ship, the better. We've got a lot to discuss."

We hurried through well-lit hallways. They weren't ornately decorated, but it was clear we were in the current incarnation of the temple by their width alone.

By the time we reached the door Will remembered, I felt as though we'd been wandering for hours, but the position of the sun showed hardly an hour had passed since I'd entered the temple.

Strange. It had felt like so much longer.

Vegetation hid the door from the outside and when we exited, I realized this would have made a better entry point, had I been permitted to find it. Everything up until now had been a test of one sort or another, which I'd apparently passed. But now I wanted to know who or what was testing me, and why. Was it simply because of my desire to stop Dag'draath? Or was something else going on, beyond the obvious?

When I spotted Sel, waiting across the road, hiding behind a refuse pile, I pushed the thoughts aside. Later would be soon enough to sit down and unravel new mysteries. Right now, we had to get back to the ship.

With the key and the goblet in hand, tomorrow couldn't come soon enough.

Continue reading this series, Legends of the Fallen with book 8, *Heart Stone*

Grab the free prequel to the Legends of the Fallen series, *Falling Suun* here:
https://books2read.com/u/3R1ElD

Like the series Facebook page to stay up to date on all new releases
https://www.facebook.com/LegendsoftheFallen

ABOUT THE AUTHOR

J.A. Culican is a *USA Today* Bestselling author of the middle grade fantasy series Keeper of Dragons. Her first novel in the fictional series catapulted a trajectory of titles and awards, including top selling author on the *USA Today* bestsellers list and Amazon, and a rightfully earned spot as an international best seller. Additional accolades include Best Fantasy Book of 2016, Runner-up in Reality Bites Book Awards, and 1st place for Best Coming of Age Book from the Indie Book Awards.

J.A. Culican holds a master's degree in Special Education from Niagara University, in which she has been teaching special education for over 13 years. She is also the president of the autism awareness non-profit Puzzle Peace United. J.A. Culican resides in Southern New Jersey with her husband and four young children.

For more information about J.A. Culican, visit her website at: www.jaculican.com.

ABOUT THE AUTHOR

I'm a full-time worker bee, mother, and writer by the wee hours of the day. I would write all the time if I had my way, but alas, life and family come first!

Somewhere in the last few years I've managed to carve out just enough time to write the trilogy that has spawned it all, based on a recurring dream I've had since my teens.

I hope you enjoy this world as much as I do.

For more information about H.M. Gooden, visit her website at: https://www.hmgoodenauthor.com/

ACKNOWLEDGMENTS

Editor: Frankie Blooding
Cover Artist: Christian Bentulan
Formatting: Dragon Realm Press

Printed in the USA
CPSIA information can be obtained
at www.ICGtesting.com
LVHW011516211023
761548LV00006B/111/J